AN UNEXPECTED KISS

Captivating Kisses
Book 1

Alexa Aston

© Copyright 2025 by Alexa Aston
Text by Alexa Aston
Cover by Dar Albert

Dragonblade Publishing, Inc. is an imprint of Kathryn Le Veque Novels, Inc.
P.O. Box 23
Moreno Valley, CA 92556
ceo@dragonbladepublishing.com

Produced in the United States of America

First Edition February 2025
Trade Paperback Edition

Reproduction of any kind except where it pertains to short quotes in relation to advertising or promotion is strictly prohibited.

All Rights Reserved.

The characters and events portrayed in this book are fictitious. Any similarity to real persons, living or dead, is purely coincidental and not intended by the author.

ARE YOU SIGNED UP FOR DRAGONBLADE'S BLOG?

You'll get the latest news and information on exclusive giveaways, exclusive excerpts, coming releases, sales, free books, cover reveals and more.

Check out our complete list of authors, too!

No spam, no junk. That's a promise!

Sign Up Here

www.dragonbladepublishing.com

Dearest Reader;

Thank you for your support of a small press. At Dragonblade Publishing, we strive to bring you the highest quality Historical Romance from some of the best authors in the business. Without your support, there is no 'us', so we sincerely hope you adore these stories and find some new favorite authors along the way.

Happy Reading!

CEO, Dragonblade Publishing

Additional Dragonblade books by Author Alexa Aston

Captivating Kisses Series
An Unexpected Kiss (Book 1)

The Strongs of Shadowcrest Series
The Duke's Unexpected Love (Book 1)
The Perks of Loving a Viscount (Book 2)
Falling for the Marquess (Book 3)
The Captain and the Duchess (Book 4)
Courtship at Shadowcrest (Book 5)
The Marquess' Quest for Love (Book 6)
The Duke's Guide to Winning a Lady (Book 7)

Suddenly a Duke Series
Portrait of the Duke (Book 1)
Music for the Duke (Book 2)
Polishing the Duke (Book 3)
Designs on the Duke (Book 4)
Fashioning the Duke (Book 5)
Love Blooms with the Duke (Book 6)
Training the Duke (Book 7)
Investigating the Duke (Book 8)

Second Sons of London Series
Educated By The Earl (Book 1)
Debating With The Duke (Book 2)
Empowered By The Earl (Book 3)
Made for the Marquess (Book 4)
Dubious about the Duke (Book 5)
Valued by the Viscount (Book 6)
Meant for the Marquess (Book 7)

Dukes Done Wrong Series
Discouraging the Duke (Book 1)
Deflecting the Duke (Book 2)
Disrupting the Duke (Book 3)
Delighting the Duke (Book 4)
Destiny with a Duke (Book 5)

Dukes of Distinction Series
Duke of Renown (Book 1)
Duke of Charm (Book 2)
Duke of Disrepute (Book 3)
Duke of Arrogance (Book 4)
Duke of Honor (Book 5)
The Duke That I Want (Book 6)

The St. Clairs Series
Devoted to the Duke (Book 1)
Midnight with the Marquess (Book 2)
Embracing the Earl (Book 3)
Defending the Duke (Book 4)
Suddenly a St. Clair (Book 5)
Starlight Night (Novella)
The Twelve Days of Love (Novella)

Soldiers & Soulmates Series
To Heal an Earl (Book 1)
To Tame a Rogue (Book 2)
To Trust a Duke (Book 3)
To Save a Love (Book 4)
To Win a Widow (Book 5)
Yuletide at Gillingham (Novella)

King's Cousins Series
The Pawn (Book 1)
The Heir (Book 2)
The Bastard (Book 3)

Medieval Runaway Wives
Song of the Heart (Book 1)

A Promise of Tomorrow (Book 2)
Destined for Love (Book 3)

Knights of Honor Series
Word of Honor (Book 1)
Marked by Honor (Book 2)
Code of Honor (Book 3)
Journey to Honor (Book 4)
Heart of Honor (Book 5)
Bold in Honor (Book 6)
Love and Honor (Book 7)
Gift of Honor (Book 8)
Path to Honor (Book 9)
Return to Honor (Book 10)

The Lyon's Den Series
The Lyon's Lady Love

Pirates of Britannia Series
God of the Seas

De Wolfe Pack: The Series
Rise of de Wolfe

The de Wolfes of Esterley Castle
Diana
Derek
Thea

Also from Alexa Aston
The Bridge to Love (Novella)
One Magic Night

PROLOGUE

London—July 1805

JULIAN WATTS PRESSED a cold compress to his mother's brow. He felt the heat of her fever through the cloth, singeing his fingers. She had been ill for close to two months now, the cough worsening, and the weight falling off her. Weight she didn't have to spare.

"I will stay home with you," he said gently.

"No," she protested weakly. "Mr. Piper is expecting you. You don't want to ruin your chances of working for him full-time. He is your way out of poverty, Julian."

He hoped she was right.

At seven and a score, he had worked on the London docks and in one of its warehouse for over a dozen years now, moving heavy cargo, and had the muscles and calluses to show for it. A year ago, however, his mother had sewn a few gowns for a Mrs. Piper, whose husband was a solicitor. Somehow, Mother had convinced Mr. Piper that Julian was the clerk he was looking for, though Mr. Piper already had two clerks working for him. Still, the solicitor had met with Julian and had been impressed, hiring him on as a night clerk.

Nowadays, after putting in a full day laboring with his muscles, Julian reported to Mr. Piper's offices. Most of the work he did in his second job was reproducing legal documents, such as marriage settlements, in order for all parties involved to have their own copy of the agreements. Mr. Piper thought Julian's handwriting impeccable, and he'd begun staying late, teaching Julian various things about his business. One of Mr. Piper's clerks was close to retiring, and the solicitor had told Julian if he were interested, he could assume that position.

Eager to do anything to better himself and help his mother, he had agreed to wait for the slot to open. In the meantime, he worked his usual backbreaking job, grabbing a meal of meat pies from a street vendor before heading to Mr. Piper's offices. He would get home shortly before midnight and fall into bed, only to repeat the long day after a few hours of sleep.

He didn't often see his mother due to his long hours, but she left him sweet notes and set out food for him. Despite their infrequent encounters, he saw how rapidly she was declining. Fear of losing her filled him. Instead of reporting to Mr. Piper's office tonight, he had come home to check on her and found her in terrible shape.

"I could leave you for a while and tell Mr. Piper you are unwell," he told her. "Then come home and sit with you."

Her gaze met his. "No," she said firmly. "I am done, my boy. You must look to your future without me."

Taking her hand in both of his, he brought it to his heart. "I cannot lose you."

She shook her head. "I am so tired," she admitted. "I have felt death coming for me. I am ready for it. You must promise me, Julian, that you will continue with Mr. Piper. Do all you can to move up in the world."

Suddenly, a choking sound came from her. Alarm filled him. He squeezed her hand tightly, not wanting to ever let go. She was all he knew. The only friend he had. It had always been the two of them against the world.

"I am sorry I could not do more for you," she apologized, trying to catch her breath.

"Never say that," he said fiercely. "You sacrificed everything for me."

A sad smile crossed her face. "You were always my world, Julian. I love you so very much."

Her eyes closed. He sat on the bed next to her, hearing her labored breathing, knowing no doctor could help her. Not that they could afford one. The poor did without many things, and that included medical assistance.

He listened as her breathing slowed, his heart aching, and then it ceased. For a moment, all seemed well. She looked at peace. It was almost as if the corners of her mouth turned up in a slight smile. While she was still warm, he kissed her brow, then he took her hands and placed them atop one another on her chest.

"I love you," he said, grief sweeping through him, mingled with frustration, knowing he had not been able to save her. "I will do my all to be the best person I can be. For you."

Rising, he felt hot tears spill down his cheeks. Already, an emptiness filled him, knowing how alone he now was. He would go directly to Mr. Piper and explain what had happened. He knew the solicitor would allow him to miss work for a few days in order to handle the burial arrangements and mourn his mother's passing.

Before he left, though, he went to the chest his mother called a bottom drawer. In it, she kept a few treasured mementos from her girlhood, along with her sewing patterns and lists of clients, including their measurements. Inside it was a small, lidded box that contained their combined earnings. He hadn't a clue how much it would cost to bury her and worried what he would do if the box did not contain enough coin to do so.

She was the one who always put aside their meager earnings. Julian almost felt as if he invaded her personal property as he opened the chest. He found the box and removed it but noticed a small bundle of parchment tied together with a ribbon. Curious, he pulled it out as well, wondering whom his mother might have corresponded with. From the little he knew, her family had disowned her when she became with child, tossing her out on the street. Julian had never asked who his father might be, and she had never revealed the name to him. He had supposed either the man was already married or that when she told him of the coming child, he had abandoned her.

Opening the box first, he counted what was within, knowing how careful she had been with their savings. His gut told him it wasn't enough. Anger simmered through him, knowing how hard the both of them worked and how little they received for their efforts. Julian refused to put her in a pauper's grave. Perhaps Mr. Piper might give him an advancement on his salary so that he might bury his mother in a proper fashion.

Setting aside the box, he picked up the bundle and untied the ribbon. Though it seemed wrong to read what was there, he hoped it might give him insight into her past—and where he came from.

As he read the first letter, his belly twisted.

Miss Watts –

I cannot have you come here again to my parents' house, even to pass along a letter. You could cost me everything. I regret to hear there is to be a child. It is most unfortunate.

I will meet you in the usual place tomorrow afternoon at three o'clock to discuss this matter.

The brief note was unsigned, but Julian knew his father had written it.

Who had he been? What had he been like? From the wording, he gathered his father had been of a different, better class than his mother, who had been a tailor's daughter.

Hesitating a moment, he set aside the note and opened the second one, wondering what it might reveal. This time, it bore no declaration or signature, but he assumed it was for his mother since she had kept it. He recognized the same hand that had written this note.

You have what you want. The marriage will allow you not to bear a bastard, but you know I can never claim him, much less you. Speak of it to no one. I advise you to call yourself Mrs. Watts and style yourself a widow.

I have paid three months' rent on the place I took you to after the ceremony. It is all I can give you. I leave now for my Grand Tour and expect to be gone the requisite three to four years. When I return, I will live my life—and expect never to see nor hear from you again.

The coldness in the tone struck Julian more than anything. Obviously, his mother had somehow met a young man from the aristocracy, and they had engaged in a brief affair. He was the result of their liaison. How heartless, though, for his father to have brushed aside his mother, leaving her alone, soon to bear a child, without family or even a single friend to aid her.

The last piece of parchment was larger. He unfolded it and saw it was, indeed, a marriage certificate. His mother's name was displayed, as well as that of Henry Barrington. The name meant nothing to him, but it gave him slight satisfaction to know he was not the bastard he had always thought he was. Still, he wanted nothing to do with the stranger who had gotten his mother with child and then blithely went off to sow his wild oats in Europe.

Julian left their rented room and hurried to Mr. Piper's offices. Using his key, he let himself in since he arrived long after the other two clerks had ended their day. He did spy a light coming from his employer's office, though, and made his way there, hesitating a moment at the open door.

Looking up, Mr. Piper said, "Ah, Julian. Do come in. I have some—"

"My mother is dead," he said flatly.

The solicitor's concern for him was immediately obvious. Mr. Piper rose. "My dear boy. I am so sorry to hear of your loss." He patted Julian on the back. "How can I help?"

"I don't know if I have enough to cover the costs of her burial," he admitted. "Is it possible to receive an advance on my salary? I won't place her in a pauper's grave."

"No, you cannot do so. I agree. Tell me what you have done so far."

He raked his hands through his hair. "Nothing. I arrived home, going there instead of straight here, because she had been so poorly yesterday. She was quite ill, Mr. Piper, but ready to meet her Maker. I have no idea what to do next."

"I can help with things, Julian," Mr. Piper said in a soothing tone.

"She was married," he blurted out, surprising himself. "I mean, she pretended to be a widow. Mrs. Watts. But there never was a Mr. Watts."

Frustration filled him, and the story spilled from him. The discovery of the two letters. The marriage certificate.

"I hate him," he said. "My father. He was in a position to help her. Instead, he ignored her."

Mr. Piper looked thoughtful. "But you say he wed her? There is proof of that?"

"Yes. Much good it'll do her now. She struggled her entire life. Cut off from her family for the transgression of bearing a child out of wedlock. Worked her fingers to the bone, especially when she sent me to school. She insisted I go. That I must learn to read and write and grasp maths."

"She was right to do so, Julian. I know you have done physical labor your entire life, but you have a fine mind, especially for numbers. I am happy your mother and my wife came into contact, else I would never have met you. I was going to tell you I am ready to hire you on permanently, beginning next week, but I am curious now as to your parentage."

He glared at the solicitor. "I want nothing to do with my birth father," he said angrily.

"Calm yourself," instructed Mr. Piper. "Let me come home with you now. I will assist you in handling matters."

Regret filled him, seeing how kind his employer was being. "I apologize for my outburst, sir. I was taught better manners than that."

The solicitor placed a hand on Julian's shoulder. "You have just lost your beloved mother. No apologies are necessary."

They returned to the tiny flat. Mr. Piper had assured Julian during the hansom cab ride over that the burial costs would be handled. When the solicitor looked over the marriage license and notes, he nodded to himself.

"We should summon the undertaker now. Do you have a gown you'd like for your mother to be buried in?"

Mr. Piper left Julian, saying he would see that the undertaker arrived shortly, and took the correspondence and license with him, instructing Julian to go to the docks first thing in the morning to quit his job.

"With no notice?" he asked.

"Tell them your mother has passed," the solicitor advised. "Ask for any wages due you. If those in authority are reluctant to give those to you, use my name. When you have done so, come to my offices afterward."

An hour later, the undertaker arrived, taking with him the gown Julian had set aside for the burial. He mentioned to Julian that Mr. Piper would help to arrange services for Mrs. Watts on the morrow.

Julian fell into a restless sleep, awakening at his usual hour of four. The room was silent except for the squeaking of a small mouse, which he chased away. It was the first day of his life without his mother in it, and sadness permeated him.

He did as his employer had requested, however, explaining his mother had passed the previous evening and asking for the wages due him. When the dock foreman tried to put him off, Julian tossed in Mr. Piper's name. Apparently, the solicitor was known to the man. Miraculously, he was told to report to the warehouse offices, where he received what he was owed.

That took a few hours, however, and by the time he reported to Mr. Piper's offices, it was half-past nine. The solicitor was out on business, and Julian was told by his clerk to wait.

When Mr. Piper arrived, he was in good spirits, asking for Julian to accompany him to his office. There, the solicitor explained he had been to the parish church listed on the certificate and had asked to see their registry.

"I found the lawful marriage recorded between your mother and Mr. Henry Barrington."

Puzzled, he asked, "Why would you do so?"

Eyes gleaming, Mr. Piper said, "We are going to right a terrible wrong today, Julian. We are going to see your father."

"No," he said firmly. "I want nothing to do with him."

"Ah, but I think you will," Mr. Piper said mysteriously. "Humor me. But first, we shall call upon a colleague of mine."

Knowing he had quit his job and that his only one would be with Mr. Piper, Julian decided to go along. It didn't mean they would actually see his father. The man had never wanted contact with his son, and he doubted they would be able to see this Barrington.

They called at the offices of a Mr. Welby. Mr. Piper asked Julian to wait in the hansom cab, and a quarter-hour later, both men returned. Mr. Piper introduced Julian, and he noted the other solicitor studied him with open curiosity.

"The very image," Welby muttered, and nodded to himself. "Well, let us do this."

They went to an area of London Julian had never seen before. Elegant homes lined the streets. Mr. Welby mentioned the area was called Mayfair, and Julian knew this was where the wealthiest of London's citizens resided.

The cab turned into a large square. Three huge townhouses sat on it, two opposite one another with a small park in between, and another at the far corner. The driver drove to that residence, where Mr. Piper paid the driver but asked him to wait for them.

Feeling terribly out of place as they moved to the door, Julian wanted to return to the hansom cab. He wore his usual clothes, that of a dock worker, and saw the odd look the butler gave him as he spoke with Mr. Welby.

The butler admitted them, however, and led them up a grand staircase. Julian clamped his mouth shut to keep from gaping at the marble floor and beautiful paintings on the wall. They moved along a corridor with thick carpeting and furnishings the likes he had never seen. When they reached the end, the butler had them wait inside an anteroom.

"Are we going to see him?" he asked nervously, wishing he were back outside. Or back unloading a ship. Anywhere but here, a world so unfamiliar to him.

"Yes. It is important you do this, Julian," Mr. Piper said firmly.

"He *must* see you," Mr. Welby agreed. "Your future depends upon it."

Before he could question what that meant, the butler appeared again, grim-faced. "You may come in. Dr. Wheeler is with him." He opened the door and stepped inside the bedchamber, ushering them inside a bedchamber four times the size of the room Julian and his mother had lived in.

The two solicitors entered first, with Julian bringing up the rear. Immediately, the stench of death hit him, and he thought of the irony of both his parents passing within a day of one another.

Yet glancing at the bed, he saw the man in it—and he was alive. Barely. Propped up with pillows behind him, his skin was sallow, his eyes burning bright from fever.

Julian's feet propelled him closer, and his gaze locked on that of a man he had only just learned about and yet despised with every fiber of his being. Henry Barrington, a name he would never forget.

"Bloody hell . . ."

Though the words he rasped were weak, Julian heard the wonder in the man's tone.

He stopped next to the bed, rage filling him. "I have no sympathy for you," he uttered. "I only learned of you because my mother just passed."

Barrington winced. "Ah, so she is gone." He swallowed. "Your mother was an angel."

"She was," he agreed. "Far too good for the likes of you."

"I see you inherited none of her gentleness. Nor her looks." Barrington paused. "Do not look so surprised. You are obviously my son. I was hale and hardy as you thirty years ago. Saw your mother when I visited my tailor and wanted her from that very moment. She was so beautiful. Kind. Unassuming."

"You put a babe in her belly and then ran off like a coward," Julian accused, not mincing words.

Sighing, the man in the bed nodded. "I agree. I am despicable. I was young. Foolish. Cowed by my own father. He never would have accepted such a woman as my wife."

"And yet you wed her," he said.

Barrington closed his eyes for a long moment. Julian thought he might be dead. Then he opened them again.

"I did. It was important to her. She wanted none of my wealth. Only a name for you. Even then, I advised her to use her own."

"She did. I am a Watts. And proud of it. We did just fine without you."

"I had three other wives," Barrington lamented. "None of them legal marriages, of course, but they were none the wiser. All barren. That was my punishment for leaving your mother. For not standing up to my father and making things right. At least you found me. I was too spineless to ever seek you out."

Mr. Welby stepped forward. "My lord, the moment I saw this young man, I knew he was yours." He indicated his fellow solicitor. "Mr. Piper has shown me the marriage certificate, and the marriage has been confirmed by the church registry. Julian is your legal heir."

Barrington sighed. "I affirm everything. The marriage. The birth. My heir."

Julian's mind whirled. "What . . . what do you mean?"

"Too tired," Barrington murmured. "Tell him . . . everything."

With that, his father took a final breath and fell still.

The doctor stepped forward, checking his patient. "I am afraid his lordship is no longer with us."

"You will attest to his deathbed confession if we have need of your testimony?" asked Mr. Piper.

"Of course." Dr. Wheeler looked at the butler. "Grigsby here will do so, as well."

Julian stared open-mouthed, no words coming to him.

Mr. Welby said, "You are now Julian Barrington, only heir to the Marquess of Aldridge. You will inherit his lordship's title and holdings."

Dumbfounded, he could only stare at Welby.

Mr. Piper clasped Julian's elbow. "I know this is a lot to take in, my lord."

Shrugging off the man, he said, "I am not a lord. Not a marquess. I refuse to take part in such a sham."

Mr. Welby cleared his throat. "I am afraid there is no choice in the matter, my lord. I knew the minute I saw you that you were the marquess' son. With the proof in hand, not to mention Lord Aldridge's acknowledgment, you are the recognized heir. This disclosure will be made public, and you will need to take your seat in the House of Lords."

"House of Lords! This is balderdash," Julian declared.

Sympathy filled Mr. Piper's eyes. "This is who you are, my lord. Though it is difficult for you to understand, you are the rightful heir."

"But he never acknowledged me. Or Mother," he protested. "I can't take anything from a man I despised."

"Whether you loathe him or not, you are still the Marquess of Aldridge, my lord," Mr. Welby insisted. "And you wouldn't be the first member of the *ton* to despise his father."

"No more struggling," Mr. Piper said gently. "You have a title. Property. Wealth."

"Yes, all of that," Mr. Welby encouraged. "This London

townhouse. Aldridge Park in Surrey, which is south of Guildford, about thirty-five miles from town. I can meet with you to discuss your investments. Your holdings."

"This is madness!" cried Julian. "Why, I am wearing one of two sets of clothing I possess. I rarely eat enough to fill my belly. I can't be a lord."

"But you are," Mr. Piper insisted. "I will, along with Mr. Welby, guide you, but you have responsibilities now, my lord."

"Yes," Mr. Welby insisted. "Aldridge Hall has a good number of tenants you'll need to look after."

He grew nauseous. "So, I'm to sweep away the past. Forget where I came from. This is my world now?"

"Yes, my lord," both solicitors replied in unison.

Head spinning, Julian asked, "Where is he to be buried?"

"Why, in Surrey," Mr. Welby said. "All Barringtons are buried in the churchyard there."

Determination filled him. "Then I want both my parents buried there, side-by-side. And Mother's tombstone will be engraved with Lady Barrington on it," he demanded. "She might not have lived the life of a marchioness, but she deserves what is rightfully hers."

"I will see that happens, my lord," Mr. Welby said. Looking to the butler, the solicitor said, "Grigsby, gather the staff. It is time they met the new Lord Aldridge."

From that moment, Julian knew his life was divided—into before he had become a marquess...

And what came from now on.

Chapter One

Millvale, Kent—March 1806

LADY ARIADNE WORTHINGTON looked around the dinner table. Her father and older brother were engaged in conversation, Val probably trying to talk over estate business, something their father had told his son over and over was no concern of his until he became the Duke of Millbrooke. Val argued that he could be his father's eyes and ears and visit the other ducal properties beyond Millvale, helping to prepare for the day when he did come into the title. Her brother had told Ariadne he did not wish to be completely unprepared when that time came, yet their father kept all matters of business private, frustrating Val to no end.

She turned to her left, where her younger sister Tia was complaining to their mother, begging to go to London.

"You always make us stay in the country, Mama. Why can't we go to town with Ariadne this year? Lia and I will be making our come-outs next year. We should see something of what it is like so we can be ready."

The duchess sniffed and looked to Lia, Tia's twin. "Do you feel the same as Thermantia, Cornelia?"

Her parents always referred to their children by their full Christian names. While Ariadne liked the name she had been given and hadn't wanted it shortened, her three siblings had all gone for a more diminutive form.

Lia, always a peacemaker, diplomatically said, "While it would be lovely to go to town and see more of it, I am content to stay at Millvale. There is so much to be done here."

"Lia!" Tia said, her exasperation evident. "What happened to a united front?"

She couldn't help but laugh. Her twin sisters favored one another in the face, but everything else about them was different.

"I mean it," Lia insisted. "I can always help on the estate while Mama and Papa are gone."

"But in town, we could go to the parks. The museums. Gunter's!" Tia countered.

They had only been to town as a family once, many years ago, when they met all their cousins. Aunt Charlotte, her father's sister, had three children of her own, as did Uncle George, their cousin who also had three children. Uncle George was deceased now, but she knew his widow continued to come to town each spring. The ten cousins had enjoyed being around one another, but they lived too far apart to get together on a regular basis.

The only cousins in the group who saw one another were Val and Constantine, Viscount Dyer. Her brother and Con were the same age and had attended school together, even sharing rooms at university. Ariadne looked forward to getting to know Con better when she made her come-out.

"It will be enough to manage your sister's come-out without having to worry about the two of you," Mama said. "Your governess will keep you occupied. It is your last year to have a governess, Thermantia, and you still have much to learn from Miss Nixon."

Tia sighed dramatically. "I suppose I shall have to settle for letters." She looked to Ariadne. "You had better write. In detail. Of all the balls and parties and what your gowns look like. The gentlemen you are interested in. The ones you kiss."

"Thermantia!" roared the duke. "That will be enough from you."

"Yes, Papa," Tia said meekly, turning her interest to the plate in front of her.

Dinner finished without any more drama. Val and their father remained at the table with brandy and cigars, while the twins accompanied their mother and sister to the drawing room.

Sitting next to Ariadne, Tia said, "I mean it. You do not have to write the both of us. You can address letters to one or the other, and you know we will share." More quietly, she said, "I want to know what kissing is all about."

"I will write when I can," she promised, avoiding the topic of kissing.

Her mother overheard that remark. "Ariadne will be too busy for much correspondence, Thermantia. You girls may write to her, but do not expect answers to your letters. The social calendar fills up quickly, and I assume that Ariadne will prove to be quite popular with her looks."

She knew she was pretty, but she did worry about her hair. It was copper, an interesting blend of red and bronze. Somewhere, she had heard red hair was not considered fashionable, and men did not like it much. If so, all three Worthington sisters would be in trouble during their come-outs since they all got their varying shades of red hair from their father. Lia's was a lovely shade of auburn, more red than brown, while Tia's was a beautiful strawberry blond. Even Val's hair, while appearing brown indoors, was russet, and shone red in the sunlight. Of course, he was a man and the Marquess of Claibourne, heir to a dukedom. It didn't matter what color of hair he had. When he decided to wed, Val would easily have his choice of ladies.

Papa and Val joined them. The twins begged off, promising to get up early to see her off tomorrow morning. Val took her aside, and they went to sit in chairs by the window.

"Are you excited about taking part in the upcoming Season?" he asked.

"A part of me is. It will be fun to make new friends and wear pretty gowns. Go to the different events. But I worry about disappointing Mama and Papa."

He frowned. "How so?"

She shook her head. "It is different from you. You aren't expected to wed right away, while I will be looked upon as a failure if I do not. After all, I am the daughter of a duke, with fair looks and a hefty dowry." She hesitated. "What if I cannot find a gentleman I like?"

Val smiled. "You don't have to worry, Sis. I guarantee there are plenty of eligible bachelors who will vie to meet you. I will personally find out everything I can about the ones interested in you and inform you of all you need to know about them. Just tell me which ones you fancy, and I'll make certain they are good enough for you. I won't have you wedding someone irresponsible or a man who will treat you unfairly."

She took his hand, squeezing it. "I am grateful you will be looking out for me. I fear Mama will push me toward men who possess the highest titles or those with the greatest wealth. Papa will be just as bad." In a gruff voice, imitating the duke, she said, "A man must be worthy to wed my Ariadne."

They both laughed, and Val said, "His Grace is intimidating. That will cause some to shy away. Others will also learn how protective I am of you. That might frighten a few more away."

Laughing, she said, "Will there be anyone left to woo me?"

"Only those brave enough to face the wrath of the Duke of Millbrooke and the Marquis of Claibourne. If they can, they may be found suitable." His gaze met hers. "Do not be in a rush, Ariadne. If you find no one to your liking this first Season, regardless of how Mama pushes you, then wait for the next. Not every girl weds after her come-out Season. You want to be certain you have found the right husband."

"I fear my inexperience will lead me to the wrong person," she said worriedly. "I do not want to make a mistake. Marriage is for life."

"True," Val said, his brows knitting together. "But you aren't looking for love, are you?"

"Goodness, no," she said quickly. "Even I am not foolish enough to think I would make a love match. Do they really even exist?"

"Not that I know of," he said breezily. "Still, I believe you can find a man who will treat you kindly. One who will be generous toward you. I would never allow you to be stuck with someone who is cruel or overbearing. Just take each event one at a time. Meet as many people as you can. And do not merely search for a husband. Have fun. Make new friends. Live a little. I believe if you do, your path will cross with the man meant for you."

Ariadne hugged her brother. "I am so glad you will be there. Con, too. I am looking forward to getting to know him better. It seems so odd that we have so many cousins, yet we have only been in their presence that one week."

"Con is reliable. You will not find a more dependable man in the city. I will have him help me to scrutinize your beaux."

"Ah, so now I have the two of you looking after me. What more could a girl wish for?"

Shortly after, Ariadne retired to her bedchamber, where her maid helped her to undress.

"Ready to go to town, Tally?" she asked.

"Yes, my lady. I've been a country girl all my life. It's exciting to get to go to town." The servant paused. "And hopefully, we can stay together."

"Why wouldn't we?" She hugged the maid. "I assumed you wished to go with me whenever I wed. Of course, it might not be a ducal household. I know some servants are very conscious about their employer's status."

"Oh, no, my lady. I don't care a thing about that. I just want to serve you. If you and your husband want me, that is."

"Tally, I will refuse to marry any man who would dictate to me who I can have for my maid. My husband will not even care about household matters. Those will be left up to me, his wife. I shall be in charge of hiring and firing staff. You will always have a place with me."

"Thank you, my lady," the maid said, tears swimming in her eyes. "You've put my mind at ease."

After Tally left and Ariadne lay in bed, she found her mind whirling and sleep impossible.

What *would* her life in town be like? What would the Season truly entail? She hoped she would make new friends and enjoy the social gatherings. Once the Season ended, she might well be engaged. Then the ceremony would take place, and she'd be off to her new home.

A wave of sadness passed over her. Kent had always been home. What if she wed a man who lived far away from Millvale? She might only see her brother and sisters each year during the Season. If they came. Not everyone in Polite Society participated in the Season. Some lived far from town and did not come often. Women, in particular, skipped the Season if they were increasing. It was hard to imagine not seeing Tia and Lia on a daily basis, something she had always taken for granted.

She wished now that she had fought to have her sisters accompany her to London. Maybe after they had been there a few weeks, she might tell her mother she missed her siblings and ask if they could join them. Yes, that was definitely a good plan. It would certainly please Tia, and Lia would happily accompany her twin to town. That decided, Ariadne dropped off to sleep easily.

In the morning, she rang for Tally and dressed quickly before going downstairs for breakfast.

Pulling Tia aside, she said, "Do not react to what I say, but I am going to ask Mama to send for you and Tia after the Season has started. You are right. I feel a bit ill-prepared, and I want better next year for you and Lia. While you will not be able to attend any social events, I can tell you about them. You can also help me choose what to wear on different occasions."

Tia looked at her without a trace of a smile. "That would be lovely, Ariadne. You are a wonderful sister. I am sorry I have to look at you as if I am bored, because all I want to do is jump up and down and throw my arms about you."

"Perhaps you should go on the stage," Ariadne mused. "I never knew your acting skills were so good."

"There is a lot you do not know about me," Tia said, sounding as regal as a queen.

She hugged Tia. "I already miss you."

Once they had breakfasted, she said her goodbyes, both to servants and her sisters. She accompanied Val to the first coach of three, and he handed her up. Mama and Papa joined them. Ariadne leaned out the window as the coach started up, waving the entire way down the lane, until everyone turned to specks.

She settled herself, seeing Mama already leaning against the window, softly snoring. Val and Papa were talking about one of the estates in Essex, so she passed the time staring out the window at the lovely countryside they passed. She wondered when her aunts and uncle would be arriving in town. At least with her being of age now and able to come to London each Season, over the years she might get to know her younger cousins. Besides Con, Aunt Charlotte had two daughters, Lucy and Dru. Uncle George had had a son named Hadrian, who now held the earldom, and two girls, Verina and Justina. From what her mother said, Ariadne gathered Aunt Agnes continued coming to town each spring to see friends, though Mama said she doubted Agnes would ever remarry.

They switched horses halfway through their journey, getting out to stretch their legs a bit. Mama immediately dropped off to sleep again once they were back on the road, her snoring louder this time. Ariadne kept studying the view outside, eager when she caught sight of London. As they approached, she thought it was possible this might be last time she did so as an unmarried lady. By next spring, she could well be a married woman, entering the gates of the city with her husband.

She knew the Worthington townhouse was in Mayfair. Parts of the city seemed familiar to her, and she supposed her one visit years ago had made an impression upon her.

What bothered her, though, was catching sight of the poor as the vehicle moved through London. She had been too young to notice before, but now Ariadne saw children on the streets, many without shoes, though the temperature for March was brisk. Looking with a critical eye, she also saw adults dressed in rags. Her heart ached, thinking of families who went cold or hungry.

Determination filled her. She would do something about this situation. Though she was only one person and her efforts would only touch a few lives, she believed it was her duty to help the less fortunate. How she would go about doing so would be tricky, especially since she was under the impression that her hours would be filled with social activities. Still, she could carve out time for the less fortunate. She could make this happen.

And would.

When they turned into a square, she caught sight of their townhouse. Three houses occupied this square. Two faced one another, with a small park in the middle. Another house sat at the end of the square. Their carriage went down one side, turned, and then went back up the other, coming to a halt.

"We're here, Mama," Ariadne said, shaking her mother gently.

Mama blinked. "Already? The drive used to take so much longer."

She caught Val's eye and had to turn away, covering her laughter with a cough.

Her brother leaped from the vehicle, assisting his father out. The duke strode into the house without a word to anyone. Val helped Mama out next, with Ariadne coming last. She smiled at the servants, greeting them.

"You are Parsons," she recalled. "And Mrs. Parsons."

"Yes, my lady," the housekeeper said. "We are ever so happy to have you in town for your come-out Season."

"Tea, Parsons," Mama commanded, sailing into the house.

Val looked at her. "I've had enough of them for now. I will see you at dinner. I am off to my club."

"Why don't women have a club to go to?" she called after

him, seeing him grin over his shoulder as he hurried away.

She went to her room, happy to see how large it was. Tally unpacked for her, chattering away.

"I had better go have tea with Mama," she told her maid, traveling downstairs, where Parsons directed her to her mother's sitting room.

"We shall meet with the modiste tomorrow," Mama told her. "I have booked her for the entire day."

"It will take that long?"

Mama smiled. "You will spend more time with her than anyone this Season, Ariadne."

Once they had a cup of tea, she decided to go and see the park across the street, ready to be outdoors after having been cooped up in the carriage on their drive to town. She went to her room and claimed her cloak, since it was a bit chilly, and a book. Making her way out the front door, she told the footman where she would be.

"Enjoy your reading, my lady," he told her. "There's a gate to enter the park. Faces the single house."

She thanked him and walked directly there, glad he had informed her of where the gate was located. Entering, she decided to explore its entire length before finding a bench to sit upon. When she came to its center, however, she spied a man sitting and stopped in her tracks.

His eyes were closed, his booted feet stretched out in front of him, crossed at the ankles. His arms rested against the back of the bench. His face was turned up to the sun, his eyes closed.

Ariadne approached him, not certain how to handle the situation. Mama had told her she was never to speak to any stranger and that at every societal affair, she must be introduced to anyone she did not know by someone she did know. Here, alone in the park, though, it seemed rude if she avoided this man. After all, he must live in one of the two other nearby townhouses, else he wouldn't be here.

He must have sensed her presence because his head moved,

his eyes coming to rest on her. His dark, thick hair and thick brows were a direct contrast to his pale, blue eyes. His face was handsome, but he had a look about him, as if he were a hungry tiger on the prowl for a meal.

"Excuse me," she said, taking two more steps toward him. "I did not mean to disturb you."

"Talking to me disturbs me," he said bluntly.

His words took her aback. She frowned deeply. "I am Lady Ariadne Worthington. My father is the Duke of Millbrooke. Our family townhouse is next to this park. I assume it is for us and all our neighbors to enjoy."

An amused look crossed his face. "Not afraid to scold me, are you?" he asked.

She felt her cheeks heat, knowing her tone had been harsh, but she wasn't going to apologize to this man.

"Just because you hold a title does not mean you have the right to be discourteous," she countered.

"How do you know I hold a title?"

"First, because you are present here and must live in one of the two other townhouses on this square. Second, you are not a second or third son because they are not nearly as surly. Not all men who hold the rank of peer are uncivil, but I will venture those who are as boorish as you do hold a title and *feel* entitled. I am sorry I spoke to you, especially since we are strangers. I should have waited for a proper introduction, as is required. I will continue to investigate this small park, and then I shall find a spot to sit, far away from you. I will never speak to you again, my lord. Even if our paths do cross."

"Assertive," he said, studying her lazily, making her cheeks burn. "You are entitled yourself, Lady Ariadne, being a duke's daughter."

"Others might believe that true, but I value those with good manners who seek to be kind to all. I cannot help my parentage, but I will not apologize for it. Good day, my lord."

Ariadne forced herself to continue walking to the part of the park she had yet to see, knowing she would eventually have to turn around and come across this man again. Though dreading it, she hoped he would be gone by the time she came around a second time.

Unfortunately, that was not the case. In fact, this time, he stood as she drew near.

"Forgive my insolence, my lady," he said, surprising her with his gentle tone, as well as the apology. "Though it is not an excuse, I am new to the world of Polite Society and have an innate sense of inferiority."

His revealing words shocked her—and drew her curiosity.

"Then I would have us start by introducing ourselves again," she said.

"Good afternoon, my lady," he said, sounding civil and courteous this time. "Might I introduce myself to you? I am Julian Barrington, the Marquess of Aldridge. My townhouse sits at the bottom of the square. I gather we are neighbors."

He took her ungloved hand in greeting. Something raced through her, a wild, wonderful feeling that had her catch her breath. She knew he felt it, too, because he looked at her, puzzled, and then released her hand.

Recovering, she said, "I am pleased to meet you, my lord. I am Lady Ariadne Worthington, daughter of the Duke and Duchess of Millbrooke." She paused. "See? Wasn't that better?"

"Forgive my previous brusqueness. I was a bit out of sorts and took it out on you. It was ungentlemanly of me."

"I will forgive you. In fact, let us pretend it did not occur and that we met just now."

Lord Aldridge smiled at her. "I think I will be very happy to be your neighbor, Lady Ariadne."

"Likewise, my lord. Have you held your title long?"

"I came into it last summer, so I would say almost eight months now."

She was interested in learning more about him, but said, "I believe I will go and read now, my lord. I hope to see you at the

Season. That is, if you are attending it."

"Yes. Invitations are piling up on my desk as we speak. Even though no one knows me, they all wish for the Marquess of Aldridge to attend their little social affairs."

"Perhaps you might come to dinner one evening. I will speak to my mother and father about it."

He studied her. "Have you attended the Season before, my lady?"

"No. I am to make my come-out this spring."

A knowing look came into his eyes. "That means you are on the hunt for a husband. I have heard it called the Marriage Mart."

Blushing again, she said, "You need to learn to curb your tongue, my lord, and not speak your every thought aloud. Members of Polite Society do not go about saying such things."

He shrugged nonchalantly, making him look rather appealing. "I see I have much to learn about this new world. Perhaps you could—"

"It is not my place to teach you of such things, my lord. Find someone at your club to do so."

"I suppose I have a club. I will have to ask."

For a moment, it struck her how lonely he looked. Perhaps that was why he acted so disgruntled. Pity moved her to say, "My brother belongs to White's. I will have him come around and meet you. He is the Marquess of Claibourne."

"Ah, another marquess. Then we are destined to be friends."

"Is that sarcasm, my lord?"

His eyes gleamed at her. "You are most perceptive, my lady."

Irritation filled her. "I am trying to do you a favor by sending Val your way. My brother," she added when his brows arched in question.

"Then send Claibourne. I fear I am going to need all the help I can get."

Afraid if she stayed in the park, it might lead to more conversation, she abruptly said, "Good day, my lord," and hurried away.

"You don't have to be afraid of me, you know," he called

after her, causing Ariadne to laugh.

She wasn't afraid of him—but her interest was certainly piqued by him. Ariadne would definitely have Val make Aldridge's acquaintance.

And find out his story.

Chapter Two

After dinner, Ariadne told Val she needed to speak with him. Her mother retired to her bedchamber, and their father said he was going out. That left them alone, for which she was grateful.

Settling themselves before a fire in the library, she said, "I made the acquaintance of a most unusual man this afternoon."

Val scowled in disapproval. "Hasn't Mama discussed with you the rules of social engagement, Ariadne? You are not to address anyone—male or female—whom you do not know. It takes a formal introduction from someone who knows both you and the other party before it is acceptable for you to—"

"Would you stop?" she demanded. "I do not need a lecture. I am not a child. What I am trying to do is confide in you."

Stubbornness remained in his eyes. "And I am your older brother. I am here to protect you. I will not see you ruined before you can even set foot in a ballroom."

"Hush, Val, and let me speak freely. It is because you are my trusted brother that I am confiding in you."

Looking somewhat mollified, he nodded for her to continue.

"I was ready to stretch my legs after our travels today." Before he could interrupt, she added, "Yes, I know to take Tally with me if I walk, but this was merely across the way. I wanted to investigate the park on our square. I did not think I needed her to do so. I took a book and thought to sit and read a while."

"Go on," he said.

"The park is lovely. A little oasis where I am certain to retreat to when I am overcome by all the excitement of the Season. It has some delightful landscaping, and I cannot wait to see what flowers will bloom when warmer weather comes. Scattered benches are available, so I will have a place to think or read."

"I have been inside it and am familiar with it. Is this where you met this man?"

Ariadne nodded. "He was sitting, lost in thought. I did not want to appear rude, so I introduced myself."

Val grimaced. "First mistake. If it ever happens again, either nod politely without speaking and move on or simply avoid eye contact and turn around to go home. The park is only for residents of our square, so either it was Viscount Burgess, whose townhouse is directly across from ours, or Lord Aldridge. I have heard he has been in ill health for some time, so I doubt it was he."

"It was Aldridge," she confirmed. "The *new* Lord Aldridge."

"Then the old man must have passed away. I did not see the death notice in the newspapers. Hmm. He had no children, despite being wed thrice. I wonder who this heir is?"

"That's the thing, Val. He was a bit cryptic, but he mentioned not being of this world. Our world. His manners were certainly lacking." She hesitated. "Yet I felt a bit sorry for him. He dressed the part of a marquess, but he seemed so out of place. He did not even know if he belonged to a club."

"He sounds rather odd. Not someone I would have you around, Ariadne."

"I told him I would send you over to meet him."

"Me? Why?"

"He needs a friend, Val. I do not know his background, but I think he is lonely."

A knowing look came into his eyes. "You have always had a tender heart, Sis. Looking after strays. Injured birds and animals. Do you think this peer is your new undertaking?"

"Would you do this for me? Help him? Please?"

"I see he made an impression upon you."

She laughed. "To be truthful, not a very good one. He was beyond prickly. Yet I think he's a bit lost. I have no idea as to what he did before he inherited his title, but he could use some polish. And a friend. He is going to attend the Season for the first time. I wouldn't want him to blunder or make a misstep that would haunt him."

Val chuckled. "You want me to befriend him and then make certain he's presentable for Polite Society?"

"Well, yes."

"What if I don't like him?"

"You might." She smiled at him.

"You think one smile, and I will do your bidding?" he teased.

She shrugged. "It always has worked before."

He hugged her. "You are too hard to resist. All right, Sis. I shall send a note to Lord Aldridge."

"Find out if he is a member of White's. If he is, take him there. Introduce him to others."

"Oh, the Marquess of Aldridge is most definitely a member of White's. The former marquess was."

"Thank you for taking care of him, Val."

He studied her a moment. "Why is this so important to you?"

Ariadne bit her lip in thought. "I cannot say why. Something about him touched me. I think he will be lost if no one takes him in hand."

"I'm not a wet nurse, you know," he grumbled, but she heard the teasing in his voice.

"No. You are a wonderful big brother who has lots of friends and can guide this new peer. After all, he is our neighbor. You would be doing a neighborly thing."

Val laughed heartily. "Only you would find a stray your first day in town and then expect me to care for it."

"He's not some mongrel off the streets," she told him. "He is a marquess. Lord Aldridge merely needs a little guidance."

"You will owe me for doing this."

"What price shall I pay?" she mused. "Oh, I suppose I could introduce you to several of the lovely girls making their come-outs with me. Mama said I should make several friends within this group." Ariadne laughed. "She told me be nice to the pretty ones, for they will be the ones who claim the most eligible bachelors and will one day rule Polite Society. Then Mama said I could be friends with the plainer ones because they would never be a threat to me."

"My advice?" he asked. "Never listen to a word that comes out of Mama's mouth. Make friends with those you wish to be friends with. While I know the finish to your Season is most likely to end in matrimony, I do believe you will find some girls who will become lifelong friends to you."

"I hope so. I adore Tia and Lia, but I would like to meet others and become friendly with them."

"I will write to Lord Aldridge first thing tomorrow morning," Val promised. "Of course, I will keep you apprised of the outcome."

"Thank you, Brother. Now, would you like to lose to me in chess?"

"Just because you beat me the last time we played, you do not have to lord it over me."

"It was the last three times—but who is counting?" Ariadne said, heading to the chessboard.

She was glad her brother had agreed to her request, and hoped Val could take Lord Aldridge in hand and help get him ready for what lay ahead.

※※※※

JULIAN ALLOWED PAULSON, his valet, to dress him. When he had first inherited the valet from the previous marquess, his thought had been to dismiss the man. It appalled him that the rich thought they needed someone to dress and undress them. Yet Paulson had proven to be a fount of information, subtly guiding his employer. Paulson had explained to him how to handle servants and tenants, which had proven invaluable. He also had given Julian advice on what was appropriate for a marquess to wear.

He had opted to use the Alderton village tailor when he first assumed the marquessate. Even that word had been unknown to him. Paulson had gone along with Julian, advising him on the appropriate materials for the tailor to use as well as for the pieces to be made up. The valet explained to Julian that he must look the part of a marquess as well as act as one, whether he believed he deserved the title or not.

Paulson had also limited the wardrobe the tailor made, saying when they got to town, Julian would need to see a tailor there for the latest fashions. When he protested that he didn't care about fashion, Paulson rejected his argument, once again saying he owed it to the title to appear properly dressed. The valet stressed that for a great many members of the *ton*, appearance was everything. If he were to be accepted, he must dress in an appropriate manner.

Julian would have argued that he didn't care for acceptance, but he would be lying. Now that he had unimagined wealth, he wanted approval from others, and that included his peers. He also wanted to do good with his fortune, but he hadn't acted upon that just yet. He needed to feel his way and not rashly spend his fortune unwisely.

His thoughts drifted to Lady Ariadne as he dismissed Paulson and ventured downstairs for his breakfast. He had been disagreeable during their encounter, which he now regretted. The park had become a retreat for him in the brief time he had been in London. No, town. That was another odd tidbit Paulson had shared. Those in Polite Society always referred to the great city as town and never by name. He hated these strange, unwritten rules.

As he perused the morning newspapers as he dined, he

thought Lady Ariadne must be different from most ladies of the *ton*. She had called him out for his poor behavior. He doubted other ladies would have done so. Because of that, she intrigued him. He assumed their paths would cross when the Season began next month, but he doubted she would show any interest in him. In fact, she would probably tell others of their brief encounter and what a boor he had been.

No, that was assuming the worst of her. She had seemed kind. She had even offered to have her brother come and visit him. That probably would not come to pass. Why would some duke's son want to know him?

Grigsby approached, a silver tray in hand. "Today's post, my lord."

"Thank you," he said, taking the stack and setting it next to his plate as a footman refreshed his coffee. "Thank you," he said again, knowing it wasn't expected of him to thank a servant for something, but happy for the small service he received. The fact he had all he could eat and drink still astounded Julian at times.

He finished his meal and took the newspapers and mail with him to his study. A fire was already lit, and he sat in a chair close to it, finishing his reading. Paulson had emphasized that Julian must learn about daily affairs, both in England and the world, saying it would help him as he listened to debates in the House of Lords and voted accordingly. The newspapers were a constant surprise to him, as full of news as they were gossip.

Finally, he went through the post. He had no secretary to do so for him, and his valet had encouraged him to hire one. The old marquess had let his go when his health grew worse, and he no longer attended social events.

Most were invitations for upcoming affairs of the Season. He set those aside, not certain which he would attend. One note intrigued him, however. Glancing at the signature at the bottom, he saw it was from the Marquess of Claibourne, Lady Ariadne's brother. So she had spoken to her brother after all.

My dear Lord Aldridge —

It has been brought to my attention that you have recently inherited your title. Since we are neighbors here in town, we should at least become acquainted with one another.

I shall be going to White's this morning and am inquiring if you wish to accompany me. The coffee and tea are plentiful, the newspapers and journals always updated, and you never know who will be there that you might find interesting.

If you are agreeable, I shall leave our square at eleven o'clock. We can stroll a few blocks and catch a hansom cab to White's.

Your most humble servant,
Valentinian Worthington,
Marquess of Claibourne

Julian's heart began racing. "Why am I excited as a schoolgirl?" he asked himself aloud. "It is only an invitation to a club."

But it was the only one he had received. He knew not only was business done at these clubs, friendships also could blossom. He was sorely in need of a friend. At eight and twenty, he had never had a single friend.

It was time that changed.

Quickly, he dashed off a note to Claibourne, accepting his invitation. Julian took it a step further, however, saying his carriage would call for the marquess at eleven o'clock, hoping that wouldn't be too presumptuous. He sealed the note, pressing his insignia to the warmed wax.

Ringing for Grigsby, he handed the note to his butler, saying, "This is to be delivered to the Marquess of Claibourne at once. Make certain my carriage is readied, for I will be taking Lord Claibourne to White's with me this morning at eleven o'clock."

Even Grigsby could not hide a smile. "Very good, my lord."

Glancing at the clock, he saw he had three-quarters of an hour before his engagement with Claibourne. He was grateful the marquess was following through with his sister's request. He looked forward to seeing Lady Ariadne again in person.

Because he intended to also convey his gratitude to the very intriguing young woman.

CHAPTER THREE

"THE CARRIAGE IS out front, my lord," Grigsby informed Julian as he entered the foyer, handing his employer his hat.

Placing it on his head, he went through the front door, opened by a footman, and climbed into his carriage. Four bays pulled it, and while Julian didn't want to become caught up in material possessions, he did take pride in the look of those horses.

The vehicle drove to the nearby townhouse, and he didn't know if he should get out and fetch Claibourne or if that was something a footman did. He waited, seeing a footman dash to the door and knock. Julian couldn't help but be eager and yet apprehensive at meeting the marquess.

The door opened for a moment and closed again. He assumed the butler would inform Claibourne of Julian's arrival. Moments later, the door opened again, and a man strode out, confidence evident in his step. Not wanting to be caught staring, Julian looked away as Claibourne approached and was admitted inside the carriage, sitting opposite its passenger. Only then did he take in his neighbor's appearance.

Claibourne looked to be in his mid-twenties, handsome, with penetrating green eyes. His build was muscular and if he'd been dressed in a meaner fashion, Julian could have seen this man as a fellow dock or warehouse worker.

"I am Claibourne. Then again, you already know that," the

marquess said, his eyes twinkling. "My sister warned me that you would be a bit prickly, so what say you put that aside as we simply become acquainted?"

"I will apologize to Lady Ariadne again when I see her," Julian said. "I was deep in thought and not expecting company when she stumbled across me yesterday. The park is private and from what I'd been told, neither of my neighbors was yet in residence. I am Aldridge, by the way." He grinned. "But you already knew that. What else did your sister say of me?"

Lord Claibourne shrugged. "I would rather gather my own opinion of you and not parrot that of my sister."

He liked hearing that. He liked this man, who seemed open and friendly. Yet Julian knew to be wary of others in the *ton*. Both his solicitors and valet had told him as much, and so he would remain guarded for now. All three men had urged him to keep his background to himself, and so he did not think he would be sharing his previous life with those he met.

"Then you sound as independent as Lady Ariadne," he commented, causing the marquess to chuckle.

"If you think Ariadne has a mind of her own, you should meet Tia, another of my sisters. Lia, on the other hand, is much sweeter."

"Do you have any brothers?" he inquired.

"I do not. I am the eldest and my father's heir apparent. I will warn you now that I am a bear where my sisters are concerned, though. I will protect them from any threat." He eyed Julian neutrally. "I haven't decided if you are one or not."

"I'm no threat to you or your sisters," he insisted. "I was grumpy and made a bad start with your sister. I will not make that same mistake with you, my lord."

"Good." Claibourne offered his hand. "It is nice to meet you, Aldridge. How long have you held your title?"

"Since last summer," he replied. "The previous Aldridge passed away, and the title came to me, a distant relative." That was the story Paulson had encouraged him to tell, emphasizing that Julian should be vague when asked about his background, assuring his employer that most people wouldn't press him for more information.

"I am sorry you lost your relative. Were you close?"

"Truthfully, I had not met Lord Aldridge until just prior to his death." Turning the conversation away from that, he added, "I have spent these last several months in Surrey. Aldridge Manor is south of Guildford, and I wanted to see to my new tenants and the estate itself."

"You enjoy the country?"

While his time in Surrey had been his first ever trip outside London, Julian had soon grown fond of it.

"Very much so. I enjoy the quiet of the country. This city never seems to sleep. It is nice to escape the noise and filthy streets and soak up the greenery of the countryside."

"I couldn't agree more," Claibourne said pleasantly. "Though I enjoy town, I prefer spending my time in the country."

The marquess launched into details regarding his father's estates, and Julian realized this man liked to work the land.

"You sound as though you are an active participant when you are in the country," he noted.

"I am not shy about tossing off my coat and rolling up my shirtsleeves, if that is what you mean. Too many gentlemen in Polite Society do not know the nature of physical labor, nor do they appreciate the hard work their tenants put in on the land. I have worked alongside many of mine." Claibourne paused. "By the look of you, I gather you have done the same."

"I have no qualms participating in physical labor. I would not ask any of my tenants to do something that I am not willing to do myself."

Claibourne smiled. "I find I already like you quite a bit, Aldridge. You are a man who says what he means."

"Is there any other kind?"

His companion frowned. "All too often, I am afraid." He glanced out the window. "I see we are here. Ariadne tells me you have yet to visit White's."

"I wasn't sure if I held a membership."

"You most certainly do. Probably at Brooks's, as well, though I suggest you stick with White's. Of course, both clubs revolve around gaming, gossip, and how well dressed you are."

He frowned. "Then I'm not certain I'll like either place."

The door opened. Claibourne said, "Come on, Aldridge." He descended the stairs which the footman had placed beside the door, and Julian followed him.

They went to the door and gained admittance, where Lord Claibourne told the man who greeted them, "This is the Marquess of Aldridge. He has been in the country seeing to affairs since he took up his title, but he is in town now for the Season and will be a frequent visitor here."

"I am Pollard, my lord," the man said. "I will help see that your needs are met any time you step inside White's."

When Julian looked blankly at him, Claibourne said, "He means in your choices of beverages. Newspapers. Games of chance. That sort of thing."

Relief filled him. Having grown up in abject poverty in London, he was all too aware of certain types of houses which catered to the sexual needs and tastes of gentlemen.

"I prefer coffee over tea, though I will drink either provided to me. I read the newspapers voraciously, so you may always bring whatever is available. As for gaming? I don't."

Julian had seen too many others gamble away their wages, falling deeper and deeper into debt, being carted off to the poorhouse or worse, falling victim to violence when they could not repay their gambling debts. He had no interest in learning how to play various games, much less lose money over them.

"Very well, my lord." Pollard took their hats. "And for evenings if you dine here? Any preference in food or drink?"

"I'm certain I'll like whatever is brought to me."

"I will show Lord Aldridge around, Pollard. Thank you. When we are done, please have coffee ready in the morning room by the staircase."

"Yes, my lord."

Claibourne gave him a tour of the club, which was fairly empty, introducing him to a handful of peers. While he was good at remembering faces, Julian had always had a hard time with names and was glad he only met a limited group of men. They visited the upper level, seeing an enormous coffee room, hall, gaming room, and dining hall. Returning to the ground floor, he viewed two more halls, a billiards room, and two morning rooms.

They settled into chairs. Immediately, a servant appeared with a tray. He placed cups and saucers in front of them, pouring for Claibourne first and adding cream to the beverage. Then the servant looked at him.

"How do you wish your coffee prepared, my lord?"

"Two sugars and a splash of cream, please."

The servant added the requested items, stirring Julian's coffee. "Anything else, my lords?"

"A couple of the raisin scones, Tommy," Claibourne requested. "You know I have a weakness for them."

The servant grinned. "Right away, my lord."

They sipped their coffee. Soon, the scones arrived. Julian bit into his.

"I can see why you requested this. It's delicious."

For an hour, they talked of his estate and its particulars, with Julian sharing things he had done to improve it since his arrival. Claibourne mentioned traveling to several of his father's estates and talked about the various crops and livestock raised on each. He couldn't recall ever spending such a pleasant hour and didn't feel the least bit inferior. If anything, Claibourne had made Julian feel most welcome.

"As more people arrive in anticipation of the Season, White's will fill up. I will help introduce you to others if we are in one another's company."

"I truly appreciate you accompanying me today, my lord. I

hope to be a frequent visitor here."

"My closest friend is my cousin, Viscount Dyer. He will be here in the next week or so."

"Then I look forward to meeting him."

As they left White's, Claibourne pointed out the betting book, noting it was a record of some of the more outrageous bets placed by members.

"As I mentioned, I am not one for gaming, so it's of no concern to me."

They returned to his carriage and pulled up in front of the duke's townhouse.

"If you are free this afternoon, we would love to have you to tea," the marquess told him. "I will tell my sister that you were a perfect gentleman during our time together. She will be curious and want to see if that behavior can last more than a few hours."

Julian realized the man joked with him. "I'd be happy to come to tea, my lord, and I'll be on my best behavior."

Before he exited the vehicle, Claibourne said, "I know nothing of your background, Aldridge, and it is not my nature to pry. A word of advice, however. Stop using contractions. Others will take notice."

He felt his face burn in embarrassment. Paulson had gotten onto Julian for that very thing, but it was a hard habit to break.

"I say it in all kindness," Claibourne added. "Ariadne told me you had mentioned you were not of the world of Polite Society. Its members have sharp claws. I think you will do quite well when the Season begins. You are handsome and affable. You do possess good manners. And of course, you are a marquess. It is merely a bit of friendly advice."

Nodding, Julian said, "Thank you, Claibourne. I'll—I will be more conscious of my word choice in the future."

"Then come at four for tea, Aldridge. I am looking forward to getting to know you better."

As the door closed, Julian wanted to kick himself, yet he thought Claibourne had handled the matter delicately. If anything, he decided to model himself after the Marquess of Claibourne, who seemed to be a most decent fellow. He vowed to make a wonderful impression at tea this afternoon. If his neighbors, being a duke and duchess, could say kind things about him to others, it would ease Julian's entry into Polite Society.

He would need all the help possible marching into that unknown world.

CHAPTER FOUR

A RIADNE HAD BEEN happy to hear that her brother had invited Lord Aldridge to accompany him to White's today. She hoped the marquess would accept the invitation. It was hard to explain why she even cared about a man she had only meet briefly, especially since he had appeared so disgruntled. It wasn't as if a marquess were one of her abandoned strays she took in and tried to find homes for. Then again, she had always been the one in her family to try and solve problems. Lord Aldridge wasn't her responsibility, yet she felt a need to help him.

Whether he wanted her help or not.

She watched out the window as their carriage rolled along the busy London streets as they traveled to Mama's dressmaker. Her mother claimed Madame Laurent was the best modiste in town. While Ariadne would have been happy for their village seamstress to have made up her come-out wardrobe, Mama insisted it must be Madame Laurent and no one else. She did look forward to choosing the material for a few ball gowns, knowing several balls would occur this Season. It would be enjoyable to discuss the type of gowns the modiste would create for her.

They passed many other vehicles and carts, and she saw the streets lined with vendors selling their goods and food. Ariadne caught the scent of hot pies, causing her mouth to water.

Then she saw a group of ragamuffins, children who were dirty and poorly clothed. None of them wore shoes, and the girls' legs and feet were stained with the mud of the streets. It broke her heart to think of the dismal lives these children led. She wondered if they were orphans, which caused her even greater pain.

"Finally, we are here," Mama said as the carriage began to slow and then came to a full stop. "Traffic is terrible these days. It takes forever to reach a destination."

They were handed down by a footman, and Mama told the driver what time to return for them. Ariadne supposed her father had need of the carriage, and that was why Mama allowed it to return home. She still didn't understand why it would take so many hours to decide upon a few designs and materials but decided to keep silent. Mama had made her come-out years ago and would know what needed to be done.

They entered the dress shop, and a tall, slender woman with kind eyes greeted them.

"Ah, Your Grace, Lady Ariadne. I am so happy to see you. I will do everything I can to make your wardrobes the best of all the *ton*."

She had not thought about Mama needing new gowns since she already had so many to wear. That must be why they would take so long today. Her mother could be quite particular about things, especially her clothing.

"See to my daughter's measurements, Madame Laurent. We have a busy day ahead of us."

A young woman appeared, and the modiste said, "This is Giselle, my best assistant. Please come with us, Lady Ariadne. We will need to measure you before we begin discussing the designs for your gowns and the best fabrics to use."

They went to rooms in the back, where her measurements were taken and recorded, and then returned to the front of the store. Mama sat at a table, flipping through samples of cloth.

Ariadne and Madame Laurent joined her. The modiste picked up a sketchbook.

"What are you looking for in your gowns, Lady Ariadne?"

"I... have not really given it much thought, Madame. I was hoping you would advise me," she replied. "If it makes sense, I would like to feel pretty and yet comfortable. I know balls go on for many hours."

The modiste nodded as she began sketching. "We will have to be careful with the shades of your gowns because of your rich hair color. Copper can clash with many colors. We want your gowns to be in harmony with both your complexion and your hair."

Mama sighed. "It is their father's fault. All four of my children suffer from inheriting his red hair, which is so unfashionable."

Ariadne had worried about the shade of her hair, but the way Mama spoke, it would be troublesome. Her usual confidence now deflated.

"Are they all copper-headed?" Madame inquired.

"No. My two youngest girls, the twins, have strawberry blond and auburn hair. Fortunately, my son's hair is chestnut. It appears brown most of the time. It is only in strong light that the red tint is evident."

"Will this be a problem, Madame?" Ariadne asked, worrying her bottom lip.

"Bien sûr que non. You have a lovely figure, my lady. We will select the right shades for your gown, as well as flatter your frame. Leave everything to me and Her Grace."

Over the next two hours, the dressmaker sketched numerous gowns, with Mama giving her approval or turning down the design. The drawings went on and on, which puzzled Ariadne.

Finally, she asked, "How many gowns are to be made up for me this Season, Madame?"

When the modiste told her the number, Ariadne nearly fainted.

"Why so many?"

"Well, you will have the sixty or seventy ballgowns," Madame Laurent began. "Those are the most important. You will also need gowns for all the many parties. Garden and card parties.

Routs. Musicales. Venetian breakfasts. And then you must have appropriate gowns for morning calls." The woman smiled. "You are very pretty, my lady, and the gentlemen will fill your drawing room each afternoon."

"But . . . it is too many!" she proclaimed. "Why would I need sixty ballgowns?"

"For each ball?" Madame said, her brows knitting together as if she were confused.

"You mean I am to wear a different gown each time?" she squeaked.

"Of course, Ariadne," Mama said smoothly. "Why, you cannot be seen in the same gown twice during a Season! Think of all the harsh gossip that would occur. You are the daughter of a duke."

"It seems so wasteful," she said. "When I see the hungry children on the streets, barely clothed, I—"

"That is none of your concern," Mama said, cutting her off. "We have decided on the designs. Let us look at materials now, Madame Laurent."

Stunned at the sheer number of gowns that must be purchased, Ariadne sat, dumbfounded, as her mother and the modiste evaluated different materials, deciding which would be suitable for a particular gown. All the while, it almost made her nauseous, seeing the amount of money which would be spent on her wardrobe alone. To think, this would be happening all across town, with numerous girls of ranking peers making their come-outs.

"Mama, will you also have as many gowns made up as I will?" she asked at one point.

Her mother stared at her disapprovingly. When she spoke, her tone was frosty. "I am the Duchess of Millbrooke. I set the standard for Polite Society. Naturally, I will have a new wardrobe for the entire Season, the same as you, Ariadne. Now, you need to participate more. After all, this is your come-out. Have a care choosing some materials for yourself."

She did as requested, trying to put aside the picture in her mind of those hungry children, but the entire process had fallen flat for her now.

"We are off to a wonderful start," Mama declared. "You are to begin at once on my daughter's wardrobe, Madame. When may we expect the first batch of gowns to be finished?"

As her mother and the modiste talked about fittings and timelines, Ariadne wondered how she was going to enjoy this Season. She decided it would be the right thing to do, looking her best, because she wanted to attract a husband. He must be the right kind of husband, though. One who shared her concerns regarding the poor. She wanted to make her mark in the world and not simply be known for being pretty and fashionably dressed. She needed to make a difference and help others less fortunate than herself.

"Quit your woolgathering, Child," Mama chastised, bring Ariadne out of her reverie. "We are ready to leave."

"Thank you, Madame Laurent," she said earnestly. "I know you and Giselle will be working very hard on my behalf."

The modiste smiled warmly. "We will do our best to make you the best dressed girl of your come-out class, my lady."

They left the dress shop and entered the waiting carriage.

Immediately, Mama said, "There is no need to thank tradespeople, Ariadne. They are being paid quite well to do their jobs. Madame Laurent's is to provide you with a spectacular wardrobe. She is being amply compensated."

"Yes, Mama," she said meekly, thinking she shouldn't worry about the many gowns being sewn for her because it was the way Madame and Giselle earned their living. "Will you return to her shop for your own wardrobe needs?"

"I have an appointment with her the day after tomorrow," Mama replied. "I will have to think on your sisters' come-outs. Since there are the two of them next year, we might have to come to town earlier in order for Madame to have ample time to make up two come-out wardrobes." Her mother smiled. "Of course, you will be free to choose Madame Laurent or whomever you wish to design your wardrobe next Season, Ariadne. I am certain you will wed a generous husband, and he will wish to see you clothed in style."

It struck her anew that come this time next year, she very likely would be a married woman, no longer under her parents' roof. Why, she might even be with child.

"Do women who are . . . . increasing . . . attend the Season?" she asked.

"It depends how far along they are," Mama told her. "The style of gowns in fashion now allows women more time before they reveal their status. If they are not showing, many do come for the social events. As they grow larger and more tired, however, they stay home. Are you thinking of yourself?"

Heat filled her cheeks. "I suppose I am. If I am to be married, I will have children. Is that something a couple . . . plans?"

Mama snorted. "It simply happens."

"How?" she asked, wondering for the first time about the process.

This time, her mother's color rose high in her cheeks. "It is not something to discuss."

"Why not?" she pushed. "I should be prepared for what to do. How does it occur?"

Mama cleared her throat. "A man and woman . . . come together. The details are unimportant, Ariadne. Suffice it to say, your husband will know what to do and tell you what you are to do to please him. You will couple. A child is the result. Enough of that."

For the rest of the ride home, they did not speak. She couldn't tell if her mother were angry or embarrassed—or perhaps both. It did make her curious about how things worked between a husband and wife, however. Perhaps Val might tell her more and help her prepare for her wedding night and beyond.

They entered their townhouse, handing off their cloaks to Parsons.

"Tell Cook we are famished," her mother told the butler.

"You are to have a guest for tea this afternoon, Your Grace," Parsons informed his employer.

"A guest? I invited no guest."

"I did, Mama," Val said, coming down the stairs. "I had an opportunity to meet our neighbor, Lord Aldridge."

"Aldridge?" Mama said. "Oh, the new one, I suppose. What is he like?"

"You can judge for yourself when he comes to tea," Val said airily.

Mama glanced to her. "You must change, Ariadne. Wear the green gown you favor."

"Why, Mama?"

Looking exasperated, Mama said, "Aldridge is a marquess and quite wealthy."

The reply stunned her. "You are thinking of him as a suitor for me?"

"He is a marquess," Mama said dismissively. "Of course, he will be considered a suitor. It will be good for you to meet him before the Season begins. I must change myself. Where is His Grace, Parsons?"

"In his study, Your Grace," the butler said.

"Get him to tea on time," Mama commanded.

"Certainly, Your Grace," Parsons said.

Mama left them, and Val said, "You had better go change, Ariadne."

"I like what I am wearing," she protested.

"You do not want Mama upset with you."

"All right," she said, admitting defeat. "But how was Lord Aldridge? What did you think of him?"

"Actually, we got along splendidly," her brother said. "We had a decent conversation about his country estate and shared ideas about farming and livestock."

"I am glad to hear it. And happy you invited him to tea, Val. But Mama is wrong. He will not be a suitor to me. He does not like me."

"You cannot know that for certain."

"He was quite dismissive of me yesterday."

Val grinned. "Yet you wanted him to make friends with me."

She shrugged. "He seemed in need of a friend."

"Perhaps you, too, can become his friend, Sis."

Being friends with a gentleman was a foreign concept to her. "Do you have friends who are female?" she asked.

He chuckled. "I am not going to answer that question, Ariadne. Go change," he urged.

She went to her bedchamber and rang for Tally, asking her maid for the green gown which went so well with her hair. Once she wore it, Tally checked Ariadne's hair and repinned a portion of it.

"You're fit as a fiddle, my lady. Have a lovely tea."

Ariadne made her way to the drawing room, aware she was breathing more rapidly and her heart raced. Surely, it couldn't be because of their guest?

Yet when Lord Aldridge entered the drawing room five minutes later, she realized he was exactly the reason she was both excited and on edge.

CHAPTER FIVE

JULIAN PACED IN his study, awaiting four o'clock, full of nervous energy. He had been delighted Lord Claibourne had invited him to tea, but now that reality approached, he wasn't sure of himself at all. He had never been in the presence of a duke and duchess. This would be his first exposure to one of the handful of couples who held those lofty titles.

He plopped into a chair, telling himself he was as good as any duke, but failed to convince himself. The fact was, he was a laboring man and had the calluses to prove it. Yes, his mother had insisted upon him getting a bit of education, so he was able to read and write. It had come in handy when he had taken over Aldridge Manor and talked with his steward regarding the estate records. At least knowing how to read and write and do maths, he could not be cheated.

But entering Polite Society and being around distinguished, titled, well-educated gentlemen caused him to be wary. His gut—which he had always trusted—told him Lord Claibourne was a rare man. His openness and generosity to Julian would not likely be the case with others he met. Hopefully, Claibourne's parents wouldn't press Julian overmuch about his background.

He did look forward to seeing Lady Ariadne again. She intrigued him, from her copper-colored hair to her frankness of speech. He also believed she was unlike many of the *ton* beauties. He hoped she would form a second, better impression of him this afternoon.

A knock sounded at the door, and he called out, "Come."

Grigsby entered. "You wished to be made aware of the time, my lord. It is five minutes until four o'clock."

"Yes. Thank you," he said, rising and collecting the walking cane and hat his butler offered.

As he went out his townhouse's front door and moved along the pavement, he hoped he wasn't making some error by not having his carriage deliver him the short distance. It seemed a waste to have the team saddled when he could walk to his destination in under two minutes.

Julian knocked at the door, which was immediately answered by the butler.

"Good afternoon, Lord Aldridge. Their Graces are expecting you. Might I take your hat and cane?"

He handed them over, and the butler passed them along to a footman.

"If you would follow me, my lord," the butler said, moving toward the staircase.

Trying not to look around but doing so all the same, he took in the furniture and paintings, all of which seemed even more luxurious than the ones in his townhouse. Naturally, a duke would have the best of everything.

"One moment, my lord," the butler said, holding a hand out slightly, stopping Julian's forward progress before opening the door to the drawing room and stepping inside. He realized the servant would announce him and thought how much he had to learn. Then he began to panic, thinking he had no idea how to greet a duke and duchess, but it was too late.

"Lord Aldridge, Your Graces," the servant's voice rang out.

Thankful the servant had kept him from barreling into the room, he thought to act—and react—in a calm fashion to prevent a future mistake such as this. He would try and take his cues from Lord Claibourne.

Crossing the enormous drawing room, he saw its four occupants rise as one to greet him. The older couple had to be Their Graces. He kept his eyes on them, knowing in the pecking order, they would always come first.

Lord Claibourne stepped in to make the introductions. "Mama, Papa, this is our new neighbor, Lord Aldridge. My lord, my parents, the Duke and Duchess of Millbrooke."

Lady Ariadne had stepped slightly behind her father, out of the line of vision of her parents' eyes. She made a bowing motion, and he quickly imitated her.

After he did so, the duke offered his hand, so Julian took it, shaking it firmly. "Ah, good to meet you, Aldridge. I knew the previous marquess. This is my wife."

Not knowing if he should shake the duchess' hand when she offered it, he again glanced slightly to Lady Ariadne. She lifted her hand to her mouth and kissed it, cluing him in on what to do next.

Taking the duchess' hand, he raised it to his lips. "A pleasure to meet you, Your Grace."

Lord Claibourne held out a hand, indicating his sister, who had quietly slid back into place beside her father. "And this is my younger sister, the eldest of my three sisters. Lady Ariadne Worthington. Lord Aldridge, Sis."

She held up her hand to him, mischief dancing in her eyes. "My lord," she said, her voice low.

Once more, he took the hand, bringing it to his lips. Where he had bent over the hand of the mother, barely making contact with her knuckles, this time he pressed his lips to the fingers of the daughter. Instantly, he felt a jolt rush through him at the contact, the same as before when he had taken her hand yesterday.

"Lady Ariadne," he said, their gazes meeting.

She tugged slightly, and he realized he still held her hand. Releasing it, he said, "It is a pleasure to meet you all. Lord Claibourne was kind enough to extend an invitation to me to take tea with you this afternoon after we met at White's. I am delighted to become acquainted with my neighbors in town."

Julian was selecting his words carefully, especially after Claibourne's suggestion regarding word choice. Usually, he would have said it was nice to meet you. Instead, he mustered the most formal attitude, posture, and language he possessed.

"Do have a seat, my lord," the duchess said, indicating a settee.

Lady Ariadne settled herself onto it, and he took his place beside her. Immediately, he caught the faint scent of vanilla, causing his skin to tingle.

The butler appeared again, supervising two maids who rolled in a teacart. The duchess filled a teacup, asking, "How do you take your tea, my lord?"

"Two sugars, Your Grace. And a bit of cream."

He kept to himself that he'd always drunk his coffee black and his tea plain until he came into his title. He and his mother hadn't been able to afford such luxuries as sugar. Now that he could, Julian had found he had a bit of a sweet tooth.

She added those to his cup and passed the saucer to him. He sat motionless, watching her provide tea to everyone else. When Claibourne took a sip, Julian figured it was fine for him to do so, as well.

"Shall I fix a plate for you, Lord Aldridge?" Lady Ariadne asked. "Our cook is quite talented."

He looked at her, seeing she nodded imperceptibly at him. "Yes, my lady. I would appreciate you doing so."

He watched her choose a couple of sandwiches, a teacake, and a scone. All looked mouthwatering. She passed the plate to him, and he thanked her, knowing if he would have chosen, his plate would have been much fuller. He would need to practice restraint in everything he did and said.

The talk seemed boring to him after that. The duke and duchess dominated it, saying much but not really saying anything at all. He suspected this was a preview of what future conversations with his peers would be like. Their Graces mentioned the weather. The flowers which would bloom come spring. Social affairs which would be held. He recognized none of the names they dropped and figured he wasn't supposed to contribute to this conversation. It was as if he were a child and should not speak unless spoken to. Right now, they spoke at him.

Fortunately, Claibourne spoke up when his parents seemed to wind down. They picked up their previous conversation, discussing Julian's estate and those of the duke's. It was refreshing to be able to contribute something.

Then he realized Lady Ariadne had been totally left out and turned to her, asking, "Do you enjoy the country or city, my lady?"

She gave him a warm smile. "I have truly only known the country, Lord Aldridge, having only been to town one other time, many years ago."

He frowned. "You stayed at home during the Season?"

"Why, yes. I was not old enough to attend and be presented. Where else would I be?"

Julian bit his tongue, but what he wanted to say was she should have been with her parents. How cruel they were to leave her and her siblings behind each year while they came to London and cavorted for months on end.

"I am hoping to get to know more of town, however," she continued. "I enjoy walking, and London does have an abundance of parks."

"Oh, you will ride through Hyde Park with your suitors, Ariadne," the duchess insisted. "Five o'clock is the fashionable hour when gentlemen drive through with the lady whom they are interested in."

"While I do like to ride in an open vehicle, Mama, I will also want to walk some. I want to get to know the city. See some of the museums and bookshops. I also might want to volunteer some of my time."

"Doing what?" the duke growled, biting into a sandwich.

He saw determination cross her face. "I have witnessed many

of the poor in the streets, Papa. I would like to do something to help tend to their needs, much as we do our tenants at Millvale."

"That is totally unacceptable, Ariadne," her father said, his tone voicing his disapproval.

"You will not have time for charitable doings," the duchess added. "Why, the Season will take up all your time. You will barely have a moment to write a letter to your sisters, much less traipse about the meaner parts of town."

"But I—"

"Enough!" the duke boomed. "Listen to your mother, child."

"I am not a child, Papa," she said stubbornly, earning Julian's respect. He doubted the duke ever had anyone talk back to him, much less his eldest daughter.

"You are a child because I say you are," His Grace said dismissively. "As you are under my roof and my responsibility, I will tell you now that there will be no going to questionable areas of town. No giving away coin to the poor. You are here to find a husband, Ariadne. When you do, you may tend to *his* tenants."

Julian saw the fire spark in her eyes and admired her spirit. He also respected that she did not continue to push her father, especially in front of company.

"Yes, Papa," she said, though he heard the edge to her voice.

"You know, you might wish to look at our conservatory, Aldridge," Claibourne said, out of the blue. "You mentioned wanting to make a few improvements to your own. Ariadne, would you take Lord Aldridge to our conservatory and show him about?"

He had never spoken of a conservatory to the marquess, but he saw the man was trying to give his sister a place to go and cool off.

Rising, Lady Ariadne said, "I would be happy to show it to you, my lord."

He sprang to his feet. "That would be delightful."

And he meant it.

"If you will excuse us, Mama, Papa," Lady Ariadne said.

The duchess waved a hand vaguely. The duke sat looking disgruntled, reaching for another sweet. As they left the room, he heard Claibourne speaking, smoothing things over.

In the corridor, Lady Ariadne said, "Are you truly interested in our conservatory? You do realize Val was trying to separate me from our parents so that my temper might cool."

"I would be happy to see it, my lady."

She sighed. "All right."

They went downstairs again. He walked beside her, not trying to engage her in conversation. When they arrived, she entered and he followed, immediately feeling the warm, moist air.

Leading him about, she showed him various plants and flowers, speaking knowledgeably of them.

"Do you have any questions?" she asked when they finished their tour.

"None. But if I do, I will know whom to ask in the future."

She blushed. "I am not an expert. Val just sent us here to keep me from causing a scene in front of a guest."

"Your brother is perceptive."

"I am *not* a child," she reiterated. "If I am old enough to wed, I am old enough to express my opinions. My father simply does not believe women should hold any. As a duke, he is never challenged."

"I gathered as much." He cleared his throat. "I am glad we are alone, however, because I wish to apologize to you, my lady."

She frowned. "Whatever for?"

"My rudeness in the park yesterday. I fear I made a terrible impression upon you. I was out of sorts. The park has come to be a place I can get away from everyone and simply be."

"I understand that." She grinned. "I have been known to be disagreeable myself on occasion."

"I also want to express my gratitude for today when I first arrived."

She looked blankly at him, and then nodded. "Oh, you mean

the introductions."

"I had no idea how to greet your parents. They are the first people from Polite Society I have met, besides you and your brother. You saved me from a great embarrassment."

"I was happy to come to your aid," she replied. "Might I ask where you lived and what you did before you came into your title? Most well-bred people would never ask you this, but I must admit I am curious."

Julian hesitated a moment. "Would you promise this goes no further than between the two of us?"

"If you think I would share a confidence with my parents, I would never do such a thing." She hesitated. "But keeping something from Val does not sit right with me, my lord."

He considered her words and made a decision, one with his gut which he hoped he would not regret. "I promise I will speak to him about my background. I sense your brother is not a typical member of the *ton* and that he will judge me for who I am, and not where I came from or the title I now hold."

Lady Ariadne nodded in agreement. "Val is the most fair-minded person I know. All right, my lord, I will keep what is said between us. Only if you tell Val, as well."

"I have lived in London all my life," he told her. "I shared a room with my mother, who passed away last summer. I have a bit of education, but I have spent my life—until now—at hard labor, earning my living."

Raising his hands, palms facing up, Julian showed her his calluses. She took one of his hands in hers, holding it steady, as the fingertips of her other hand danced lightly across those calluses.

It made his head spin.

Dropping his hand, she said, "There is no shame in having worked for a living, but I believe you should keep this to yourself, my lord. Those you will meet during the Season will not be openminded." She paused. "Might I ask how you even became a marquess?"

"I never knew who my father was," he told her. "My mother never mentioned him, and I knew well enough to leave it alone. I did know she was the daughter of a skilled tailor who made clothing for gentlemen of the *ton*. When she found herself... with child, her family turned her out."

Lady Ariadne gasped. "How cruel!"

"It is not unusual to do so. She raised me alone. We had very little. Barely enough food to eat, and we lacked many things you would take for granted. When she died, I found a few letters to her." He paused. "Letters from my father."

Immediately, her eyes lit up. "*He* was Lord Aldridge."

This woman was perceptive.

"Yes," Julian confided. "Though he wasn't the marquess when they knew one another. To make a long story short, he wed her. Gave her a small sum, and then left on what he wrote of as his Grand Tour."

"Ah, those used to be popular," she said. "Before the war with Bonaparte began. Young men would go, often with their tutors, and see the Continent for a few years."

"Yes, that is what his letter revealed. He knew his parents would never accept her, so he left London for the Continent and cut her from his life."

"So, you never saw him. Never heard from him."

"I have no evidence of any contact between them after his departure. I would have been born several months later. Mother was a seamstress, having learned from her own father. I started working when I was young. Cleaning chimneys. Selling newspapers. When I grew into my full height and size, I found work in the warehouses and on the London docks."

"No wonder you are so muscular," she said, her cheeks slowly reddening as she realized what she had said.

Though he was secretly pleased at her compliment, Julian politely ignored it. "He married her, you know. I found their marriage certificate, along with the letters. Proof of the marriage was found in the parish registry. I had the help of a solicitor I worked for and—"

"I thought you did physical labor."

"I did. I also took on a night job as a clerk to a solicitor. He was ready to offer me regular employment when I shared with him what I had found. Needless to say, the old marquess was on his deathbed by the time we confronted him. He admitted everything, with his solicitor and butler as witnesses, and claimed me as his heir."

"And here I am."

"That is fascinating," she said. "No wonder everything seems so strange to you."

"It has taken all these months, since last summer, for me to get used to owning a large estate and having servants wait upon me. Coming to London, however, has truly been strange."

"Why do you want to partake in the Season?" she asked, clearly curious.

"For the same reason as you, my lady. I wish to find a wife. The man who sired me had three of them, all of them barren. I do not take any of my responsibilities lightly. I know I must provide an heir, so I will do so as soon as possible."

"Will you tell your wife all this, my lord?"

"I don't know," he said honestly. "If I do, I doubt any lady in Polite Society would have me. I especially can't tell her parents."

"But you told me," she said softly. She reached and took his hand, squeezing it. "Thank you for sharing your story with me, my lord. Thank you for trusting me."

Lady Ariadne released it, and Julian felt bereft.

"I will never tell a soul," she promised him. "You can count on my discretion. And do not underestimate yourself. You are a very handsome man. You speak and carry yourself well. You hold a lofty title, and I assume you have a decent amount of wealth. You will have no trouble finding a bride on the Marriage Mart."

Julian looked at the young woman before him. She had poise. Charm. Spirit. And she was quite beautiful, especially with her copper hair.

He wasn't ready to speak openly to her yet, but he had already made up his mind.

Lady Ariadne was the one for him. No other would do as his marchioness.

CHAPTER SIX

ARIADNE JOINED HER brother for breakfast the next morning and said, "Will you take me to the park this morning?"

"I'd be happy to, Sis. Would you prefer walking or riding?"

She considered his question a moment and then said, "I wish to walk Hyde Park this first time. I would like to see how close we are to it."

"Not far at all," he told her. "I think you will enjoy it. The park is quite large."

She had Tally bring her a spencer and bonnet, and they set out from the townhouse. Just as they were about to leave the square, a hansom cab turned the corner and came to an abrupt halt. From it leaped a nice-looking man in his mid-twenties, and Val called, "Con!"

So, this was her cousin Constantine, Aunt Charlotte's and Uncle Arthur's eldest child.

He paid the driver and then came to greet them. Smiling at her, he said, "You must be Ariadne. I remember your vivid hair color more than you. It has been much too long since we saw one another."

"I have been jealous all these years, with Val getting to be friends with you and see you at school. It is good to finally be with you again, Con. If I may call you that."

"Please do. Mama insists on calling me Constantine, which I loathe. Papa calls me Dyer. I prefer Con."

Ariadne laughed. "We were about to go walk in Hyde Park. Would you care to join us?"

"I am happy to do so," Con replied, falling into step on her other side as they continued heading toward the park.

"Did Aunt Charlotte and Uncle Arthur come with you to town?" asked Val.

Their cousin chuckled. "Mama and Papa have had one of their usual falling-outs."

"Oh, no!" she said.

Con laughed. "It is nothing, Ariadne. This happens with great regularity. My parents argue over the smallest of things and won't speak to each for days. Even weeks. It is always over trivial matters. Mama asked for me to escort her to town early because of the tension between them, and I was only too happy to honor her request."

"Will Uncle Arthur follow?" she asked.

Her cousin shrugged. "Perhaps. Papa has never been one who enjoyed the Season or sitting in the House of Lords. I suppose he will find his way here sooner or later, but Mama is always eager to come to town and be with her friends."

"Then you and Aunt Charlotte must come for tea this afternoon," she told him. "I would love to talk with her."

"She will like that."

They entered Hyde Park, and Ariadne fell silent, content to walk in nature and listen to the conversation between Val and Con. They talked about friends from school and told her a few stories about the mischief they had gotten into during their days at Eton.

"You sound like two rascals," she declared. "Hopefully, you acted in a more mature fashion while at university."

The two men looked at one another and then burst out laughing, causing her to do the same.

"I am certain you have more stories you can entertain me with about your days at Oxford."

"We could," Con said, "but they would not be fit for your

delicate ears."

"Why does everyone insist upon treating me as a child?" she asked testily.

Val looked to his cousin. "Ariadne expressed a strong opinion yesterday, and Papa put her in her place. His Grace is like most men of Polite Society, Sis. Papa believes women only have one purpose, and that is to provide heirs and spares to their husbands."

"I am more than a brood mare," she said grumpily.

"I like that you are opinionated and spirited, Cousin Ariadne," Con told her. "It will take a special gentleman to wed you. Unfortunately, most bachelors of the *ton* hold the same beliefs as Uncle Charles."

"I have told my sister that you and I will scrutinize—even investigate—any gentlemen who wish to court her."

Con smiled. "Between the two of us, we will make certain the match you make is a good one."

Quietly, she said, "My greatest fear is that Papa will take it upon himself to decide who my husband should be, and that gentleman will be cut from the same cloth. Being the first woman to wed in our family, I do not know exactly what to expect. I also want to smooth the way for Lia and Tia."

"Mama will be easy," Val told her. "She will be looking for you to wed a man with the highest rank. Money will come next in her consideration. Looks and character would not be something she would ever consider."

"You are right," she agreed. "Mama can be quite shallow in that regard. But what of Papa?"

"He is a duke," Con pointed out. "A duke's daughter cannot wed simply anyone, Ariadne. Uncle Charles, too, will also be interested in your potential husband's title and wealth."

She looked to her brother. "Do you think I will be given any choice in the matter? I worry that Papa will wish to be rid of me quickly since I am opinionated and marry me off to someone controlling and domineering. Or worse, someone ancient. I have heard that happens more often than not."

"I will not let that happen to you, Sis," Val vowed. "I have Papa's ear. He confides in me since I am his heir, and he is also willing to listen to my opinions. I will protect you the best I can."

"Thank you," she said fervently. "I am fortunate to have you—and Con—looking out for my interests. I know not every girl making her come-out shares my circumstances."

Looking to Con, she asked, "Are you interested in the Marriage Mart? Val does not seem to be in the least."

Her cousin laughed. "Val and I are only four and twenty, Ariadne. There is no societal pressure on us to wed anytime soon, especially because we merely hold our fathers' courtesy titles now. We will be much more appealing to anxious mamas seeking husbands for their husbands once we come into our own titles and wealth."

She couldn't help but pout. "At four and twenty, I would be considered long on the shelf if I were not wed. It does not seem fair how men and women are treated in such a different manner in Polite Society."

"We will help you make the best match possible," Val promised. "We will look into all the men interested in you. Actually, only those you are interested in instead. That will be a much smaller group."

Con asked, "Are you interested in making a love match?"

"I do not expect to make a love match. None of our parents did so. All I ask is that my husband is considerate and respectful of me. It would be nice if he could pay more attention to his children than our parents have to us, Val."

"You have high expectations, Ariadne," Con told her. "Val and I will do our best to see you taken care of, however."

She already liked this cousin of hers a great deal and understood why Val trusted Con so much.

They returned to the townhouse, Con promising he would bring his mother to tea with him this afternoon.

Val said, "I was going to head to White's now. Do you wish

to accompany me?"

"Yes. It would be good see who is already in town. Until later, Cousin," Con said, taking Ariadne's hand and kissing it.

She went inside and informed Parsons that they would be entertaining her aunt and cousin at tea.

JULIAN SAT AT his desk, having already breakfasted and gone through the morning's post. He was thinking of going to White's again this morning. Lord Claibourne had told him most gentlemen went to their club at least once a day. With no social events to attend and no estate matters to handle, Julian was already growing bored in London. He had only come at the urging of his valet to see his tailor in order to be fitted for a new wardrobe. He was toying with the idea of returning to Aldridge Manor now the fittings had taken place, until it was closer to the beginning of the Season.

For now, though, he decided he would go to White's. Claibourne might be there, and he would enjoy talking with the marquess again.

He asked for his carriage to be readied and half an hour later, he approached the door to White's. There, he was warmly greeted by Pollard and told that once he took a seat, his coffee and newspapers would be brought to him.

As he walked through the ground floor rooms, he spied Claibourne sitting with another man close to the same age. As Julian wondered if he should approach them uninvited, Claibourne saw him and waved him over.

"Aldridge, it is good to see you again. May I introduce to you my cousin, Viscount Dyer? Con, this is our neighbor in town, Lord Aldridge. He inherited the marquessate last summer."

Viscount Dyer offered his hand. "It is an honor to meet you, my lord."

Shaking the offered hand, Julian said, "Likewise, my lord."

"Won't you join us?" Claibourne asked, and Julian took a seat with the pair.

"I do not recall Lord Aldridge having any offspring," Viscount Dyer remarked.

"Yes, he wed multiple times and remained childless," he replied. "I am a distant relative of his."

Julian once again used the story he had planned to share with others, but he immediately felt guilty since he had promised to share his background with Lord Claibourne.

"Aldridge has a country estate in Surrey," Claibourne said. "Tell my cousin about your property."

As Julian spoke, coffee and newspapers were delivered to him, the coffee doctored exactly as he liked. It amazed him how such small details were adhered to by those who served titled peers.

The three men spent a pleasant hour talking about the land and a few issues coming up in the House of Lords. Dyer asked who Julian's tailor was, and he shared the name, saying he was waiting for his wardrobe to be made up.

"I have been a bit bored, though, being in town," he admitted. "I prefer the country," he revealed, surprised that he truly felt that way, wondering if after this Season he would ever be interested in returning to London again.

"I feel the same," Claibourne said. "Of course, I come to town for the Season each year. Some of the events can be amusing, and the company can range from dull to delightful."

"Are either of you ready to take a wife?" Julian asked.

Both men laughed aloud, and Dyer said, "Not in the slightest, Aldridge. We are still sowing our wild oats. We hold courtesy titles from our fathers and are given quarterly allowances by them. Some bachelors in the same position take rooms of their own here in town, but my cousin and I prefer to save our coin and live in our families' townhouses during the Season. I doubt either of us will consider marriage until we come into our own titles and have full control of our estates and holdings."

Claibourne said, "You are in a much different position than the two of us, my lord. I assume you will be on the hunt for your marchioness this Season."

Carefully, Julian said, "I have considered doing so," knowing he was interested in Claibourne's sister, but not ready to reveal that to anyone just yet.

"With Ariadne making her come-out this Season, she will get to know many of the other girls doing so," Claibourne continued. "My sister is an excellent judge of character. If there are any particular ladies you are interested in, simply ask Ariadne's opinion of them. She would freely share it. She might even help you in finding a wife."

From Claibourne's words, Julian took to understand that the marquess did not consider him a candidate for his sister's hand, which disappointed him. While he already respected him, Julian determined to prove to Claibourne and his parents that he would make a good husband for Lady Ariadne.

Viscount Dyer said, "You must not discount Aldridge here, Val. Why, he might be interested in Ariadne."

Claibourne studied him a moment. "Yes. I could see the possibility of that match."

Hope sprang within him. "Lady Ariadne is a lovely woman," he praised. "She seems to have not only beauty, but also a kind heart."

"You will need to meet the other girls who are making their come-outs," Claibourne said, his gaze boring into Julian now. "And I would need to know you much better before I would consider you courting my beloved sister."

Again he recalled his promise to Lady Ariadne yesterday. Julian had told her he would tell her brother of his humble beginnings.

"I spoke to Lady Ariadne about my background in the conservatory," he began. "Her concern was that I share it with you. She told me that you were a man of honor and that whatever I said to you would go no further." He looked to Viscount Dyer.

"The two of you seem quite close."

Lord Dyer nodded. "We are not only cousins, but also the closest of friends. I, too, am honorable. If you have something to share, it will stay between the three of us. That I can promise you."

Since they were in a far corner and no one could overhear their conversation, Julian decided to bare his soul. He shared the same details he had discussed with Lady Ariadne, with no interruptions from either of his companions.

He finished by saying, "Lady Ariadne told me you were a fair-minded man, Claibourne. I do hope you and Lord Dyer will keep to yourselves all that I have discussed with you."

The marquess looked at him in approval. "You may have humble beginnings, Aldridge, but your father was a marquess. You are now the same, despite the circumstances in which you grew up. I am a decent judge of character, as is my cousin, and I find you to be a good man. An honest one. You could have kept your past a secret from us, and no one would have been the wiser. I admire you for your openness."

"This will go no further," Lord Dyer promised. "No one need know how you came into your title. Your parents were legally wed, and you are the rightful heir. You have a wonderful opportunity, Aldridge. Not many men have a second chance in life to remake themselves."

"I plan to do good with my wealth," he told the pair. "I never dreamed of being in such a position, and I am grateful for it, but I will help the less fortunate."

How Julian would do so would take some thought, however. The sheer number of those who needed assistance was overwhelming. After all, he had been one of those in need not that long ago. While he could use his position in the House of Lords to possibly address some issues, he knew pressing needs such as food and clothing should take precedence.

"Then you will make for an excellent peer and addition to Polite Society," Claibourne declared. He smiled at Julian. "I think the three of us are going to be very good friends, my lord."

Chapter Seven

After her walk with Val and Con, Ariadne spent the rest of her day at the milliner's shop. Once again, she was appalled at the number of hats and bonnets which were selected, thinking how many hungry children could be fed with the money being spent to make her look fashionable. While there, Mama had also selected numerous pairs of gloves for her daughter.

"A lady simply can never have enough pairs of gloves," Mama declared.

She was glad all the shopping for that was done, but Mama had said they would also be purchasing slippers. Ariadne could only guess at the number of pairs she would need to be suitably dressed for her come-out. At least that wouldn't happen for a few days. For now, she was looking forward to seeing Aunt Charlotte again at tea today.

Entering the drawing room, she found her parents and Val already present.

"Did you enjoy spending time with Con at White's?" she asked her brother.

"I did. We also saw Lord Aldridge while we were there."

Ariadne's heart skipped a beat hearing his name. She didn't understand why.

And was afraid to think on it.

"I asked Aldridge to tea again today, Mama," Val added, smiling at his mother. "He got on so well with Con. I knew you would not mind."

Mama smiled indulgently at her son, and Ariadne shook her head. Her brother was Mama's obvious favorite, and Val could do no wrong in her eyes. If she didn't love Val so much, she would resent him. It didn't seem fair that he was so cherished simply because he was a man, while she and her sisters barely received any attention at all from their parents because they were women.

"If you wish for Lord Aldridge to come to tea, we are happy to host him," Mama said airily.

Parsons appeared. "Lady Marley, Viscount Dyer, and Lord Aldridge are here, Your Graces."

"Do show them in," the duke said, rubbing his hands together eagerly.

Ariadne knew Papa and his sister had been quite close as children. She assumed they saw one another regularly during the Season each year.

The trio entered the drawing room, and they all stood to greet them. Her eyes went straight to her aunt, who looked the same to Ariadne.

"Charlotte!" cried Papa. "It is ever so good to see you."

Greetings were exchanged, and her aunt looked closely at Ariadne. "You have grown into a lovely young lady, Niece. It is too bad you have inherited your papa's hair color, though."

Again, a mention of her hair. She had known red hair was unusual. None of their servants nor anyone in their village had red in their hair, but she didn't know it would be such a detriment as she was introduced into Polite Society. She was certainly more than the shade of her hair, yet Ariadne worried now that her copper hair was all others would see instead of who she truly was.

"Ariadne will still attract a good husband," Mama assured her sister-in-law. "Why, she is fair of face and has a lovely figure."

Aunt Charlotte pursed her lips. "True. It is unfortunate, though, that she cannot wear a wig."

"Is red truly that unfashionable, aunt?" she asked, thinking of her siblings and the varying shades of red hair they all possessed.

"All of us have varying shades of it."

"You are the children of a duke," her aunt said. "In the end, *that* is what will matter."

She felt unsure, worried now about her come-out in a way she hadn't before. All she had focused on was meeting new people and the fun she would have, participating in all the social events. Ariadne had not thought she would be judged harshly merely because of the color of her hair.

"Have a seat," Papa said. "Come sit with me, Charlotte."

Two teacarts were rolled into the drawing room, and Mama and Aunt Charlotte both poured since there were so many of them. Ariadne sat next to Con, with Lord Aldridge on her left and Val on Con's right. Papa and Aunt Charlotte dominated the conversation, and she was beginning to think she would not be fond of her aunt.

"She is a bit much," Con said quietly of his mother. "When the two of them are together, they seem to forget about everyone else."

Aunt Charlotte did ask a few questions of Lord Aldridge, including asking him if he were considering finding a wife this Season.

"Yes, my lady," the marquess said, causing a chill to run through Ariadne. "Since the previous marquess had no children of his own, I feel it is my duty to take a wife as soon as I can and provide an heir."

"A wise choice, my lord," Aunt Charlotte declared.

Her father and aunt dominated conversation for the rest of tea, and Ariadne wished she could spend more time talking with her cousin and Lord Aldridge. She glanced to Val, who knew how to effortlessly change the direction of any situation.

"Papa? If you don't mind, I think we younger people are going to stretch our legs."

"Go ahead," the duke said before looking to his sister. "You will stay for dinner, Charlotte?"

"Of course, Millbrooke."

Val rose and bent to kiss Aunt Charlotte's cheek. "We will see you later then," he promised.

They escaped the drawing room, and she stopped a passing maid, asking for her to retrieve the blue velvet spencer and a bonnet for their walk.

"We do not have to go walking, Sis," Val told her as the maid scurried away. "If we like, we can go hide in the library."

"No, a walk sounds good to me," she replied, looking at their guests. "That is, if Lord Aldridge and Cousin Con care to do so."

"After listening to Mama go on and on, I am more than happy to be outdoors," Con said. "Aldridge?"

"I enjoy walking," the marquess said.

They went to the foyer, where the men received their hats and walking canes and Tally helped Ariadne into her spencer. She tied the ribbons of her bonnet, and they were off.

Her brother and cousin were deep in conversation by then, so she fell back. Lord Aldridge offered her his arm, and she slipped her hand through the crook of it. He felt warm and smelled of a wonderful cologne that reminded her of being deep in the woods.

"Your cousin is very nice," the marquess said.

"I think so, too. I have only met him once before today, but I truly like him."

"Your families are not close? It seems His Grace and Lady Marley certainly are."

"I have heard Papa say they were thick as thieves growing up, along with their cousin, my uncle George. He is deceased now. The adults all see one another each year when they came to town for the Season. We cousins were only brought together once. It has been at least ten years ago or more, for Uncle George was alive then."

She chuckled. "That was when we all discovered why we have such unusual names."

He looked intrigued. "How so?"

"Apparently, Papa and Aunt Charlotte were fascinated by Roman and Byzantine history. They brought Uncle George into it, and they would pretend to be various emperors and empresses during play. They all decided when they had children, they would name their offspring after these people in history whom they adored."

Lord Aldridge nodded thoughtfully. "I confess I had never heard the name Ariadne before. I assume Val and Con are diminutive forms of rather fancier names."

"Yes. Val is Valentinian, while Con is actually Constantine. My twin sisters are Cornelia, who goes by Lia, while Thermantia is known as Tia."

He laughed. "That last one is a mouthful. No wonder she prefers Lady Tia."

"My other cousins also have nicknames. Con's sisters Lucilla and Livia Drusilla are called Lucy and Dru. Uncle George's daughters have done what I have and kept their given names of Verina and Justina, while his eldest, Hadrian, is now known as Tray since he is the Earl of Traywick."

"Did I count ten cousins in all?" Lord Aldridge asked.

"Yes, there are ten of us. I am hoping as more of us turn older, we will be in town each year for the Season and get to know one another better. Papa always claimed it was too far for us to visit family or for them to visit us. He despises time spent in a carriage and is forever lamenting about England's muddy, slow roads. Con's family lives in the west, in Somerset. Uncle George lived in the Lake District in the northwest of England, but he came to Millvale, the ducal estate, summers, while his parents were in town. That is why he knew Papa and Aunt Chalotte so well."

"I wonder what it would be like to be from such a large family," mused the marquess.

"Do you truly have no one since your mother passed on?"

"I suppose there is her family. The ones who tossed her aside when they learned she was expecting a child out of wedlock. Because of their cruelty, I would never wish to meet any of them, much less claim them as kin. And my birth father wed three times, outliving each wife. They had no children of their own. It is only me."

"Would you want a large family because you have been so alone, my lord?"

He grew thoughtful. "I have yet to contemplate it, but I must say I am a bit envious of your large family, my lady. I can only wonder about having so many brothers and sisters, much less all those cousins."

She smiled. "I highly recommend having a large family. "I was so happy to have Val and my sisters while I was growing up. I believe we will remain close, no matter whom we choose as spouses or where we might live in the future. For me, that is what the Season will be like in the years to come. Time to see my family and all my nieces and nephews and dote on them. The four of us made a pact long ago. We decided we would never leave our children in the country for months and months. We will bring them to town with us at the start of each Season. If later they wish to go home for some of the summer, they can do so, but I think it is a terrible idea to separate families."

"Are you close to your parents?" he asked.

Ariadne sighed. "I would like to tell you otherwise, but no, they are merely my parents. I do not feel for them what I feel for my siblings. I love Val and the twins. Mama and Papa? I am respectful to them, but I feel no true bond with them. They both adore Val, naturally, because he is the heir. Val is good-natured and does not act spoiled in the slightest, but even he realizes the favoritism shown him."

"Because he is the heir," Lord Aldridge said flatly.

"Yes. He is who is important. Girls are to be married off and in my parents' case, most likely forgotten." She grinned. "I can imagine two decades from now entering a ballroom and speaking to my mother—and her not having a clue who I am."

"What of her grandchildren? Would she not be interested in them?"

Shrugging, Ariadne said, "Possibly if I birth any boys. Mama is a bit selfish. Her world revolves around her friends and clothes."

The marquess halted in his tracks. His gaze bored into her, as if he could see down to her very soul. "You want a different life, don't you, my lady?"

"I do," she said quietly. "I want to see my children daily. Talk and play with them. I want my husband to do the same. I also want to do more than simply bear children and wear pretty gowns. I want to make a difference. How, I am not certain of yet, but I will discover what I am meant to do—and do it rather well."

Lord Aldridge smiled at her, causing Ariadne's belly to flood with butterflies flapping their wings. He had a very nice smile, one which drew a person in, ready to share confidences.

"I have every confidence you will find your chosen path, Lady Ariadne," he told her.

They gazed at one another, neither moving, until Val called, "We should head home. It looks as if a storm is brewing."

Reluctantly, she turned her gaze to the heavens, seeing the darkening clouds.

The four of them walked briskly back to the square. As they reached the ducal townhouse, a footman came dashing toward Lord Aldridge.

"My lord, a messenger just arrived from Aldridge Manor. Your steward has died suddenly, and you are requested to return to the country at once."

Chapter Eight

Shock reverberated through Julian. Mr. Smith had served the previous Marquess of Aldridge for close to twenty years. He had been instrumental in explaining the workings of a country estate to Julian. It was only because of Smith's experience and knowledge that Julian had felt comfortable enough leaving the country to attend the London Season.

Now, it looked as if that would not occur.

Looking to his companions, he said, "Please excuse me. It seems as if I will be returning to Surrey for an undetermined amount of time."

"The Season starts in three weeks," Lady Ariadne said. "Surely, you can have things sorted out by then so you may return for it?"

"It isn't that easy," he said. "Mr. Smith was a longtime, trusted retainer. I am inexperienced in running an estate, and he was quite valuable. I have no idea how to even go about searching for a new steward and while I do, I cannot leave my tenants without supervision."

He saw disappointment cross her face and wished he could guarantee his return to town, but his duties at Aldridge Manor came before anything else.

"I would be happy to assist you," Lord Claibourne said. "You know I have much experience in looking after my father's various estates. I could come with you to Surrey."

"I do not want to be left behind," Viscount Dyer added. "If you will have me, I will also come along. Val and I can help you sort out anything. Hopefully, everything will be running smoothly so that you might return to town in time for the start of the Season."

"I have an idea," Lord Claibourne said. "My father has an estate in Essex with an excellent steward. A Scotsman named Ross. Ross has a son he has been training for several years now to follow in his footsteps, but the elder Ross is simply too young to retire at this point. The younger Ross has been wanting to leave and gain experience on his own, away from his father's supervision. He's bright and innovative, Aldridge. Young. Probably only two and twenty, but I do not think you should hold that against him. I have seen what he can do. Would you be interested in Ross for the position?"

Relief swept through him. "I would be happy to interview your Mr. Ross, my lord."

"Then let Con and me accompany you to Surrey. We can see the property and while I travel to Essex to fetch Mr. Ross, Con will be there to help you in the running of the estate."

"I would be most appreciative, Lord Claibourne. I hate to draw you and your cousin away from London, however."

Lord Dyer grinned. "Val and I are always up for an adventure. We are happy to help."

"Then I accept your generous offer, my lords." He looked to Lady Ariadne. "I am sorry to deprive you of your brother's and cousin's company, my lady."

She smiled. "Oh, they would probably get into trouble if left to themselves here in town. This way, they can be more productive."

"And I will not have to listen to Mama complain about Papa," the viscount said. "When shall we leave?"

"I think at first light tomorrow," Julian suggested. "We could be at Aldridge Manor by mid-morning if we do so."

"Very well," Lord Claibourne said. "I shall have Fisham pack for me at once." Looking to his cousin, he said, "Con, we should leave our valets here in town and travel lightly. Perhaps we might borrow Lord Aldridge's valet if an emergency arises."

"Paulson would be happy to attend to the both of you," he assured his new friends. "He is quite clever."

"We will come to you tomorrow morning," Claibourne told him. "Once I have viewed Aldridge Manor, I will leave the next day for Essex."

"I hope Mr. Ross will accept the position as your steward," Lady Ariadne said. "Keep these two in line, my lord. I look forward to your return to town."

He hated leaving her, feeling there was something between them, but knowing his priority was to his estate and people.

Taking her gloved hand, he brought it to his lips and brushed a kiss against her fingers, again feeling those unusual feelings stir within him when in contact with her.

"Until we meet again, Lady Ariadne."

Julian excused himself and returned to his townhouse. He spoke with the messenger, who gave him a brief letter written by Briscoe, his country butler. The note confirmed the unexpected death of Mr. Smith, stating the steward had not previously been ill. Briscoe said the local doctor believed it to be a sudden heart attack.

Going to his bedchamber, he found he had no need to ring for Paulson. The valet was already packing.

"Almost done, my lord. I assume we'll be leaving early tomorrow morning for Aldridge Manor."

"Yes," he informed the valet. "And Lord Claibourne and Lord Dyer will be accompanying us."

Paulson looked pleased. "They offered their help?"

"They did. They wish to see my estate, and Lord Claibourne has an idea of someone who might take Mr. Smith's place. The two gentlemen will leave their own valets in town. I offered them use of your services if they are needed."

Paulson beamed. "I will be happy to serve the three of you,

my lord."

Julian took the time to write a note to Mr. Wilson, his tailor, explaining he had been called away unexpectedly to Surrey and would miss his fitting. He assured the tailor he would send word when he returned to town so that they might reschedule their appointment.

The next morning, he arose earlier than usual, dressing and having a light breakfast in his room while Paulson finished the packing and took the luggage downstairs to be loaded atop the carriage. He met briefly with Grigsby, assuring his butler he would send word when he would be returning to London.

"I hope to have the matter of a new steward settled soon."

"Everything will be ready for you when you return, my lord," Grigsby said. "I will save the post for you to go through."

He had not accepted any invitations so far to upcoming social affairs and would discuss that with his traveling companions.

The two men awaited him in the carriage as he boarded.

"Good morning, my lords. You are prompt."

"We are looking forward to our country respite before the social whirl of the Season begins," Lord Claibourne revealed.

Julian tapped his cane on the carriage's roof, and the driver set the horses in motion.

"Might I ask you about the Season while we ride?"

"Ask away," Viscount Dyer said. "We have participated ever since our graduation from Oxford."

"Tell me about it in general, and then I may have specific questions to ask."

For the next half-hour as they left London behind, his friends told Julian what to expect. They described what happened at balls, since those were the most frequently held events. He was shocked to learn they didn't commence until nine or ten in the evening, with dancing going on until four or five o'clock in the morning.

"When do you sleep?" he wondered.

"Country hours are quite different from those in town," Lord

Claibourne said. "We have always eaten dinner early in the country and gone to bed at a decent hour. Oftentimes, I am up at first light, breakfasting and then getting out on the estate."

"You will likely sleep until noon or so," Lord Dyer added. "Breakfast and then you will go to your club. Or possibly participate in morning calls if you are courting a few ladies."

"How does a lady have time for gentlemen to call upon her in the morning if she doesn't even get to bed until dawn?"

The two lords laughed. "Morning calls take place in the afternoon, Aldridge," Lord Claibourne said. "Usually between two and four. And I have no idea why it is called that, so save your breath."

"Polite Society is puzzling to me," Julian admitted.

They spoke of other events and how often clothes must be changed.

"Thank goodness, we are nothing like the ladies, who might change four or five times a day," Lord Dyer said, shuddering.

"Oh, you must send flowers," Claibourne added. "To ladies who interest you."

"What?" he asked.

"If you are interested in a particular lady—or ladies—you will wish to call upon them the day after an event. Say you dance with someone who piques your interest. You should send her a bouquet the next day, which she will display in her parents' drawing room. The larger the bouquet, the more interest you have in her. Other suitors will do the same."

"It can grow competitive," Lord Dyer said. "And expensive."

"Do you send flowers to ladies?" Julian asked.

"Every now and then," Dyer replied. "While Val and I are not shopping on the Marriage Mart for wives, if we enjoy the company of a certain lady, we will send her a bouquet and call on her briefly. Usually, that spurs her other, more serious suitors into action."

"Should I call on multiple women?" he mused.

"At first, you may very well decide to do so," Claibourne

advised. "As the Season progresses and you narrow your choices for your marchioness, that will change."

Dyer began chuckling. "I hate to tell you this, Aldridge, but the Season is like a jungle. Hungry mamas stalking eligible bachelors, trying to help their daughters win the favor of a gentleman looking to wed. You will be a new entrant into the social swirl. With your looks and title, a flood of women will be thrust at you, so beware."

Worried, he asked, "How brazen will they become?"

Laughing, Claibourne said, "Some will be bold. Others timid. We should warn you that you are never to be alone with a lady. If you are found together alone, whether or not you are in a compromising position, the assumption will be that you *have* compromised her. Either you wed her—or she is considered ruined for other gentlemen."

"There are those wily mamas who will encourage their daughters to trap a lord into marriage," cautioned Dyer. "Never accept a request to take a lady to the library or anywhere else others will not be. My advice is to stay in sight of as many people as you can at all times in order not to have your hand forced into a marriage you do not wish for."

"This is a bit frightening," he declared. "I am leery now of attending any event."

"We do not mean to scare you off, Aldridge," Dyer said. "We are simply trying to save you from an unwanted union. Keep alert. Listen to your inner voice. If it tells you something is off, then it is."

"We will introduce you around," Claibourne told him. "Con and I can let you know which ladies to avoid and which ones might be a good match for you. Ariadne can also help in that regard."

His head swirled with all he had been told. "Thank you for alerting me to so many things. I have a better idea now what to expect—and what to avoid."

They arrived at Aldridge Manor, being greeted by the Briscoes, who served as his butler and housekeeper. He also saw Mr. Smith's body and was told the funeral would take place tomorrow afternoon.

Lord Claibourne suggested after they had some refreshments that they ride the estate.

"I want to be able to tell Ross all I can about Aldridge Manor. I hope he will be interested in coming to see it."

They were gone the rest of the afternoon, seeing the land, looking over the mill and farms, speaking with tenants as they did so. To a man, they all asked Julian about a new steward, and he told them he would hire one shortly, with recommendations from the two friends he had brought with him. Both Lord Claibourne and Lord Dyer asked thoughtful questions of his tenants, and he knew the two lords had made a strong impression upon his people.

They lingered over dinner and then brandy and cigars, talking over numerous topics. For a moment, Julian basked in the glow of what he now knew was friendship. While he might never be as close to these two men as they were to each other, he believed they had formed the foundation for a friendship which he hoped would continue.

Especially if he wed Lady Ariadne.

He wouldn't mention anything to her relatives yet. First, he needed to see if she might be interested in him. While she had seemed sympathetic to him as he shared his years before the marquessate with her, she might not believe him appropriate to be the husband of a duke's daughter. Only once he returned to London and the Season began would he have a chance to evaluate her attitude and feelings for him.

As far as Julian was concerned, though, Lady Ariadne was the ideal woman to become his marchioness.

They saw Claibourne off early the next morning. The marquess had estimated it to be sixty miles or so from Aldridge Manor to the ducal property just south of Chelmsford.

"I should return tomorrow by early afternoon. I will discuss with both Mr. Rosses the prospect of the younger coming to Surrey to serve as steward at Aldridge, if that is still agreeable with you, my lord."

Julian nodded. "While I would prefer a man with more experience, I am taking your word when you say that Mr. Ross is capable and a good candidate for the position."

"I would not have recommended him otherwise," Claibourne replied.

After the marquess left, he and Lord Dyer went riding again. They spent the morning out on the land, and the viscount accompanied him to Smith's funeral, which Julian thought was a very decent thing to do, considering Dyer had never met the man. At dinner that evening, the viscount asked for Julian to call him Con.

"I have never been one for formalities," the viscount told him. "Both Val and I took to you right away. I think he would agree with me that when we are alone together, we can relax the rules of Polite Society and address one another as friends."

"I am honored to hear you think of me as a friend," he replied. "I am Julian. Julian Barrington."

Con laughed aloud. "Then you fit right in with the two of us. Because of our names, I have held an interest in history, both ancient and more modern. Did you know that Julian was a nephew of Constantine the Great and the last non-Christian emperor of the Roman empire?"

"I am afraid my schooling did not include history and geography. I wonder why my mother chose the name."

"It does not matter. You are Julian to me, as you will be to Val." Con placed a hand on Julian's shoulder. "You are a man worth knowing, Julian Barrington. You have a lot to be proud of here at Aldridge Manor."

At half-past noon the following day, Julian's carriage returned, bearing both Lord Claibourne and Mr. Ross. The two men, along with Julian and Con, went to the drawing room, where they were served refreshments.

"Thank you for coming, Mr. Ross," Julian began. "I appreciate you making the effort to come and interview for the position of steward at Aldridge Manor."

Ross, who was just under six feet, and wiry, with dark hair and eyes, responded, "It is an excellent opportunity, my lord. One which I didn't think I had a chance at for many years to come. I am three and twenty, but I was brought up assisting my father in all estate matters. I know keep ledgers of crop production and livestock births and deaths. Record sales of each. I have a good grasp regarding crop rotation and have delivered everything from horses to goats. Lord Claibourne shared a bit about your property with me, and I am eager to see the land and meet your tenants."

"I know you have not toured the estate yet, but what are your priorities, Mr. Ross? What kinds of improvements have you made or assisted with on His Grace's estate?"

Ross immediately launched into a detailed answer. His ideas were sensible, and he sounded as if he'd had all the experience he needed to step into Mr. Smith's shoes. As Ross spoke, Julian looked to Con and then his cousin. Both men nodded imperceptibly in approval.

"I have no further questions, Mr. Ross. Despite your youth, I believe you have the ability to fill my previous steward's shoes."

He had already spoken to his two friends about the salary to offer, and Julian now shared that with Mr. Ross.

"You would also have a cottage of your own. It is halfway between this house and the tenants' cottages."

"That is convenient, my lord, not only for when I am working with the tenants, but when I meet with you to discuss estate matters."

"There is an office in the house here dedicated to your work," Julian informed his new steward. "I would be happy to go over the ledgers with you now."

"I can do that on my own, my lord. I feel your time would be best spent taking me around the land and introducing me to your people. Now, if that is agreeable to you."

He liked that Ross was eager to take up his duties. All four men went to the stables, mounting horses and riding about the property. Everywhere they went, Julian could see how his tenants took to the personable young man, and he believed hiring Ross was a good decision.

As the steward was talking to one farmer and his wife, Julian said to Claibourne, "I cannot thank you enough for recommending Mr. Ross to me."

"He is eager but mature for his age. I think you will be relieved that you can return to town and not worry about what is occurring at Aldridge Manor." Val smiled. "Con told me that you are Julian to him now. I hope you would also do me the honor, as your friend, of calling me Val when we are together."

He nodded gratefully. "I am more than happy to do so, Val. I understand this is only when we are alone and not in the company of others."

"That is correct," Val told him.

Ross approached them, his face flush with excitement. "You have wonderful tenants, Lord Aldridge. I am enthused about my new position."

"I have had Mrs. Briscoe and her staff clean Mr. Smith's cottage. You may move into it at once."

"I appreciate that, my lord. I plan to write to you weekly, so that you will have an idea of the progress being made at Aldridge Manor. I am also happy to come to London if you summon me for a report in person."

They all agreed to spend another day at Aldridge Manor, with Julian in Mr. Ross' company the entire time. They spent several hours going over the ledgers and discussing the spring harvest, as well as the fall one, which would occur shortly after he had returned from the Season. He wondered if he might be bringing a wife home with him.

They left for town the next morning, all three men saying they were eager to return. Julian mentioned he would need to see his tailor since he had missed a fitting, and they made plans to meet at White's the following afternoon before they parted company.

As Paulson undressed Julian and prepared him for bed, he wondered how he might find himself in Lady Ariadne's company before the Season began, especially knowing now that he was not to be alone with her. He supposed it had been an exception, her showing him the ducal conservatory, and doubted they would have that opportunity again.

Then he recalled how they had first met in the small park on the square and determined he would go there tomorrow morning—and every morning afterward—to see if he might come across her. Of course, she would be preparing for her come-out, and he knew that must involve her wardrobe.

Deciding a chance meeting in the park might take too long, Julian decided he would ask the duke and duchess to tea, along with their daughter and son. It would be a way to return their hospitality to him.

And the opportunity to see Lady Ariadne again.

Chapter Nine

With Val gone, Ariadne grew bored, especially after another day was spent at the shoemaker's. The slippers she tried on seemed flimsy at best, and her fears of them falling apart were seconded when she asked about how long they would last.

"A night of dancing in a pair, my lady, and you'll need another pair," joked the clerk, causing her further distress. The waste of money being spent on her come-out continued to haunt her, yet she knew the various businesses she and Mama were now patronizing depended upon the *ton* wishing to look fashionable to earn their livelihood.

One good thing that came out of today's visit was a new pair of boots. Since she rode and walked so much in the country, she was not opposed to purchasing a new pair. That, however, led Mama to lament that they had not put in an order for a riding habit.

"I have two riding habits in decent shape, Mama," Ariadne reminded her mother. "I see no need to replace either of them."

"But they are not of this year's designs, Child," Mama said firmly, once again affirming how her parents disregarded the fact that she was a grown woman and could make a simple decision about a riding habit.

She knew any protests would land upon deaf ears, and they stopped by Madame Laurent's shop again to place an order for a new riding habit. All the way home, Mama talked about how the possibility of going riding with a gentleman in Hyde Park meant that Ariadne must be prepared and look her best. She kept silent, knowing if she mentioned how strenuous riding could be and how hot and sweaty she would become riding in London in the heat might cause her mother to forbid riding at all. As soon as Val and Con were back in town, she intended to have them take her riding. As of now, she had no one to go with her, which meant she was not allowed to go at all.

The next day, Mama left the townhouse. She would be spending her entire day with Madame Laurent again, seeing to her own wardrobe needs for the Season. Ariadne decided to take this opportunity to leave the house with Tally.

As they walked along the pavement, the maid asked, "Where are we going, my lady?"

"St. George's in Hanover Square."

The church was where her parents worshipped on Sundays, and Ariadne had heard it was the most popular place for members of Polite Society to hold their weddings. While she had only attended services there once during her previous visit to town many years ago, she thought the church far too grand for a wedding. In her mind, a wedding was an intimate affair. She did not want hundreds to attend the ceremony, most of them strangers to her. Her preference was to be wed in the Willowshire church, the nearest village to Millvale.

"Why are we going to church in the middle of the week, my lady?"

Patiently, she explained to Tally, "I want to see about helping with the poor. I have seen so many of them since we arrived in town. I thought if I spoke to someone at St. George's, I could volunteer my time. Even some of my pin money."

"You've a kind heart, my lady," the maid told her. "But you won't have time to do much once the Season starts."

"Then I shall try to do something now."

Not only was Ariadne determined to see what she could do to

help immediately, but she fully intended to continue helping the poor once she wed. She would have to make that clear to any man who thought to be her future husband.

When they arrived, the first person she met was the sexton, who cared for the property and rang the bells for services. He directed her inside to the church's office. Though the vicar was not in, his curate was. She introduced herself and asked if she could meet with him for a few minutes, making certain she mentioned she was the daughter of the Duke of Millbrooke.

The curate's eyes lit up. "Why, of course, Lady Ariadne. Please, have a seat. What can we do for you?"

"I am interested in helping the poor, Mr. Rogers. They seem to be everywhere I look. I feel it is my Christian duty to help ease their suffering."

He smiled benignly. "That is kind of you, my lady. You might not know that Parliament passed a series of acts many years ago for this very thing. Way back when the Tudors sat on the English throne. These laws make it the obligation of each parish to care for its poor. That includes the old and infirm. Orphans. Our parishioners pay a poor rate, a kind of tax, and that goes toward aiding the poor and orphans."

The curate paused. "Your own father participates, doing his part, by paying this on behalf of himself and his entire family. So you see, my lady, it is unnecessary for you to do so."

"But the poor are starving, Mr. Rogers. Their clothes are in tatters, mere rags. Many of the children I see are shoeless. They look scrawny and ill. Surely, I can do something myself. Volunteer my time, at the very least."

A frown knit his brows together. "What you suggest is not appropriate for a duke's daughter. Does His Grace know you are here?" His tone had turned stern.

She didn't want to lie, and so Ariadne said, "Papa knows my views regarding the poor. I have made them perfectly clear to him." She paused. "I *want* to help, Mr. Rogers."

He cleared his throat. "I am going to be blunt, my lady. The rookeries are no place for you or any member of Polite Society. They teem with gambling. Prostitution. Theft. Raging alcoholics who would tear a pretty thing like you to shreds."

She gasped.

"It is a cruel world, my lady," the curate continued. "You seem determined to me, however. The best I can do is send you to Miss Crimmins. She is the head of the orphanage St. George's sends funds to each quarter. Perhaps after speaking with her, you will see your errand of mercy is fruitless."

He took a pencil and scribbled an address on a piece of parchment and handed it to her. "Here. You can find Miss Crimmins at this address. I suggest you have an escort, however. It is in a rough part of town."

Rising, she held her head high. "Thank you, Mr. Rogers," she said curtly. "Come along, Tally."

They left the parish office, with Tally saying, "Don't get any wild ideas, my lady. You need to listen to that man. He knows what he's talking about."

Ariadne halted. "Then how are things ever going to change if no one does anything about them?"

A stubborn look came into Tally's eyes. "You heard him. His Grace pays the church, and they take that money and give it to the poor."

Her own jaw set stubbornly. "I can help on my own. I can lend a helping hand."

"Their Graces will lock you in your room and won't let you out until the Season begins if they learn of this foolishness," her maid declared.

Her eyes narrowed. "Then they will not need to hear of it."

"My lady, I'm begging you not to do this."

"And I am going to do it with or without you, Tally. Wouldn't it be better if you came along to supervise me? It is not as if I am marching into a gambling den or tavern. I want to help motherless children. Is that so wrong?"

Tally crossed her arms. "I'll go. To keep you out of trouble.

And I hope I can do that."

"Thank you. For accompanying me. For not telling Mama or Papa."

"I should. If they find out, I'll be sacked for sure."

"They won't," she promised. "And you know you are already coming with me when I go to a new household." She looked around. "We must take a hansom cab there. I have no idea how far this orphanage is, and I suppose walking might not be safe."

"At least you have some sense," Tally muttered, as Ariadne hailed a cab for them.

The driver gawked at her. "Are you sure this is where you wish to go, my lady?" he asked after she handed him the page with the address written on it.

"Yes. I am certain."

As they drove, she saw the architecture of the buildings change. The streets grew more narrow and had more refuse. Foul smells filled the air.

When they arrived at the orphanage, she paid the cab driver and then asked, "Would you wait for us, sir? We will need to return to Mayfair once my business here is concluded." When she saw his reluctance, she added, "I will pay you for your time while you wait."

He scowled but said, "Be quick about it, my lady. This isn't a part of town for the likes of you—or even me."

"Thank you."

She and Tally got out of the hansom cab and ventured inside the three-story building. They passed several boys, all dressed alike in a shirt and breeches. The clothes looked clean, even if they were too large for two of the children, and she was pleased to see all three wore shoes.

A thin, tall woman who looked to be in her late thirties stepped from a room. "May I help you?" she asked, assessing them.

"I am Lady Ariadne Worthington, daughter of the Duke of Millbrooke. This is Tally, my maid."

The woman frowned at her. "What brings you to Oakbrooke Orphanage, Lady Ariadne? We don't see any dukes—or their daughters—here."

"I wish to volunteer my time to your orphanage, Miss..." She hesitated because the woman had yet to introduce herself.

"Miss Crimmins," she said crisply. "I'm not sure we have need of your help."

"May I see the orphanage, Miss Crimmins? It might give me an idea of what I could do to support you."

"If you have money, we'll take it. Otherwise, we don't have need of you," the woman said bluntly. "I have been in charge of Oakbrooke for five years now. We see the children are clothed and fed. Teach them how to read and write. Pray they'll stay out of trouble."

"I could help in teaching," Ariadne said brightly. "I have always loved reading and writing. I could even teach history and geography."

Miss Crimmins sniffed. "Those here don't need to learn about kings and queens and wars, much less places they'll never go. If you have a donation, my lady, make it. Otherwise, you can be on your way."

Embarrassment caused her cheeks to redden. No one had ever dared speak to her so curtly. "I want to help, Miss Crimmins," she implored.

"For how long?" the woman demanded, looking her up and down. "I'd say you're on the verge of making your come-out."

"I am."

"Then you'll be caught up in all those social activities, Lady Ariadne. You simply don't have the time to be here on a daily basis, dealing with these children. Filling their heads with knowledge they'll never use and hope for a better future, which would be cruel. Now, do you have a donation or not?"

She knew by the time she paid their driver, not much would be left. Rasing her chin, she said, "I will see that my father makes a generous donation to your orphanage, Miss Crimmins. Good day."

Turning, she slipped her arm through Tally's and stepped briskly from the building.

"I won't say I told you so, my lady," her maid said, sympathy in her eyes.

"I appreciate that," Ariadne said, close to tears.

Fortunately, the driver had waited for them, and she gave him her address in Mayfair. She and Tally didn't converse on the drive home. Ariadne couldn't help but keep her gaze in her lap, unwilling to see the poverty surrounding her, knowing she could do nothing about it.

She had failed. Miserably. Humiliation filled her. And she would not be able to ask Papa for a donation. He would be furious with her for having gone to such a place. Not wanting to break her word to Miss Crimmins, though, she hoped that Val might help her contribute to the Oakbrooke Orphanage when he returned.

Was she destined to only be a pretty face in a pretty gown, marrying a nobleman and bearing his children? Or could she turn the rules of Polite Society upside down and find a gentleman willing to be more of a partner to her, one who would help her try to make a difference in the lives of a handful of those in poverty.

Ariadne would see when the Season began.

Chapter Ten

Julian's carriage reached London, and surprisingly, he was glad to be back in the city of his birth. While he had enjoyed the brief respite in the country and was pleased with his newly hired steward, being back in London meant seeing Lady Ariadne Worthington again.

"When will you be going to your tailor?" Con asked.

"I will probably see him tomorrow morning," he replied. "I had to put off a fitting while we were gone."

"My tailor retired last autumn and moved to Liverpool to live with his daughter and her family. I am looking for a new one," Con explained. "Might I accompany you on your visit?"

"Certainly. He was highly recommended by my valet, who said the previous Lord Aldridge used him. Paulson is quite particular and would not have steered me wrong."

"Well, I might as well go along," Val said good-naturedly. "I could use some new coats. What about your shirtmaker, Julian?"

"I saw him when I first arrived in town. Again, the former marquess used his services, and Parsons said no other would do."

He shared the name, and Val said, "I have heard of him. I think I will see him and say you referred me to him."

They pulled up in front of his townhouse, and the trio disembarked from the carriage. Already, footmen from the duke's townhouse scurried over to claim Val's and Con's luggage.

"Thank you again for accompanying me to Surrey and finding me a new steward. I wish to repay your kindness."

"It is not necessary," Val said. "But an invitation to dinner would be nice."

Julian had thought to ask his friend's family to tea, but he saw dinner would be a better opportunity.

"You read my mind," he told his friends. "Check your diaries for tomorrow evening. Of course, your families are also invited."

"I will speak to Mama," Con said. "If she already has plans, I will let you know tomorrow morning while we run our errand. I doubt Papa has come to town. He is most likely giving Mama time to cool her heels after their spat."

"If he has come to town, then he is welcome to come," Julian told his friend.

"Let me check with my family," Val said. "Since it is still early, I believe they will have no other engagements. I will go to the tailor's with you and let you know then, as well. What time are you leaving in the morning?"

"Ten o'clock," he threw out, thinking he would send a footman to Mr. Dalglish's shop to let him know to expect them.

"We will meet you here at the appointed time," Con said.

His friends headed toward Millbrooke's townhouse, while Julian went inside his own.

Grigsby awaited him. "Were you successful in engaging a steward, my lord?"

"Thanks to Lord Claibourne, Aldridge Manor is in good hands once again." Pausing a moment, he then added, "I am going to have a dinner party tomorrow, Grigsby. Please inform Cook. I can give her the number of guests tomorrow morning after I have spoken with Lord Claibourne and Lord Dyer. If all can attend, it will be seven of us total."

"I shall speak with Cook now, my lord. Do you have any requests?"

"No. Leave that up to her."

His cook worked magic with food. At least, that was what Julian thought. Having eaten a limited diet before coming into his title, though, he hoped her cooking would be good enough to please the Duke and Duchess of Millbrooke.

"Also, send a footman to my tailor. Tell him I will call at a quarter past ten tomorrow morning."

"Of course, my lord."

Julian headed to his study. As he thought, the post had piled up during the days they had been gone. More invitations had arrived. He would need to speak to his friends about them. He had thought to do so when they were out of town, but he changed his mind, thinking if Val and Con went through them with him, they could give insight into the various hosts and tell Julian a bit about those who might attend the events.

A knock sounded at the door, and he said, "Come."

Grigsby entered, looking apologetic. "Cook would like to speak with you, my lord."

He had never met with her before in person and had only spoken to her once when he first inherited his title.

"Have her come in."

Grigsby retreated and then Cook appeared in the doorway. She was a stout woman, with graying hair and kind eyes.

"Come in, Cook. What do you wish to discuss?"

She crossed the room and he indicated for her to take a seat. Reluctantly, she did so.

"Since you have no wife, my lord, and this is the first time you'll host a party, I wanted to go over a few preferences with you."

"Truly, Cook, whatever you have in mind to serve will be fine."

She frowned. "I know you like my food because your plates are returned to the kitchens scraped clean."

Julian wondered if that was a mistake on his part. "I enjoy what you prepare."

She seemed to relax and smiled. "I like hearing that, my lord. Tell me who is coming."

"If everyone accepts my invitation, it will be the Duke and

Duchess of Millbrooke, my neighbors on the square, and their son and daughter. Also, the duke's sister and nephew."

Her eyes widened. "A duke, you say?" She thought a moment. "Then here's what I'd like to serve."

Cook launched into a lengthy menu, which including everything from a white soup to rabbit, house lamb, various vegetables, and something he was unfamiliar with.

Seeing him frown, Cook said, "Fanchonettes are a dessert, my lord, not something everyone is comfortable attempting. Never fear, though. Mine come out delightful."

"What does it include?" he asked, curious.

"It's a custard tart, my lord, made with lemon. That makes it rich and creamy. I also pipe meringue atop it in the shape of pearls and then brown the meringue slightly. Believe me, it will be a wonderful way to end the meal, certainly fit for a duke and his duchess."

Julian smiled approvingly. "Everything you have suggested sounds wonderful, Cook. I will only hope Their Graces do not try to steal you away from me after they have dined on your food."

The woman giggled like a young girl, and he was glad he had paid her a compliment. Servants should be praised for a job well done, and he knew his cook would put an outstanding meal on the table tomorrow night.

※

"Do you have to go to the tailor's?" Ariadne asked Val at breakfast. "You only got home yesterday. I was hoping we could go for a ride this morning. Besides, you will see Lord Aldridge tonight at dinner."

Yesterday when Val had arrived home, he had shared at tea that the marquess had asked the four of them to dinner this evening. Her parents had agreed to accept the invitation, as had Aunt Charlotte, who had joined them for tea.

"How about we ride this afternoon, say one o'clock?" Val countered.

She snorted. "Then I have nothing to do until then."

"What, no shopping?"

"Thank goodness that is over with. At least for now."

Her brother chuckled. "Most women adore shopping, Sis."

"All I can think about is that I am like a doll Mama is dressing up and putting on display for others to admire."

Val stroked his chin. "Actually, that is a fairly accurate description of the Marriage Mart. You are to look your best and act your most charming, luring in a husband."

"That sounds so nefarious," she declared.

"You will have no trouble attracting men, Ariadne," he assured her.

"But will they be the right kind of men?"

He shrugged. "Aldridge seems to like you."

Her heart skipped a beat, hearing the marquess' name. "You think so?"

"I do. He is a decent fellow. I know we are sworn to keep his background a secret, and I hope you would not hold it against him."

"Oh, I would never do that," she said, a bit too enthusiastically, causing Val's brows to shoot up.

"Do you like him, Sis?"

"He seems nice," she said, tempering her words. "Of course, I would need to get to know him better. Actually, I want to get to know a good number of people better before I even begin to think about taking a husband."

Val thought a moment. "How would you like to go to the tailor's shop with us this morning?"

Excitement filled her. "Truly?"

"I do not see why not. I am your brother and will be your escort to most events this Season. It will give you something to do, and you can be around Con and Julian and get to know both a bit better."

"Julian? You are calling Lord Aldridge by his first name, Val?"

"Con and I like him. I will be very honest with you, Sis. Con and I get along with most everyone we meet, yet as far as close friends go, we have always stuck only with one another. There is something about Julian, though. Something we both feel. I believe he will be a good friend to each of us for many years to come."

The thought of Lord Aldridge and her brother and cousin all being friends made the marquess appeal to her even more, but Val did not need to know that just yet. Besides, she did want to have her come-out and experience all the fun of a Season. Still, it wouldn't hurt to get to know Lord Aldridge—Julian—better. Especially before he had met other eligible ladies.

"I would be delighted to accompany you. Just keep it from Mama."

"You think she would disapprove."

"I know she would. She does not rise until noon unless we have an appointment, and we have none today. We will most likely be home before she even stirs."

They walked to Lord Aldridge's townhouse, seeing Con pull up in a hansom cab, which parked behind the marquess' carriage.

"You skipped tea yesterday," Ariadne chided.

"I had a previous appointment," Con said, a gleam in his eyes.

"That means you went to see a woman."

Both men cleared their throats, and Val said, "You are not supposed to know of things such as that, Sis. And definitely not supposed to bring up the topic."

Lord Aldridge stepped from his front door and came to greet them.

"I hope you will not mind, but Ariadne is going to the tailor's with us," Val informed the others.

She saw the tips of Lord Aldridge's ears pinken slightly and bit back a smile. "I hope you do not mind my presence, my lord. I have never been to a tailor's shop. Val is trying to keep me entertained since I complained of being bored while the three of you were out of town."

"Do ladies go to the tailor?" the marquess asked.

"They do if they wish to," Con said, taking Ariadne's hand and helping her into the waiting carriage.

On the way, she asked about the new steward, and Lord Aldridge eagerly told her about Mr. Ross and his qualifications.

"His father serves as steward on one of your father's estates, my lady. Mr. Ross has been in training his entire life, ready to take the reins at an estate of his own. He may be young, but he has some innovative ideas. It pleases me that we will have a partnership for many years to come."

"A partnership?" she asked.

"Why, yes. That is what I think of it as. As my steward, Mr. Ross is there to take care of my land and my tenants when I am absent and care for them as I do even when I am there. We are both in league to make certain the land prospers, which helps my coffers and makes my tenants happy. I look upon him as a fellow associate. A colleague, so to speak."

"That seems a unique way of viewing your relationship, my lord."

Lord Aldridge nodded thoughtfully. "Perhaps it is. I believe it will lead to success, however."

If this man were willing to make his steward a partner, he might take the same attitude in marriage. Ariadne hoped he did. Not only was Lord Aldridge attractive, with his dark hair and brows and contrasting blue eyes, she was drawn to the person he was. She wondered if her very different views regarding marriage would make sense to him.

Somehow, she needed to devise some kind of test. If he passed, then she would definitely consider him a viable candidate for her hand.

They arrived at the tailor's shop and entered.

"Ah, Lord Aldridge. Good morning." A man headed toward them, about forty years of age. He had dark hair and watery blue eyes and looked to have a congenial nature. He had an air of familiarity about him, but Ariadne knew she never could have met him and dismissed the notion.

"I brought along a few friends, Mr. Dalglish. Lord Dyer is searching for a new tailor and would like to see examples of your work."

The tailor nodded eagerly. "If you would care to try on some of the pieces I've already completed for you, his lordship can see how they fit you and then examine them more closely for the details. If you would come with me, my lord."

The two men disappeared into what Ariadne thought would be rooms similar to those at Madame Laurent's. While they were gone, she strolled about the shop, examining samples of materials, while Val and Con spoke with an assistant.

Lord Aldridge appeared, looking quite dapper in dark gray trousers and a lighter gray coat and vest. They went to get a closer look at him as he stepped up on a slightly raised platform.

"You look splendid, Aldridge," Con praised.

Ariadne had thought the marquess handsome, but she had looked mainly at his face. Now, she saw how well he filled out his clothes, his shoulders broad and quite appealing. Something inside her stirred, and she grew a bit dizzy. She dug her nails into her palms, but her gloves were too thick to make a difference, so she bit down on her tongue, helping to clear her head.

"I am very pleased, Mr. Dalglish," Lord Aldridge said. "Do you have anything else ready for me?"

The marquess changed clothes several times, growing more attractive each time he came out. She thought he looked best in a midnight blue coat and fawn riding breeches which were molded to his muscular legs. She wished she could lift the tails of his coat and see how he filled out the backside of those breeches and found her cheeks growing hot.

Once he was done, Con asked for Mr. Dalglish to measure him. He got Ariadne involved by asking her to look at bolts of material with him. Even Val and Lord Aldridge joined in, helping Con to select several different colors and patterns. Con arranged a day to return to the tailor's shop, and they left, with Mr. Dalglish saying he would have everything ready delivered to Lord Aldridge that afternoon.

In the carriage, the marquess said, "I suppose I can wear something new to dinner this evening. Thank you again for saying you will come tonight. It will be the first time I have entertained guests, either here or in the country."

"Thank you for inviting us, my lord," Ariadne said demurely, her pulse pounding as she looked at him.

Why was she suddenly so attracted to him?

She didn't understand why something about this man touched her so, but she was ready to spend more time in his company. Suddenly, she was the one who wanted him to have a good impression of her before the Season began and other ladies drew his attention.

When they reached home, Val asked if she still wanted to go riding.

"Most definitely," she told him.

Ariadne needed something to keep her mind occupied. Riding took a great deal of physical effort and mental concentration, else you'd be tossed from the saddle. An hour or two atop a horse was just the thing she needed.

Only then would she take time to examine these new, blossoming feelings for the Marquess of Aldridge.

Chapter Eleven

Julian greeted his guests, pleased that everyone invited had been able to attend. The meal, under Grigsby's supervision, went smoothly. He was fortunate to have inherited such dedicated servants and decided his entire household should receive an increase in salary, especially his butlers, housekeepers, and valet. They had been instrumental in helping him acclimate to his new position.

Lady Marley said, "Your cook has outdone herself, my lord. This dessert is positively divine."

"I will pass along your kind words to her, my lady," he said, thankful each course had gone so well.

The duke and duchess had been talkative, and along with the duke's sister, they had dominated much of the conversation. He hadn't minded, trying to listen for names and other specifics, filing them away for the time when he would meet those mentioned.

Looking around, Julian saw everyone had completed their meal. He now rose and said, "I am so glad you could join me this evening."

Quickly, he saw Grigsby approach and knew he had somehow erred. He didn't know whether to sit or remain standing and would take his cue from his butler.

"If you wish, my lord, I shall take the ladies to the drawing room while you and the gentlemen have your port and cigars."

Putting on a smile, he said, "Thank you, Grigsby."

The other men at the table rose as the ladies were helped from their seats by footmen. Grigsby led them away. The footmen sprang into action, knowing what was expected, and soon the men all had drinks and cigars. Julian had never smoked in his life and waved away the offer of a cigar. The duke, Con, and Val all accepted, however, and soon the sweet smell of tobacco filled the dining room.

After half an hour, Grigsby took the lead again, saying, "If you care to join the ladies in the drawing room, my lord, I can have tea brought."

"No tea," said the duke. "Another snifter of brandy will do."

Julian had drunk spirits before becoming the marquess. He found them not to his liking but did sip a single brandy each evening, knowing it would be expected of him once he moved about Polite Society. He did think it rather forward of Millbrooke to decline tea for everyone when it wasn't even his household. Then again, the man was a duke and probably used to everyone fawning over him and accommodating his every request.

"Go ahead and bring tea," he told his butler. "The ladies may prefer a cup."

"Yes, my lord," Grigsby said, an approving smile crossing his lips.

They joined his other guests, and Julian saw the ladies each sipped a sherry. He only knew what the drink was because Grigsby had walked him through the various spirits and mentioned sherry was a popular drink amongst women.

Once they were seated, Her Grace said, "Ariadne, you should play and sing something to entertain us."

She looked to him. "Would you care if I played your pianoforte, my lord?"

He had never heard the instrument played before and said, "You may play for as long as you wish, my lady."

"I play rather well, but I sing abominably," she admitted cheerfully. "I will refrain from torturing you with my voice."

Her mother frowned disapprovingly, but Julian found Lady Ariadne's candor refreshing. He suspected he would be placed in situations many times where a young lady had no talent and was still encouraged to perform for others.

He didn't know what piece she played, but it was soothing to his ears. Since no one spoke and gave her their full attention, Julian was able to study her at length without distractions. The shade of her hair was remarkable, and he longed to unpin it and run his fingers through her tresses. She had a flawless complexion and lips which tempted him beyond measure. He even liked the small crease in her brow as she concentrated on the keyboard.

What would it take for this beauty to wed him?

She finished playing, and Val said, "Bravo, Sis. Your playing could soothe any savage beast."

"Then perhaps I should play for Bonaparte," she quipped. "He might not be so bloodthirsty and eager to gobble up all of Europe if he could hear me play."

Everyone chuckled, and Con said, "It certainly would be a new strategy for our government to employ. Perhaps Parliament can take it under consideration."

"Would you play something else for us?" Julian asked. "Just one more."

"All right," Lady Ariadne agreed.

This time her song was livelier, and his spirits soared. He had a feeling he would never grow bored in her company, but he was afraid he couldn't say the same about himself. He reminded himself that she was the daughter of a duke, whereas he had been a laborer all his life. While she seemed sympathetic to his background and he knew she would never reveal what he had shared with her, most likely she would not consider him as a husband, wanting a true blueblood instead.

After she finished, Her Grace said, "Charlotte and I are to spend all day at the modiste's tomorrow. Thank you for your hospitality, Lord Aldridge."

As everyone rose, Val said, "It is still early. Perhaps we

younger folk might stay on a while." He looked to Julian. "We could play a few hands of cards."

He was eager to be in their company and agreed. "You are welcome to remain, my lord."

Their Graces and Lady Marley took their leave, and Val called, "Break out the cards!"

"I know we must have a deck or two available. I will have to find where they are kept." He hesitated. "I must apologize in advance. I have never played cards and have no interest in picking up gambling."

"Oh, we do not have to wager, my lord," Lady Ariadne said. "But you must learn a few card games. You will be invited to card parties during the Season. They can be quite fun."

"Only because you win so much," her brother teased affectionately. "I do agree with my sister, though, Julian. Cardplaying should be added to your repertoire of social skills."

"You might wish to escape to the card room at a ball," Con added.

"Cards are played during a ball?" he asked, puzzled.

"Most married couples only engage in a few dances," Con told him. "Why, I doubt my own parents have danced once since they were wed. Many men retire to the card room where, yes, they do play and wager. Bets can be a pittance—or they can add up to a small fortune."

He shook his head. "I don't see the point in throwing my money away. Even if I knew how to play games of chance, they are exactly that. Pure chance."

"Still, ducking into the card room might save you from an insistent mama wishing to corner you and demand that you dance with her wallflower daughter," Val pointed out. "You can always spend some time there and not play. Have a drink. Watch the action."

"I shall teach you how to play cards, my lord," Lady Ariadne said. "I have taught several people how, even my younger sisters. Knowing the strategy behind choosing certain cards is vital." She paused, obviously thinking. "While you eventually need to learn other card games—piquet, vingt-et-un, or loo—most hostesses at card parties have their guests play whist. That is what we will concentrate on now."

He rang for Grigsby, who led them to the card room, a place he had yet to see in his own house. Soon, Lady Ariadne was explaining the rules of whist to him.

"It takes four players, working in teams of two, who sit across from one another. Here is how you shuffle the cards, which you will be called upon to do when it is your turn."

She demonstrated how to do so and had him practice a few times. Julian quickly picked up the skill, but he told himself he would continue to practice so he could shuffle with ease when at a card party.

Lady Ariadne then shuffled the deck again, had her brother cut it in half, and then dealt the cards in a clockwise manner. When she reached the last card, she placed it face up.

"The dealer always shows this last card, which belongs to him or her," she explained before setting it atop her own stack. "Most times when players receive their cards, they will pick them up each time until all thirteen are in their hands. My advice is for you to place them in numerical order, with any card being a two placed first. Do not worry about the suit."

"Suit?" he asked, unclear what that might be.

Quickly, she named the four suits. "I think it would be best to play a few hands with all of us having our cards face up. Arrange your cards in front of you gentlemen, so we can all see them. My lord, after any tens you hold, the jack, then queen, and king are the next highest, with an ace being the most valuable card of all."

They did as she asked, and he made a decision. "Would you please call me Julian? Your brother and cousin do, and we are in an informal situation here. It seems odd to my ears to hear you referring to me as my lord."

She studied him a moment. "I can do so, but only in a rare circumstance such as this."

Pleased at the progress he had made with her, Julian arranged his cards accordingly.

"Now, the player to the dealer's right is the first to select and place a card in the middle of the table. This is called leading. The point of whist is to try and take as many tricks as you can, meaning the highest card played wins that round, known as a trick."

Val played an eight of diamonds.

"If you have any diamonds in your hand, Julian, you must play one of them. If you want to take the trick, play a high diamond." She looked at his hand. "You have the king of diamonds, but that means someone else holds the ace of diamonds. I would wait to see if that were played before relinquishing my kind. I would play a low diamond to see if the ace is drawn out. If a player does play that ace of diamonds, then you would win any other round where all diamonds are played."

He took a three of diamonds and tossed it into the middle of the table. Con played the ace he held, which led Ariadne to play the five of diamonds.

"See, I am playing my lowest diamond. I can sacrifice it, knowing it is a low card and it would be less likely to win another round of diamonds."

Con claimed the four cards in the middle, neatly stacking them and setting them aside.

"Con now gets to lead since he won the trick," she continued. "He might wish to take charge and play another high card, or he might decide to sit back and draw other high cards from his opponents."

Her cousin played a two of spades. They each played a spade, and Julian had the trump card, so he collected the four and set them aside.

"If I were you, I would now play that king of diamonds. You are certain to win the next hand since you know the ace has already been played."

He did as she requested. "I have a question. What if someone leads with a card, but I have none in that suit?"

"Ah, you are catching on," she declared. "If you no longer hold any cards of the suit played, choose the lowest card of another suit and play it. You do not want to waste a high card which might win a round for you. Since I can see that you are already done with diamonds since you hold no more of that suit in your hand, then you know others at the table hold them. The odd thing is, since you took the last trick, you might lead with a mid-card, say a seven or eight. You have quite a few clubs. Play one of them."

Choosing the seven of clubs, he placed it down. Val had none, so he played his lowest diamond. Con only had the six of clubs and played it.

"Now, here is where your partner comes in handy. We are sitting opposite one another, and I should have a good idea that you are trying to win this trick. I would never trump you by playing a higher card in the suit you played. Our collected tricks won will win us points at the end of play. So, I will choose a five of clubs, even though I hold the ace of clubs."

Ariadne played her card, and he said, "I am beginning to understand. You explain things well."

They continued playing the remainder of their cards, and he won four of the hands, with Ariadne winning five.

"That means our total score is nine tricks taken," he said.

"The losers score no points, despite the fact they may have won a few tricks. Winners must subtract six from their score."

He frowned. "We only get three points?"

She laughed, and he loved the musical sound of it.

"The winning team at the table is the one which reaches five points first. We are already off to an excellent start. Most winning teams only score a point or two each round."

"Are you confident enough now to play with cards hidden?" Val asked.

"I believe so," Julian replied.

Val collected all the cards and shuffled them several times, having Julian cut them. As Val dealt, Julian lifted a card at a time, organizing his hand so by the time all cards were given out, he was ready to play.

"You will learn more about strategy each time you play," Con told him. "And your partner. You might even speak beforehand so each of you has a good idea what the other is up to."

They played several more rounds, becoming tied at four apiece. Ariadne rejoiced—loudly—when they claimed victory in the final hand.

"I should hope I could partner with you in the future, Ariadne," he said, loving how her unusual named rolled off his tongue.

"I would be happy to do so, Julian. You caught onto whist quickly."

"Next, she will be teaching you how to play chess," Val said. "Our Ariadne is skilled at the game."

She stood. "We should be getting home. Thank you for having us, Julian."

"Thank you for coming—and for teaching me a social skill I lacked."

He accompanied his guests down the stairs, falling beside Ariadne, who asked, "I do not been to be impertinent, Julian, but do you know how to dance?"

It had not struck him he would need to know how to do so, despite the repeated mention of balls.

"I do not possess that particular skill," he said quietly. "I am ashamed I have not thought about it."

As they reached the foyer and the butler began handing them their things, Ariadne asked, "Are the two of you doing anything tomorrow afternoon? Say, one o'clock?"

"No," Val and Con replied in unison.

"Good. Because we are going to teach Julian how to dance."

CHAPTER TWELVE

A RIADNE AWOKE, SURPRISED she had finally fallen asleep last night. Already, excitement filled her, knowing she would be seeing Lord Aldridge today.

No, Julian.

She had been thrilled when he asked her to call him by his Christian name. She doubted there would be many times they would be in a situation similar to last evening, but she already felt a bond of intimacy forming between them.

He had caught on quickly to whist, but that had not surprised her. Despite his saying he had had the barest of education, she found him to be intelligent. She wanted good things for him. He had lived in poverty for most of his life, only coming into his title by accident. She wondered if his father would have sought out his son if Julian had not found those letters from the Marquess of Aldridge after his mother's death. Something told her Aldridge never would have done so.

That meant she never would have met Julian.

She rang for Tally and dressed for the day, a spring in her step as she made her way down to the breakfast room, and she found her father at the table, something she never saw. Glancing to Val, he merely shrugged.

"Good morning, Papa. Val."

A footman seated her, and another poured her tea. She placed cream and sugar into it, stirring well. Her father continued to read his newspaper while Val and she talked during their meal. Neither of them brought up the dance lesson which would occur this afternoon. It wasn't as if she hid anything from her parents. She simply did not think Papa would be interested.

Surprisingly, he set aside his newspaper and directed his attention to her. "What do you think of Lord Aldridge, Ariadne?"

She didn't know if this was some kind of test, but she answered as honestly as she could without giving away her growing interest in the marquess.

"I find his lordship to be a gentleman, Papa. I know Val has become friends with Lord Aldridge, and I am glad he is enjoying time with our new neighbor."

"He will need a marchioness," Papa commented.

"Yes, Papa. He will," she replied, wondering where this conversation was leading.

"The old Aldridge never had any luck with wives. Each time he wed, his bride was younger than the previous one. He never could get a child off any of them. I cannot know if it was their fault—or his." Papa paused. "Or if that kind of thing runs in a family."

"I doubt it does, Papa," Val said, entering the conversation. "There have been numerous Marquesses of Aldridge over the years. They cannot all have had barren wives, or the title would have died out and been returned to the crown. As far as the current Lord Aldridge goes, Con and I like him a great deal."

Her father's attention swung to his son, and the duke nodded thoughtfully. "You will know more about the eligible bachelors this Season than your mother or I ever could. I am leaving things up to you, Claibourne, to make certain your sister marries well."

"Rest assured, Papa, that Con and I both have Ariadne's best interests at heart. Why, we have already discussed a few of the gentlemen we wish to introduce her to when the Season begins."

Val paused a moment before adding, "So far, the Marquess of Aldridge is at the top of our list. I have been impressed with his integrity and intelligence. Con and I even went and visited his country estate in Surrey."

"You did?" Her father's eyebrows arched in interest. "Tell me about it."

Her brother spouted numerous details regarding Aldridge Manor. The amount of farmland and number of tenants it held. The crops grown and what the yield had been the past several years. He spoke of the livestock and mill.

All the while, her father listened carefully, finally saying, "That is a good deal of information to possess, Claibourne. I am grateful you have taken such an interest in Aldridge."

Ariadne couldn't help herself. "Are you saying that you would approve a match between myself and the marquess, Papa?"

"It is much too early for that, Ariadne," her father said dismissively. "Your brother will recommend a suitable husband, and I will have the final approval. I expect you to be wed—or at least betrothed—by Season's end."

She knew her mother would favor a smart wedding held at St. George's, and Ariadne wanted to be heard now before Mama could influence Papa regarding the ceremony.

"I would like to be betrothed, Papa, but I would prefer not to wed in town. I know a great many couples speak their vows at St. George's, but I have always thought marriage to be a solemn, intimate occasion. I would prefer my marriage to take place in Kent, at the Willowshire church near Millbrooke."

Before Papa could respond, her brother came to her rescue. "That is a splendid idea, Ariadne. So many wish for an invitation to the wedding of a duke's daughter. If you hold the ceremony near Papa's ducal country seat, it could become the most exclusive invitation following the Season. Papa and Mama could choose only the cream of Polite Society to attend your vows."

She mouthed *thank you* to him, and he beamed at her. Glancing to her father, she saw him nod.

"I agree wholeheartedly," he said. "Only a handful of my closest friends should witness the marriage of my daughter and her betrothed. It will be as you wish, Ariadne. We will make certain your betrothed understands the family's wishes regarding where the ceremony is to be held."

And Mama, she thought silently, thrilled that the large obstacle had been so easily removed before it even surfaced.

Her father rose. "My sister tells me Lord Marley is in town. I am going to meet him at White's now."

The duke left the breakfast room, and she said to Val, "Thank you so much. I did not want Mama to plan for a wedding which involved hundreds in attendance. You speaking up approvingly swayed Papa. You know once he gets something in his mind, he is determined to have his way. Now, no matter what Mama says, I will have the luxury of marrying at home."

"It seems he thinks Lord Aldridge might be a worthy candidate for your hand. What do you think, Sis?"

"Just as I said to Papa, I like Lord Aldridge quite a bit, but I am looking forward to the Season and meeting many others. If Lord Aldridge is interested in courting me, however, I would be open to his suit once the social whirl begins."

"Despite what Papa just said, it is not for me to tell you whom to wed. I want it to be your choice, though I am happy to share my opinions with you regarding your suitors. I will say that Aldridge has a good heart. He is a good man. I hope you will give him your full consideration."

Ariadne planned to do that very thing.

"I need to speak to your valet."

"Whatever do you want with Fisham?" Val asked.

"He still has his fiddle, doesn't he?"

Understanding lit her brother's eyes. "You wish for him to play for us this afternoon during the lesson."

"Exactly."

Val looked to Grigsby. "Would you have Fisham join us in the ballroom now? And have him bring his instrument."

The siblings went to the ballroom, drawing back several of the curtains. By the time they had done so, Fisham joined them.

"I brought my violin, my lord," the valet said, looking rather confused. "Do you wish me to play for you?"

"I do," Ariadne said. "I am going to be giving a dance lesson to our neighbor this afternoon, Fisham. I would like you to play for us while I do so. I know I can count the beat, but once Lord Aldridge gets the steps down, it would be more pleasurable to see the marquess dance to music."

"I am more than happy to accommodate you, my lady," the servant replied.

"Then come to the ballroom at one o'clock promptly," she said. "You may leave your violin here until then."

Next, Ariadne went to her bedchamber and rang for Tally. When the maid arrived, she said, "I have need of you this afternoon. As a dancer."

Her maid's eyes lit with interest. "And where might I be dancing, my lady?"

"I am going to help teach Lord Aldridge how to dance. Fisham has agreed to play for us. I need another woman to participate."

"You know I love to dance, my lady. I am happy to join you and his lordship."

That afternoon, she went to the ballroom a few minutes before one o'clock, finding both servants already present. They opened more of the curtains, and minutes later, Val and Con appeared with Julian in tow. She would have to remember to call the marquess by his title since servants were present.

"Thank you for coming, Lord Aldridge," she said formally.

"Thank you for agreeing to this lesson, my lady."

"I was going to have Val or Con play the part of another lady, but I have convinced my maid Tally to assist us today."

Con immediately said, "That means you only need Val and not me. I am off then."

Ariadne had a good idea that her cousin was going to see a woman and gave him a knowing smile.

"You should not look at me that way, Cousin," Con said,

laughing as he exited.

She turned her attention now to Julian. "The most important thing is to feel the rhythm of the music, my lord. Just about every country dance occurs in a four-count. One, two, three, four. One, two, three four." Looking to Fisham, she said, "Play something."

The valet took up his bow and began playing. Ariadne waited a moment and then started counting aloud, nodding for Julian to participate, as well.

"Good, my lord. It seems you can identify the beat. Many people have no rhythm. I am happy to learn that is not the case with you."

She motioned for them to go to the center of the room. The only person who remained farther away was Fisham, who seated himself in a chair.

For the next quarter-hour, Ariadne went over the steps of a popular country dance that she knew would be played at upcoming balls. She had all of them do the four-count aloud as they moved through the steps. Julian caught on quickly to the pattern.

"You have an excellent memory, my lord," she praised.

"Memorizing has always come naturally to me," he shared.

"Then it is time we tried our steps set to music." She looked at Fisham, telling him what to play, at about three-quarters the usual tempo.

"Aye, my lady," the valet replied.

They went through an entire dance, with Julian faltering only once. Even Tally praised the marquess, telling him he caught on more quickly than anyone she had ever seen dance.

"This time, play the same tune, but at its usual tempo," Ariadne instructed.

For the next couple of hours, they danced to Fisham's music, only stopping and moving to a new dance when Julian had down the steps for that particular dance. Ariadne was able to teach him several different country dances, and she knew he would be a popular dancer at balls come the Season.

"Dancing has worked up a thirst," Val proclaimed. "It is close to teatime. I am heading to the drawing room."

"And I have a gown to hem for you, my lady," Tally said.

Fisham stood. "Do you still need me, my lady?"

"No. Your contribution made a huge difference, Fisham," she said.

"Thank you all for participating this afternoon," Julian told everyone. "It made things make sense to me, having others participating in the dance and showing me where to go."

He turned to Ariadne. "I do think I'm a bit confused about a few steps, my lady. Might we go over them once more before you go to take tea?"

"Certainly, my lord."

As Val left, she called, "His lordship and I will be in the drawing room in a few minutes."

Her brother waved a hand in response as he exited with Tally and Fisham.

"I do not know which steps you are having problems with, Julian. I think you have danced beautifully this afternoon."

He stepped toward her, and Ariadne sensed an electricity in the air. Her heart began beating rapidly as she gazed up at him.

"You saved me a great deal of embarrassment," he said, his voice low and husky, sending a tingle dancing along her spine. "I cannot imagine what I was thinking, ready to turn up at a ball without having danced a step in my life."

Swallowing, she said, "You are more than prepared now, Julian. With more practice, you will be an accomplished dancer and in demand."

Suddenly, his hands rested on her shoulders, and she could feel the heat from his fingers through the material of her gown.

"You have taken care of me in several ways, Ariadne. I only wish there were something I could do for you."

Kiss me...

His eyes widened slightly, and she realized she'd voiced her thought aloud. Before she could scramble away, his head bent, and he lowered his lips to hers.

Chapter Thirteen

Even though Adriane had inadvertently asked for the kiss, it still proved to be unexpected.

And oh, so delightful . . .

She had never been kissed before and only knew a couple pressed their lips together. As Julian did so now, his touch brought sensations roaring within her. She was aware of his hands still gripping her shoulders. The spice of his cologne. The heat of his body so very close to hers. And his lips against hers, soft and yet somehow firm at the same time.

His hands slid down her back, bringing her closer to him, enveloping her in a wonderful warmth as her heart beat wildly. Her palms pressed against his chest, which seemed harder than stone, reflecting the laborer he had been until only recently. She grew dizzy as he lifted his mouth from hers, then kissing her again, this time harder.

Something awakened deep within her, a yearning she had not known existed. Something that she realized only this man could fill.

He broke the kiss again, despite her murmuring a protest. His lips brushed her brow tenderly, and suddenly she felt like a prized treasure he valued above everything else. He kissed her eyelids. Her cheeks. The tip of her nose. Each kiss was sweet and playful.

But she wanted more of what had come before. Gripping the lapels of his coat, she yanked him down to her again, their lips colliding, bruising. His kiss was more demanding than before, frustrating her because she did not know what he asked of her. Whatever it was, she was too inexperienced to give him. She sought to end the kiss and ask him what he needed from her, but as she did, his tongue stroked her bottom lip. Sizzling need rippled through her. Instinct took over, and she opened to him. That was all the invitation he needed, because Julian's tongue suddenly swept inside her mouth in a new kind of kiss. One extremely intimate and daring. Lovingly, he stroked her tongue, exploring, searching.

For her part, Ariadne determined not to be a passive observer, but rather an active participant. Boldly, her tongue met his, and a war as old as time began between them, only she realized both of them would be victors.

Her hands slid up his chest, moving past his shoulders, one hand gripping his nape. She found her fingers playing with his silky hair and heard the growl come from him. For the first time in her life, she knew she exercised her feminine powers.

And liked it.

The kiss went on and on, many kisses which blurred together. Heat rose within her until Ariadne thought she might burst into flames. Her breasts grew heavy. The place between her legs began pulsating in need. A wicked thought occurred to her.

She wanted him to touch her. There.

How had she turned so wanton, so quickly? Is this what kissing did? And still, she kissed him back, the unexpected first kiss now becoming one which she knew she could not live without.

"Ariadne!"

Hearing her name startled her, and she jerked away from Julian, seeing Val headed toward them, a thunderous look darkening his face.

Reaching them, he demanded, "What the bloody hell are you two doing, kissing like that?"

She found herself tongue-tied as her brother glowered at them.

Julian spoke up. "It is my fault. I apologize to you and Lady Ariadne."

Anger sprouted within her, and she turned to him. "You are apologizing?" she accused. "*I* was the one who asked for the kiss. And I was enjoying it very much until my brother interrupted us."

She felt Val clasp her elbow and turned to face him.

"You *asked* to be kissed?" he demanded.

Her face flamed. "I did not quite realize I was asking aloud," she amended. "I was thinking it, and somehow, the words slipped from me."

His eyes narrowed. "You might have asked for a kiss, but Lord Aldridge did not have to accommodate your request," Val said coldly. "Go to your bedchamber, Ariadne. You are in no condition to be seen at tea. I will tell Mama you have a headache."

The bold woman who had kissed Julian with abandon now vanished, being replaced by the timid, obedient girl she had always been.

"Yes, Val," she said, glancing to Julian and quickly away again. Her kissing partner looked incredibly guilty. "I will see you another time, my lord," she told him, not wanting to know what her brother was going to say to him.

Fleeing the ballroom, she returned to her bedchamber and fell upon the bed. Her fingertips went to her swollen lips, touching them in wonder. She lay there, reliving every moment she'd had with Julian. Every kiss. Every sigh.

She must have fallen asleep because the next thing Ariadne knew, Tally had entered the room.

"How are you feeling, my lady?" the maid asked. "I wish you would have rung for me. I could have massaged your temples for you."

She pushed herself to a sitting position. "I had no need of you, Tally. I merely took a nap and feel much better now."

"Do you feel well enough to dress for dinner?"

Ariadne regretted having been a meek lamb. "Yes. I shall wear the pale blue silk."

Once dressed, she went to the drawing room and found her parents and Val already there, each of them sipping a drink.

Parsons approached her, bearing a silver tray. "Would you care for a sherry, my lady?"

"Yes, thank you," she said, lifting the crystal glass from the tray and sipping it, feeling its warmth fill her.

But not the warmth she had experienced being in Julian's arms, participating in those drugging kisses.

Mama asked, "Are you feeling better, Ariadne?"

"Yes, Mama. It was just a slight headache. I napped a bit and feel completely myself now."

Her gaze shifted to her brother, and she looked defiantly at him.

They were called into dinner, and she forced herself to act as if nothing had happened. Ariadne knew, however, that her world had changed radically with that unexpected kiss.

After dinner, she decided to speak with Val privately and asked, "Would you care to play a game of chess with me?"

"All right," he said neutrally, accompanying her to the winter parlor where the chessboard sat, ready for them to begin their game.

They took a seat opposite one another, and she said, "We need to speak about what you saw this afternoon."

Val frowned deeply. "You were fortunate that I am the only one who saw the two of you and not a servant, who might spread gossip. What were you thinking, Sis? You know very well how much I like Julian, but finding him gobbling up my sister was too much."

"I do not wish to come between the two of you," she told him. "I hope you will still remain friends with him, Val, but I have felt something growing between us, almost since we met."

"You realize if I had told Mama and Papa what I had seen, he would be forced to wed you, even before your come-out."

"I understand. I am grateful you kept silent. Thank you."

"What were you thinking?"

"You are just like our parents, Val. You are treating me as if I were a child—and not a woman. I wanted to kiss Julian. I have never kissed a man before. I needed to see what a kiss was like."

"There are many kinds of kisses, Sis, and the one I saw you participating in was dangerous. What are your feelings toward him?"

"Confused," she admitted. "I do like him, Val. That is what led to the kiss. I have sensed an electricity between us. It is as if I am drawn to him in some inexplicable way."

His face softened. "So, you do have true feelings for him."

"I suppose I do, but they are so new and fragile, I do not know quite what to make of them." She hesitated. "I know you have coupled with women. Can you tell me what that experience is like? I asked Mama, but she brushed me off. She merely said I would need to do whatever my husband told me to do and will not prepare me in the least."

Her gaze bored into him. "I need to know more than that. You are the only person I can turn to."

"Coming together with someone is a most intimate experience," he began. "It does not have to involve kissing, but it can. You will touch one another. Caress. Stroke. You may or may not remove your clothes. I suspect many wives of the *ton* keep their night rails on during the act, but it is the deepest level of intimacy which can occur between two people."

Feeling awkward, she asked, "Where would my husband touch me? Be specific, Val. I do not want to go into a marriage blind."

For the next few minutes, her brother explained to her the mechanics of lovemaking. The process surprised her. Some of it even shocked her.

When he finished, she said, "Thank you. I needed to know all that. I fear too many mothers of the *ton* do not inform their daughters about what to expect." Then she asked, "Do you do this with regularity?"

He nodded. "Men have needs, Ariadne. Women do, as well. It is perfectly natural. Not every woman is comfortable with what occurs in the marital bed, however. It can cause some husbands to look outside their marriage for satisfaction. In town, there are places men can go in order to have their needs met. Some men even keep a mistress, setting her up in a household so she is available whenever he wants to see her."

She gasped. "Have you done that?"

Val laughed. "No, I am not one to make such a commitment to any woman." He paused. "I am going to tell you things now that you must be made aware of. To keep you from being hurt later on. Many husbands stray from their marital vows. It is commonplace within Polite Society."

"You mean . . . after they wed?"

He nodded grimly. "Moreover, once a wife has provided an heir and spare, many of them do the same, as well."

"That is awful, Val!"

Shrugging, he said, "It is the way of Polite Society. Now, if you find a man you truly like and he has a fondness for you, in return, that may not be the case. I do want you to be prepared all the same because there is a strong likelihood that your own husband will follow this practice."

"I would not take kindly to my husband going elsewhere and doing such . . . things . . . with another woman. Why, I might claw his eyes out. And hers, too."

He grinned. "I see a passion within you, Sis. I am certain you will keep your husband happy and at home. But will that husband be Lord Aldridge?"

"I cannot say at this time, Val. The way he made me feel when we kissed, though? It was heavenly. But would other men also make me feel the same?"

"You are already friends with him. I think friendship is an excellent foundation for a marriage. I would not commit to Julian yet, though. You are right in that you are inexperienced. You must make your come-out and see a bit of society."

"Should I . . . kiss any other men?"

"It wouldn't hurt to do so and compare how you feel about them, versus Julian. However, I must warn you to be most careful in doing so, Sis. I have already told you that if you are caught kissing anyone—actually, even being alone with a gentleman—you will be ruined unless he weds you, amidst much gossip."

"You have given me much to think about, Val. I will make my come-out as planned, but I already think very favorably of Julian. Will you promise me you will be kind to him? I am almost afraid to ask what you said to him after I rushed from the ballroom."

"I let him no in no uncertain terms that he is to keep his hands and lips off you." He smiled. "I will tell him tomorrow that we are still friends, though."

"Thank you," she said fervently. "I would never wish to come between you and your new friendship."

"I think you should not see him for a while, Sis. Put a little distance between the two of you. The Season starts in two weeks. You need to keep busy with other things."

"I miss Lia and Tia," she said forlornly. "Do you think you could convince Mama to allow them to come to town to be with me?"

He studied her and then nodded. "I think having our sisters here would be good for you and them. I will speak to Mama tomorrow regarding the matter."

She reached for his hand and squeezed it. "Thank you, Val. You are the best brother ever." Then Ariadne smiled broadly. "Are you ready to lose to me?"

"Never!" he said, laughing.

They played two games, with Val winning both. Her mind had not been on the game—but on Julian Barrington instead. Her brother was right, though. It would be wise to keep to herself and not see Julian until the Season began.

Chapter Fourteen

Ariadne cried, "Lia! Tia!" as her sisters were handed down from the carriage.

She ran toward them, embracing them both at the same time, tears of happiness running down her cheeks.

"We missed you so, Ariadne," Lia said, tears welling in her own eyes.

"We want to hear about everything you have been doing," Tia added.

"I have been beside myself without being able to see you every day," she told the twins. "Come inside. You need some tea after your journey to town."

She looked to Parsons, who stood nearby, and the butler nodded. "I will see to tea at once, my lady." He looked at her siblings. "It is delightful to have you here with us, my ladies. If Mrs. Parsons or I can do anything for you, please let us know."

They entered the foyer, where Mrs. Parsons greeted them, saying, "I have prepared a large bedchamber for you, my ladies. Her Grace suggested that you share one."

"We are used to doing so," Tia said. "In fact, we prefer it."

"We have always shared," Lia confirmed. "Thank you, Mrs. Parsons."

They went to the drawing room, her sisters pointing out pieces of art and furniture they remembered along the way.

"It has been many years since we have been here, Ariadne,"

Lia said. "Have you seen anymore of Con? Your last letter mentioned how much you have enjoyed talking with him."

They took their seats, and she said, "Our cousin is wonderful, like another brother to me already. I can see why he and Val have been the closest of friends all these years."

"Where *is* Val?" Tia demanded. "I thought he would be here to greet us. Mama, too. How on earth did you ever convince her to allow us to come to town?"

"I missed the both of you terribly and told Val so. He is the one who persuaded Mama to have you come for a few weeks to be with me. Val said it would not hurt to have the two of you see a little of what a Season is like. Of course, you cannot accompany me to any events. Mama also said you will not be allowed in the drawing room if I have any suitors call upon me."

"It does not matter to me," Tia declared. "We are here. In town. It is so nice to be somewhere different for once."

She looked to Lia. "What of you? Are you happy to be here?"

Lia smiled. "I am happy to see you and Val."

"Is your governess coming?" she asked.

Tia's nose crinkled. "Miss Nixon is coming in the next carriage, along with a maid to care for us. She has said we will have our lessons in the mornings, but we will be free in the afternoons to ride or walk and see a bit of town."

Tea arrived, and Ariadne poured out for them.

Lia said, "You will soon be doing this in your own household. Are you excited about finding a husband?"

It was on the tip of her tongue to tell them about Julian, but Ariadne decided to hold back for now. She assumed at some point the twins would meet the marquess, and she would seek their opinion about him after they had done so.

"Papa has let me know his expectations are that I should be betrothed by Season's end."

"That does not seem fair!" Tia cried. "What if you do not find any of the eligible bachelors amenable to you?"

"The assumption is I will find a husband—or one will be

found for me."

She watched both her siblings shudder at that thought and wanted to reassure them.

"It is not as bad as it sounds. Val and Con are already thinking about gentlemen they are friendly with, and they will introduce them to me. In fact, Papa has told Val that he will be the one responsible for helping me to find a husband."

"Our brother will not let you down," Lia said, patting Ariadne's hand. "He has always been protective of the three of us."

"And if Con is helping him, that makes it all the better," Tia added.

Once they finished their tea, the twins went to their room, with Ariadne telling them to be in the foyer in half an hour because they were to go to her modiste's appointment with her and Mama. That news excited both twins.

Ariadne made her way downstairs, finding Mama already waiting in the foyer.

"I was not in favor of your sisters coming to town," Mama said bluntly. "I have enough to worry about, launching you into Polite Society, without having to worry about them."

"They will not be a bother to you, Mama," she reassured. "Val only wanted them to see a little of what they can expect for their own come-outs next spring. They will be leaving in a few weeks. Val and I will take responsibility for them."

"Do so then," Mama said dismissively.

Sometimes, Ariadne wondered why her mother had even borne children since she never seemed interested in them. Then again, the only child she did seem to care about was her son, the heir apparent. She supposed when her parents tried to have the obligatory spare, they had been disappointed when three girls followed. One time, she had overheard Mama speaking with one of her friends, saying birthing the twins had almost killed her and that the doctor had told her there were to be no more children after that. Ariadne decided her mother's disappointment in not providing another son was why she treated her daughters so callously. It caused her to vow to treat her own sons and daughters as equals, loving them no matter what their gender.

She only hoped she could find a like-minded husband who would not favor his sons over his daughters, at least overtly.

That caused her to think of Julian again. Because he had not been brought up in the world of the *ton*, she believed he might be different from other men. She only wondered if they were meant to be together.

Tia and Lia came downstairs in high spirits but tempered them once they saw Mama's frowning disapproval.

In the carriage on the way to Madame Laurent's, Mama told them, "You are to be seen and not heard while we are at the modiste's shop. It is only because Valentinian insisted you be here that I had the goodwill to allow you to come to town for a short while."

"Yes, Mama," the twins said in unison, casting their gazes downward.

Once they arrived, however, Mama saw one of her friends and abandoned the three of them. The woman was choosing fabrics and insisted that Mama assist her. That left them on their own, and they went to the rear of the shop as Giselle fitted Ariadne.

Lia looked at the rack of gowns which her sister would be trying on. "These are beautiful," she said, wonder in her voice. "The materials are so luxurious."

Giselle aided Ariadne in slipping from her gown and then placed the first of the ballgowns to be fitted on her.

"Oh!" Tia exclaimed. "You look like a princess from a fairytale." She looked to her twin. "Just think, Lia. This is what we shall be wearing this time next year."

Tia began dancing about the dressing room, causing the others to laugh.

An hour later, Giselle helped Ariadne dress again and told her, "You may come for a final fitting for these in a few days, my lady. I have already started cutting the material for the next round of gowns."

"The next round?" Lia asked, round-eyed. "How many gowns are they making up for you, Ariadne?"

She thanked Giselle and led her siblings from the dressing room and said, "It is an obscene number, Lia. Do you know that I will only wear each of those creations once?"

"No!" both twins exclaimed.

"I had no idea that was how things worked," she confided. "Apparently, it is a great sin to wear a ballgown more than once, and Polite Society looks down upon you if you do so."

Lia nodded in understanding. "That would lessen your chances of making a good match because others would speak ill about you. Gossip spreads quickly, and it might reach the ears of your suitors and their families."

"Exactly," she confirmed. "While I am unhappy about the expense and waste, I do understand that is how Madame Laurent and Giselle earn a living. Mama has emphasized that more eyes are upon me than most girls who are making their come-outs because I am a duke's daughter. It will be the same for the two of you."

They returned to the center of the dress shop, where Mama was still sitting with her friend and Madame Laurent.

Mama glanced up. "Are you pleased with the gowns, Ariadne?"

"Very much so, Mama. Madame Laurent and Giselle have done a fine job. I will be superbly dressed this Season wearing their creations."

"You may take the carriage straight home," Mama said. "Lady Charworth still requires my advice. Have it sent back to me."

"Yes, Mama," she said, surprised that her mother would allow them to return home unescorted. Then again, they had both their driver and a pair of footmen who would see to them.

She instructed their driver to take them home and then return for Her Grace. As they journeyed through the streets of town, Ariadne began pointing out different sights to her sisters, and the happiness her siblings experienced spilled over to her. She decided once she wed, she would have both Lia and Tia come stay with her for a while. Perhaps the girls could spend Christmas with her and her new husband.

Their vehicle turned into the square, and she saw a hansom cab pulling up in front of their own townhouse.

"I see Val," Lia said enthusiastically.

"Is that Con with him?" Tia asked. "And who is the other gentleman?"

Her heart sped up as she tried to calmly say, "Yes, that is Con with Val. He is the one in the midnight blue coat and buff breeches. With them is Lord Aldridge. He is our neighbor and has held his title less than a year."

As their carriage made the circle and pulled up to their townhouse, Lia said, "Lord Aldridge is quite handsome. Have you met him, Ariadne?"

The vehicle came to a halt. "Yes, I have. He has become friendly with Val and Con and been to tea."

The door opened, and she saw that the three gentlemen waited for them on the pavement. Tia bounded from the carriage first, Val stepping forward to hand her down and embrace her. He then assisted Lia before taking Ariadne's hand and bringing her down.

Con was hugging Tia, and he glanced to Lord Aldridge, who averted his gaze. Ariadne wondered if he did so because Val had frightened the marquess with his stern warnings about kissing his sister.

Or worse. What if Julian had changed his mind about the kisses they had shared and no longer had feelings for her? Or he wanted to avoid future conflict and had washed his hands of her?

She swallowed her dismay at that thought and smiled brightly at her cousin as Val made the introductions.

"Con, you met Tia and Lia when our families were together, what eight? Nine years ago?"

As Con greeted the twins, he told them, "Just as I told Ariadne I recalled her copper hair, that is how was able to tell the two of you apart," their cousin revealed. "You favored one another so much in the face and still do, but I remember Lia's auburn hair and Tia's strawberry blonde shade. I am glad Val was able to convince Uncle Charles and Aunt Alice to have you come to town for a while."

Val said, "This is Lord Aldridge." Pointing to the townhouse at the bottom of the square, he added, "The marquess resides there and is our neighbor. May I present my younger sisters, Lady Lia and Lady Tia Worthington?"

Ariadne couldn't help but smile to herself as Julian stepped forward, now knowing how an introduction worked. He bowed and took Lia's hand, kissing it, saying, "I am happy to meet you, Lady Lia." He did the same with Tia. "I will be off now and let you become reacquainted with your cousin."

She looked to her brother pleadingly, and Val nodded. "It is teatime, Aldridge. Would you like to come in for it?"

Julian seemed torn about the invitation, but Con slapped him on the back. "I know you favor the tarts here, Aldridge. Come inside with us."

It would have been awkward for Julian to refuse the invitation after that, and so the marquess said, "I would be delighted to join you."

They went to the drawing room, and Val asked, "Where is Mama?"

"She stayed at the modiste's shop, helping to advise a friend about her wardrobe for this Season," Ariadne told her brother.

The teacarts were rolled in, and Parsons came to her. "My lady, His Grace sent word that he will not be at tea this afternoon. He is taking it with Lord and Lady Marley."

"Thank you, Parsons. I shall pour out for our guests."

She had had numerous lessons in serving tea to others and felt comfortable now as she did so. With only the young people present, it was a lively teatime although she noticed Julian barely contributed to their conversation.

"How long will you be in town?" Con asked the twins.

As always, Tia took the lead. "Val told Mama it was only for a few weeks, then we will be banished to the country once more."

"Tia, that is unkind," Lia chided. "You love Millvale."

"I do," Tia responded, "but I love the idea of an adventure in town more. We have spent our entire lives in the country, Lia. I want to go places." Then her eyes lit up. "We must go to Gunter's," she declared.

"Ah, I remember all three of our families going there the one time we were all together," Con said. "I have not been to Gunter's in ages."

Val looked to Ariadne. "Do you have any engagements for tomorrow?"

"I am seeing the milliner again tomorrow morning, but my afternoon is free."

"Then we shall make merry at Gunter's tomorrow afternoon," he proclaimed. "How does one o'clock sound?"

Everyone nodded in agreement, but she saw Julian remained quiet.

"You are welcome to come with us, my lord," she told him.

His gaze finally met hers for the first time that afternoon. "I would not intrude upon a family outing."

"Have you ever been to Gunter's?" she asked.

"No, my lady. I have not."

"Then you must come with us, Lord Aldridge," Tia encouraged. "Everyone should go to Gunter's. I insist, my lord."

Ariadne saw Julian could not turn down her sister without seeming rude. "If it will not be a burden to the rest of you, then I would be happy to accompany your party, Lady Tia."

"You are never a bother, Aldridge," Val said. He looked to the others. "We shall depart from here at half-past noon. I will ask if Papa needs the carriage or not."

"Mine is available to us," Julian said quietly. "It will seat all of us with room to spare."

"Excellent," Val declared.

Tea ended, and the marquess thanked them for the invitation, saying he had another engagement.

After he exited the drawing room, Tia said, "It will be so much fun getting to know more of you, Con," she told their cousin. "Lord Aldridge is very quiet, though."

Lia spoke up. "There is nothing wrong with being quiet."

Her twin laughed. "That is because you are one of those quiet ones. Perhaps you and the marquess will make a match during next year's Season. Unless he is already wed," Tia amended.

The thought of Julian wed to anyone else, much less her own sister, made Ariadne nauseous.

Val quickly said, "The two of you do not need to worry about matches at this point. Con and I will see that Ariadne is taken care of first. Then we will turn our attention to the two of you."

"And Lucy," Con said. "My sister is to make her come-out next spring."

Tia clapped her hands in delight. "Oh, that will be ever so much fun, doing so with our cousin."

Con took his leave, and Ariadne went to her bedchamber. She worried now what her relationship would be like with Julian.

Had that unexpected kiss changed it for the better—or the worse?

Chapter Fifteen

Julian did not want to go to Gunter's, whatever it was. It had been impossible to turn down the invitation, however. Lady Tia had appeared so eager for him to join their group. She was lively and vibrant, and he did not think she was used to being told no. Not that she seemed spoiled. Both she and Lady Lia had conducted themselves well. He sneaked glimpses of Ariadne, who looked fondly at her sisters throughout tea.

It was Ariadne he wished to avoid.

He hadn't minded Val chastising him for kissing his sister. Julian deserved the dressing down his friend gave him. Although once Val had concluded his rant, he had offered Julian his hand. For his part, Julian had apologized, saying he had not expected to kiss Ariadne and still wasn't quite sure how it had happened. Val emphasized the need for discretion, explaining that Julian should never be alone with any unmarried lady because it could lead to an instant betrothal in order to save the lady's reputation. Val had said he liked Julian too much to see his hand forced.

It was all something Val had shared with him before, but it seemed more real to him because of that kiss with Ariadne. After that, he'd vowed to himself never to be alone with her again unless several others were present and not to seek out her company.

Because he was afraid he would be compelled to kiss her again—at length—if they were alone again.

He knew she felt the attraction between them, but he was determined to put it to an end. She was the daughter of a duke. While he did possess a high rank himself, Julian had finally let himself realize the truth.

He wasn't good enough for a woman such as Ariadne.

She radiated joy and kindness and was beautiful and poised. He didn't deserve such a woman. She needed to be with a man who was her equal, not some poorly educated former dockworker that had spent his entire life in poverty. He might be a marquess now, with a fancy house and plenty of servants to wait on him, but inside, Julian still felt like that same, inadequate man. As if he were an imposter traipsing about Polite Society, fooling no one.

Because of that, he would not pursue Ariadne. No, Lady Ariadne. He had to start putting both physical and emotional distance between them. He did not want her to believe that he would vie for her hand. He was merely her family's neighbor. The sooner she understood that, the better. He would not speak of this to her, though. Julian figured once the Season started, eligible men would be lined up outside her door, competing for her attention. With a long list of suitors, he would not be missed.

He had decided after listening to Con and Val that he would pursue a wallflower. They were women who proved to be shy or unpopular and remained on the sidelines at social events. Looks were not important to him. All he needed was someone caring, a woman who would bear his children. He had always hated being an only child and looked upon Val's and Ariadne's bantering with a bit of jealousy. He hoped his marchioness would give him a large family. In turn, he would lavish attention upon both his wife and those children she produced.

Wedding a wallflower would also give a woman who might not have had a chance at marriage the ability to have a life she had always yearned for. Not that he wanted his future wife to be grateful or feel indebted to him. He simply knew that wallflowers were outcasts, and he felt like one himself. Together, he hoped he and his wife would build a strong relationship and come to like one another.

When the knock sounded on the door of his study, Julian rose, knowing it was Grigsby here to tell him that his carriage was ready.

Opening the door, he saw his butler. "Yes, I know. The coach awaits."

"It does, my lord." Grigsby paused. "I know it is not my place, but Mrs. Grigsby and I are happy that you are settling in and have made friends."

He smiled wryly. "Did you think it would prove hard for a laborer to do so?"

His butler looked taken aback. "No, my lord," he said stiffly. "I only meant it is good that you are entertaining and going places. This household was an unhappy one for many years. I hope you will bring light to it."

"I am touched, Grigsby," he said, causing his butler's face to pinken slightly. "I still don't know if I will fit in with the majority of Polite Society once the Season begins, but I have made a few friends. Good ones, I believe."

"We hope you will entertain more often, my lord. I am sorry if I overstepped."

"No. I appreciate the sentiment. And I will inform you that I do hope to bring home a marchioness at Season's end."

Grigsby beamed. "Very good, my lord."

Julian went out to his carriage, feeling pleased that his butler and housekeeper wanted the best for him. Yes, they were in his employ, but he had found the pair to be honest and honorable and was lucky he had them managing his London household.

As he reached the vehicle, he saw the group of siblings leaving Millbrooke's townhouse. At the same time, a hansom cab pulled up bearing Con, who waved in greeting and then paid his driver.

"Ready for Gunter's?" Con asked.

"Since I have no idea what Gunter's is, I cannot say," he replied.

Lady Tia must have heard his comment and said, "Why, Gunter's is the most wonderful place in the world, Lord Aldridge. At least, it seemed that way when we were children."

"You can tell me about it on our way there, my lady," he said affably, determined to enjoy the outing, even as he avoided Ariadne as much as possible.

Val handed up his three sisters and climbed in after them, followed by Con. Julian entered the carriage last. Unfortunately, the only empty spot was next to Lady Ariadne. He took it, settling himself, and then tapped his cane on the roof to signal his driver they were ready to depart. The carriage started up.

"Gunter's is a teashop, my lord," Lady Tia said. "But they are known more for their sweets, particularly their ices and sorbets."

Even Lady Lia's eyes lit with excitement. "The ices are ever so wonderful. Papa took us there the time we came to town. It was us, along with Con's parents and siblings and our uncle George and his four children." She paused. "There are only three of them now. Cousin Lucius died soon after that, along with his father."

"Have you ever had an ice before, my lord?" asked Lady Tia. "They have all kinds of flavors." Her nose crinkled. "Some are quite terrible looking, with vegetables or meat in the frozen concoction. The rest, however, are sweet and delightful."

"I am getting maple again," Lady Lia announced.

"You got that last time," her twin complained. "Try something different."

Lady Lia shook her head. "It has been years since I had it. I have dreamed about it because it was that good. I will have a maple ice. Nothing else will do."

"I will take you more than once to Gunter's while you are here," Val volunteered. "If that changes your mind about what to order."

Lady Lia grinned. "I am still ordering maple today."

Everyone in the carriage laughed, and even Julian said, "I

admire your tenacity, my lady. In fact, you have convinced me that I, too, must sample the maple and no other flavor."

When they arrived in Berkeley Square, Con said, "I hope we are eating inside today."

He frowned. "We would dine outdoors?"

Ariadne told him, "When the weather is pleasant, many people come to Gunter's in an open carriage and park. The waiters will dart across the street, trying to avoid traffic, and come and take orders, then return with them minutes later. I think we should go inside today. They have an array of sandwiches, and I am certain we are all hungry. We can save our ices and sorbets for dessert."

They entered the teashop, and he looked around, surprised to see a young man and lady sitting at a table for two.

Val must have seen his confusion and quietly said, "Gunter's is the one establishment in town where an unmarried couple might be seen in one another's company without a chaperone. I cannot explain why. It simply has always been this way."

Immediately, his mind imagined him sitting at a table with Ariadne, sharing an hour in her company as they tried various ices. Julian shook his head, trying to rid himself of such a fantasy. He would never ask her to accompany him here alone, and she certainly would never ask for him to do so.

A man greeted them. "Lord Claibourne, it has been quite a spell since we have seen you."

"I have all my sisters with me today, Charlie. They have only been here once and are pining for an ice. Also, Lord Aldridge and Lord Dyer have joined us for the outing."

Julian noticed Val mentioned his cousin last. It must be because he held a higher rank than Con. It seemed foolish, considering he had only known Val for a short time, while Con was Val's cousin and longtime friend. He doubted he would ever make sense of the rules of Polite Society.

"We are happy to have you dine at Gunter's," Charlie told the group. "Bert will take care of you today. Please follow me."

He seated them at a table for six. Julian noticed most of the tables held only two or four chairs.

Once they settled, a stout man with a ruddy face came toward them, handing out menus.

"Are we here for sweets today, or more?" he asked.

"We are a ravenous group, Bert, but also one with a sweet tooth." Val told the waiter.

"You have come to the right place, my lord. We have plenty of cakes, pies, and tarts to choose from, as well as our famous ices and sorbets."

"Give us a minute," Con said. "We will peruse the menu and let you know our orders."

After a few minutes, they decided to order a large tray of sandwiches, along with a salad for each of them. Julian was surprised when the sandwiches were brought out. They were stacked high with various meats and cheeses. He bit into one with roast beef, finding the bread soft and the beef as tender as anything he'd ever eaten.

"Gunter's is known for catering many of the *ton*'s affairs," Con shared. "I know Mama has used their services on several occasions."

"Tell us more about our cousins," Lady Lia encouraged. Turning to Julian, she added, "We live far apart from one another and only gathered once years ago. All three families spent a week in town, the cousins getting to know one another. Then we have been apart ever since, save for Val and Con, who went to school and university together."

"As I mentioned to you yesterday, Lucy will make her come-out next Season," Con began. "She is a very spirited young lady, full of joy. She loves to ride. Dru, too, enjoys riding. She is the youngest Alington and feels at home in nature. While Lucy is looking forward to making her come-out, Dru is somewhat ambivalent. I think if Lucy proves successful, Dru will take to things better, especially if Lucy is already wed and can help guide Dru through the process."

"Are you like Val and waiting to wed?" Lady Tia asked her cousin.

Laughing, Con said, "If Val weds, then I will think about doing so. Something tells me I have many carefree bachelor years ahead of me."

Bert returned. "Are you ready to order your ices?"

They debated, all except Julian and Lady Lia. Their gazes met, and her eyes sparkled.

"I am so glad we already made up our minds," she said. "You will not regret your choice of maple, Lord Aldridge."

"I rarely have eaten sweets, so I will take your word that the maple is good."

"Do you not like them?" she asked, frowning.

He should not have opened that door. How could he tell this young, innocent girl that he never had two coins to rub together? Sweets were an unknown luxury to families such as his.

Instead, he told her, "I have only recently started partaking of sweets, and I do like them. Perhaps a little too much."

Bert returned several minutes later with small serving cups. Julian was glad they were small because the ices were quite sweet. Conversation died down as everyone concentrated on their special desserts.

His gaze met Lady Lia's, and he nodded approvingly at her. "You may recommend anything you wish to me in the future, my lady. The maple ice is delicious."

"I am glad you are enjoying it, my lord," she replied.

Val insisted on paying their bill, saying the largest group at the table consisted of Worthingtons.

"With Val paying for our meal and Julian providing the transportation, I must think of some way to contribute," Con said. "How about a ride in Hyde Park? Would you care to explore the park this afternoon, Cousins?"

"Yes!" squealed the twins. "Ariadne has written of how beautiful it is. We are happy to do so, Con."

They returned to his carriage, sitting again in the same places they had before. Julian was conscious of the scent of vanilla coming from Ariadne. It caused a deep yearning within him. He told himself she was not for him and to stop wasting time being infatuated with her.

Julian knew he lied to himself, though. He wasn't infatuated with Ariadne.

He feared he loved her.

He'd instructed his driver to stop at the ducal townhouse. He watched the others climb from the carriage except him. Ariadne was the last to leave.

Turning to him, she asked, "Are you going riding with us, Julian?"

Just hearing his name on her lips caused his pulse to leap. He knew now was the time to put a stop to everything.

"No, Lady Ariadne," he said formally, even though the two of them were alone for a moment. He wanted her to understand things were not going to progress between them. "I have other matters to attend to. In fact, I will be leaving for Aldridge Manor in the morning and not returning until the Season begins."

Disappointment reflected in her sky blue eyes. "I am sorry to hear that, Julian."

"Please. Lord Aldridge. I fear we have become too familiar with one another."

"Because of our kiss?" she asked softly.

"Are you coming, Sis?" called Val.

"Yes," Julian told her. "I was wrong to kiss you. I regret doing so. I promise it will never happen again."

He saw hurt spring to her eyes now, knowing he had put it there. Knowing he must hurt her in order to push her far away.

"I see," she said, swallowing. "Then I wish you a good day, my lord."

She stood and took her brother's waiting hand, not looking back. The door to the carriage shut, and he closed his eyes, knowing he would have to live with the damage he had done to her.

And the damage to his own soul.

CHAPTER SIXTEEN

IT WAS THE night of the opening ball of the Season.
And Ariadne was miserable.

The previous two weeks had inched along, and she had kept all her hurt inside her. No one knew what Julian had said to her. His words in the carriage that day had dashed all her dreams. Thankfully, she had her sisters with her. Even though they were unaware of her distress, they had been a balm to her soul.

She had done more fittings, not only of ballgowns, but of gowns she would wear to other events, as well as ones she would don to receive visits from suitors during morning calls.

The twins had been with her each step of the way, their enthusiasm unbridled. Mama had told them they could remain for the first week of the Season before returning to Millbrooke.

They had gone to Gunter's an additional time with Val and Con, but the place seemed to have lost its charm without Julian being in their party. Lia had asked about him, and Ariadne told her the marquess had business to attend to in the country and that they would not see him until the Season began.

Tally finished dressing Ariadne's hair in an elaborate coiffure, and she caught sight of her maid smiling at her in the mirror.

"You have outdone yourself, Tally," she declared, causing the maid to blush. Standing, she turned so the twins could see her.

"Every man in the ballroom will fall in love with you this evening, Ariadne," Tia exclaimed.

"Your dance programme will be filled," Lia predicted. "Oh, what fun to dance every dance at a ball."

She only wished one of those dances could be with Julian. She told herself to stop thinking of him that way. He had expressed his feelings. He was no longer interested in her, for whatever reason, and she would never question him regarding it. She needed to stop moping about, hoping he might change his mind. Julian was a man unlike others, and she would not be able to replace him easily in her heart. Still, she would be meeting many others this evening. The Season had been something she looked forward to for a long time.

Yet something told her that she would never find a man of Julian's character, much less one whose kiss affected her the way his had.

Mama swept into the room, ordering the twins aside. "Let me look at you, Child."

Her words rankled Ariadne, but she put a placid look upon her face as Mama scrutinized her daughter's appearance.

"Madame Laurent has done her job well," her mother proclaimed. "The gown is flattering. It will attract the eyes of others. Your hair is also suitably dressed."

Mama turned to the twins. "Go to bed now. We will speak with you tomorrow."

"But we want to wait up for Ariadne," protested Tia. "We want to hear all about tonight's first ball."

Mama clucked her tongue. "We will not arrive home until at least four or five o'clock in the morning. You may hear about the ball after Ariadne has slept."

"You will be out all night? Into morning?" Lia questioned.

"Of course," Mama said dismissively. "The dancing will be broken up when our hosts serve a midnight buffet. Dancing will then resume for several more hours. Everyone in Polite Society makes a point to attend the first ball of each Season, which makes it so difficult to find your carriage and driver afterward. It will take a good hour or longer to return home."

Ariadne had known none of this. In fact, she thought her mother had done a poor job in preparing her daughter for the Season. Yes, they had gone around to the various shops so that she was dressed impeccably, but as far as anything else went, Mama had neglected her duties. Only Val had filled in a few blanks for her regarding social etiquette and the behavior expected from her.

"Come," Mama ordered. "His Grace is waiting for us."

Lia went to embrace her, and Mama shrieked. "Get back, Cornelia! Do not wrinkle or muss Ariadne in any way. She must be perfect tonight."

"Yes, Mama," Lia said meekly. She looked at Ariadne and said, "I hope you have a wonderful time at your first ball."

"Remember every detail because we want to hear about everything," Tia reminded her, taking her twin's hand and leading Lia from the room.

Ariadne followed her mother down the stairs, and they accompanied Papa to the carriage awaiting them.

Traffic was brutal. They only had a few blocks to travel, and she thought they could have easily walked the distance more quickly. Her mother would have been appalled at that idea, and Ariadne thought her slippers would not have held up to the walk.

The carriage slowly rolled to a halt, and the door opened. "This is as close as we can get, Your Graces," a footman announced.

They exited the vehicle and followed the stream of people heading to the townhouse of Lord and Lady Treeley, the host and hostess of this first event.

As they entered the stately townhouse, Ariadne saw a line before them. Her father bypassed it, going up the stairs to the very front. She and Mama followed him, and Ariadne thought it incredibly rude that he would not have them wait their turn to meet Lord and Lady Treeley. She supposed it was one the privileges of his rank, though, because no one called Papa out for doing so.

Gazing out, she saw so many beautifully gowned women and for the first time, she felt a bit insecure. How would she measure up to the rest of the girls who were making their come-outs? There also would be young ladies from last year who had not made a match and would be returning to the Marriage Mart. She prayed her brother and cousin would find a kind man for her. Val had told her he would weed out the fortune hunters, those who would be interested in her only for her large dowry and status as the Duke of Millbrooke's daughter.

Moments later, Val joined them. "I see we are at the front of the line, as usual," he quipped quietly.

"Papa marched straight to the front," she revealed. "No one called him out for doing so."

"He will not be the only one to do so, Sis." Val paused, looking at her from head to toe. "You look beautiful. I hope you are excited about this evening."

All her excitement about the Season had faded, but she smiled brightly, not wishing to betray her true feelings. "Of course. After all, I may meet my future husband tonight."

"Con and I have a list of gentlemen we expressly wish to introduce you to, as well as those we want you to avoid. I will not bore you with names now. You will be deluged hearing too many of them as it is. I have also warned off a few not to even approach you. Ones I do not believe are appropriate for you. They will not be asking you for a dance."

He looked about. "I still do not see Julian here. I know he returned from the country yesterday because he was at White's this morning."

Even hearing the name caused her to tense. Casually, she said, "I hope he was able to complete his business."

"Frankly, I do not think he had any business to see to," Val revealed. "I believe he is nervous about this evening and wanted to retreat to the country in order to collect his thoughts and gather his courage."

"He should not be nervous," she said. "After all, he has looks, wealth, and an enviable title. He will easily find a bride this Season."

Her brother studied her a moment. "I thought Julian was interested in you—and you in him."

Thankfully, Val did not mention the kiss he had witnessed.

"After I got to know him a bit better, I believe we would not suit," she explained, deliberately remaining vague. She looked across the room, feeling Val's gaze bore into her.

"I thought you would suit quite well," he said, and she knew he was pushing her to reveal more.

Before she could reply, though, a buzz filled the air, and she saw Lord and Lady Treeley had appeared. Footmen opened the doors to the ballroom, and she peeked inside, seeing it decorated with greenery and bright flowers. She turned her attention to their hosts, who were greeting her parents.

"You know my son, Claibourne," Papa said to the earl. "And this is Ariadne, my daughter who is making her come-out this Season."

She could see Lady Treeley scrutinizing her as Ariadne dropped a curtsy to her hosts.

"You will easily find a husband, Lady Ariadne," the countess said. "Your fair face and good breeding will be evident to all."

"Thank you," she murmured, a bit taken aback by the brazen statement, wondering if everyone would speak so bluntly regarding her prospects of marriage.

They moved into the ballroom, Mama directing them to the left, saying, "We will stand here. It is a prime location, and I wish for everyone in attendance tonight to see you first thing, Ariadne."

After that, a flood of people spoke to them upon entering the ballroom. She was introduced to so many others that her head spun, and Ariadne doubted she would be able to recall a single name. She saw Val nod a few times at gentlemen, who only then approached her. Her brother or mother would then make the introduction, and the gentleman would ask to sign her dance card. She knew Val would not have let things go so far unless it was a gentleman he wished for her to know better, and so she agreed every time.

Her programme filled quickly, and she knew she was foolish, holding out hope that Julian might appear and request a dance with her.

Then suddenly, he was there, greeting her parents, looking incredibly handsome in his black evening wear.

He turned to her, a wistful smile crossing his face. "You are lovely, my lady," he complimented, bowing and taking her gloved hand, bending over it and pressing his lips to her fingers. Familiar sensations rolled through her at his touch.

"Thank you, Lord Aldridge. Your tailor has done a fine job with your wardrobe, as well."

For a moment, they merely drank in one another, and she held her breath, ready to hand over her dance programme to him.

Then he bowed again. "If you will excuse me. Viscount Dyer has promised to take me about the room and introduce me to others since I am new to Polite Society."

"I will join you shortly," Val told his friend.

Ariadne watched Julian walk away, her heart shattering into a thousand pieces. He had not wanted a dance with her. He wanted nothing to do with her. She could not let anyone see how his absence affected her, however, and smiled brightly at the next gentleman Val introduced her to. He asked for a dance, and after one more introduction, her programme was now full.

"Ah, Agnes," Mama said. "It is good to see you."

Ariadne turned, immediately recognizing the woman. "Aunt Agnes, how good to see you again after so long."

Her aunt's eyes twinkled as she took in her niece. "My, Ariadne. You have grown into a true beauty. The last I saw you, you were such a sweet, caring girl."

"How are my cousins? I assume Hadrian is still at university."

Aunt Agnes smiled. "He is. He goes by Tray ever since he took his father's title. Once he graduates from Oxford, he will then take his place in Polite Society."

"And Verina and Justina?"

Her aunt talked a bit about her two daughters and then said, "I do not want to take up any more of your time, my dear. You must come see me, however."

"I will do so, Aunt," she promised, recalling how she had liked this woman very much.

The musicians had picked up their instruments and were tuning them. Val, who had disappeared for a bit, returned.

"I had to see to Julian," he apologized. "He will be dancing several times this evening." Her brother frowned. "He was most interested in meeting wallflowers, however. Of course, they were thrilled that a marquess was signing their dance programmes." Val shook his head. "I am not quite certain why he was doing so."

Ariadne didn't understand either. She told herself it shouldn't matter to her. She had only spent a brief time in the marquess' company and shared a few kisses with him.

But those kisses had been powerful. Passionate. She wondered if any man could live up to Julian Barrington.

She saw a gentleman coming her way and supposed he was her first dance partner. He confirmed it when he bowed to her.

"I believe we are to dance this first set, Lady Ariadne." He smiled, a charming smile. "I will remind you that I am Lord Leverley. I know you have met many people this evening already. My advice to you is always to ask your new partner his name again if he does not volunteer it."

She returned his smile. "That is excellent advice, my lord. I will definitely take it."

Val looked at them approvingly, and she knew her brother had left her in good hands with Lord Leverley.

"May I escort you onto the dance floor?" he asked.

She placed her fingers upon his sleeve, and they moved onto the floor. Much to her dismay, however, the group which formed included Julian and his partner. She was plain of face, but she had a beautiful smile which she was now using as she looked up adoringly at the marquess.

Ariadne turned away, gazing at her own partner. "Do you enjoy dancing, my lord?"

"I do. Especially when I have such a lovely partner to dance with," he flirted.

The music began, a lively country dance, the first one she had taught to Julian. Bile rose in her throat, and she swallowed it quickly. She tried not to look at him and concentrated on her own steps and enjoyment. At one point, though, they did join together to dance a few measures before returning to their own partners. Their gazes had met briefly, and deep yearning had filled her.

Lord Leverley escorted her from the floor, and she was quickly claimed by a handsome viscount. The rest of the evening seemed a blur. She did dance every set. She visited the retiring room twice, where she spoke with a few other girls also making their come-outs. The midnight buffet was enjoyable, but she tried not to overeat so she could remain light on her feet.

In the carriage on the way home, she closed her eyes, exhausted from the long night of activity. No one else spoke, and she was glad she wasn't pressed to give her opinion on anything or anyone. The entire night had been a tremendous disappointment to her. She had looked forward to making her come-out her entire life, and now it seemed pointless.

All because her heart had been broken by Julian.

Ariadne went to her bedchamber, where she found Tally asleep in a chair and Tia and Lia asleep on her bed. She thought it sweet that the twins had wanted to wait for her, but she had no desire to talk about tonight's ball.

Gently, she shook Tally's shoulder and put a finger to her own lips. Tally understood and quietly undressed her mistress. She left her bedchamber, Tally following her.

"I will sleep in the twins' room," she told the maid.

Once she climbed into bed and brought the covers over her, Ariadne finally gave into the tears she had held back for hours and cried herself to sleep.

Chapter Seventeen

Ariadne awoke, finding Lia and Tia perched on either side of the bed, watching her anxiously.

"You're awake!" Tia cried. "Finally. We have been waiting forever."

"Not that long," Lia amended. "But we are eager to hear about last night." She looked at her twin. "And no interruptions. Ariadne must speak freely."

She pushed herself to a sitting position, stacking her pillows behind her for support. Her sisters were very dear to her, and she would not disappoint them.

For an hour, Ariadne told them about the Treeleys' ball in great detail. She described how the ballroom was decorated. The different songs the musicians played. She elaborated on the midnight buffet and the incredible variety of foods available. She also told them about many of the gowns she had seen other women wearing, going into minute details of several dresses and the variety of colors.

All the while, her siblings sat, enraptured, their entire attention focused on her and her experiences.

Finally, Tia sighed. "It all sounds so wonderful, Ariadne, but what of the gentlemen you met? Were they handsome? Kind? Interesting?"

"Did you favor a particular one?" Lia asked.

"The ballroom was crowded with many people," she began.

"You can ask Val to estimate how many were in attendance because I cannot venture a guess. Val and Con—and Mama—introduced me to a good number of the guests. Lia was right. My programme filled quickly, and I did dance every set, but only with someone Val and Con approved of."

"You did not answer my question," Lia said. "Did you feel a special kinship with anyone?"

"This will be hard to believe, but you really do not converse much," she revealed. "That was a little disappointing."

"Well, if you were dancing every dance, I suppose you would not have time for talk," Tia pointed out. "Dancing takes a lot of effort and concentration. I rarely say much to my partners when we go to the village assemblies."

"Exactly," Ariadne agreed. "A gentleman might comment on something as he took me to the dance floor, but the rest of the time, we were dancing. Then he would escort me from the floor, where another partner awaited me."

"What about at supper?" Tia demanded. "Surely, you conversed some then with others."

"My partner for the supper dance was a friend of Val's and Con's from university. He led me to their table, where another two gentlemen also sat, along with their supper dance partners. I actually spent more time talking with a few of the ladies, and I believe I will be friendly with a couple of them."

Lia frowned. "Then how are you supposed to get to know a man, much less decide if you might wish to wed him?"

"I suppose that takes place this afternoon. Mama has told me I am to make myself available each day between two and four o'clock. Guests will call then on me. I hope I will be able to have a decent conversation with a few gentlemen at that time." She paused. "That is, if anyone shows up."

"Oh, they will," Tia assured her. "You were so beautiful last night. I think our drawing room will be crawling with eligible bachelors." Her bottom lip turned out in a pout. "I only wish we could be there, too, so we could meet some of your beaux."

"You know Mama has forbidden us from doing so," Lia said sternly. "She would send us packing tomorrow if we tried." Shuddering, she added, "I have learned not to cross Mama."

Ariadne took both their hands and squeezed them. "I will tell you everyone who comes and what we talk about." She chuckled. "If I can remember their names."

"Oh, you will eventually," Lia assured her. "You will be going to events daily for the next several months. You will see the same people over and over again."

"You are right. I am going to return to my bedchamber now and ring for Tally."

"Oh, Mama said you would not eat breakfast downstairs with us," Tia said. "That you would eat it in your room as she does since you will be sleeping later."

She hadn't known that. Rising from the bed, she said, "I will decide that for myself."

When Tally appeared, though, she carried a tray with a covered dish.

"Brought you your breakfast and some tea, my lady. I hope you slept well in another bed."

"It was fine. Will you always be waiting for me in my room when I return from an event late at night?"

"Yes. It will be easier than you having to ring for me. I hope you don't mind if I doze off, though."

"You may sleep in my bed if you wish, Tally. I would not mind."

Her maid's eyes widened. "Oh, no, my lady! I could never do that. The chair will do just fine. Now, eat something and then I'll dress you. You'll need to go see your flowers. They have been arriving all morning."

"Flowers? From who?"

"From the men you met last night," Tally said, laughing. "It's something they do if they like you. They'll come to visit you this afternoon, too. We need to think about what gown you should wear."

The maid went to the wardrobe. "How about this mint green?"

That was one of her favorites which Madame Laurent had made up. "Yes. The green will do."

"Then eat your toast points and eggs. I'll go fetch some hot water for you."

By the time Tally returned, Ariadne had finished eating and set aside her tray. She washed with the hot water and then allowed Tally to dress her.

"Keep the hair simple for daytime today," she instructed, and her maid twisted her copper locks into a neat chignon.

By now, the twins had returned, clamoring for her to come to the drawing room.

"It is filled with bouquets, Ariadne. Filled!" Tia said enthusiastically.

"If every arrangement indicates a caller, you will be busy all afternoon," Lia told her. "I have told Tia we should sit at the window and watch your suitors arrive."

She accompanied her sisters to the drawing room, finding Mama there. Her mother went from one bouquet to the next, reading the cards, nodding to herself.

Seeing her daughters, she looked at Ariadne. "You have done well, Child. I will wager no other girl receives as many arrangements today than you have. Despite your red hair, I knew you would be a diamond of the first water."

Having never heard the phrase before, she assumed it meant that she was popular. Ariadne walked from one arrangement to the next, reading the cards, trying to see if she could picture the gentleman who had sent these particular flowers. By the time she reached the last card, she squelched her disappointment, seeing none had come from Julian. She didn't know why she had held out false hope that he might be responsible for one of the bouquets, especially since he had not even bothered to claim a dance last night.

Her sisters had followed behind her, reading the cards, and

Tia now asked, "Why didn't Lord Aldridge send you flowers? I assumed he would."

"Why would he?" she asked. "We barely spoke last night. In fact, we did not even share a dance."

"I thought he liked you," Tia said. "I saw him looking at you when we went to Gunter's and would have sworn that he did."

"There is to be no swearing in this house, Thermantia Worthington," Mama chided. "You and your sister need to go upstairs. Now."

The twins knew better than to argue and quickly vanished. Mama turned to her.

"I have the same question, Ariadne. I would have thought the marquess would have been one of the first men to have signed your programme last night. The fact that he didn't—much less that he did not send you flowers—gives me pause. Did you say something to alienate him?"

She sat in the closest chair, folding her hands primly in her lap, trying not to fidget.

"I think we both came to the same conclusion, Mama. That we would not suit one another."

Her mother's lips thinned in disapproval. "But he is a marquess, Ariadne. It does not matter if you do not suit. He is quite wealthy. As a duke's daughter, you are expected to wed a man with his qualities."

"Lord Aldridge was the one to tell me that we did not suit, Mama," she said quietly, hoping that would keep her mother from speaking about him. "I cannot force him to be interested in me."

"Pish-posh," Mama declared. "You must try harder. Why, I saw the man dancing last night with girls who are the biggest of wallflowers. Plain girls with no figure and no spark. Surely, you can catch his attention again and change his mind."

Sadly, she shook her head. "I do not think he is a man to change his mind once it is made up, Mama. I will admit at one time, I was interested in Lord Aldridge, but he made it evident he is not interested in me."

Her mother sniffed. "Well, the Season is in its infancy. You have plenty of time to attract a worthy man. And if a suitable one does not distinguish himself from other gentlemen, we can always arrange for you to be found alone with Lord Aldridge."

"What?" she cried. "What are saying, Mama? You would wish me to *trap* him into marriage?"

Her mother shrugged nonchalantly. "It would not be the first time. Aldridge seems of good character. He would not see you ruined. And no eligible dukes are looking at the Marriage Mart this year, so a marchioness is the highest rank you could attain."

"Forget such a thought, Mama. I forbid you from trying to arrange anything of the kind. I will not be forced into a marriage with Lord Aldridge or anyone else."

Her mother marched toward her, jerking Ariadne from her seat. "You will do whatever I tell you to do." She paused. "How do you think I caught a duke?"

Horror filled her. "You . . . forced Papa to wed you?"

"He had shown interest in me. I was the daughter of a marquess. Meant to make an excellent match. When Millbrooke's attention began to wander to one of my rivals, I made certain it was drawn back to me." Her mother's triumphant smile made Ariadne sick to her stomach. "He was caught kissing me by my mother and her best friend. Naturally, Millbrooke did the honorable thing and wed me."

She jerked away from Mama, who said, "Oh, wipe that judgmental look from your face, Child. I brought him a healthy dowry. I gave him a son whom he worships. I have turned a blind eye to all his indiscretions for years. I have allowed him to lead his life, while I led mine."

Ariadne had always known her parents had little to do with one another and had guessed their marriage had been an arranged one. What she hadn't guessed was that Mama and her mother had done the arranging, trapping Papa for life. She would never participate in such a scheme. She cared too much for Julian to do something so vile.

"I would rather be gossiped about than force any man to wed me," she declared.

Her mother's eyes narrowed. "You say that now, but gossip flies like the wind and can cut deeper than you can ever imagine. You have a duty to this family, Ariadne Worthington. You are the daughter of a duke and will wed accordingly. I will not have you gossiped about."

She started to retort with harsh words, but Mama added, "Remember—your conduct will reflect upon Cornelia and Thermantia. If Polite Society rejects you, they will do the same to your sisters."

The words gutted her. Ariadne could never endanger her sisters' chances of making a good match.

"I will never act in a manner which will reflect poorly on my family, Mama," she said quietly. "At the same time, that means I will not conspire to force a man to wed me. I will behave honorably. Val has been charged by Papa to assist me in finding a husband. I trust him with all my heart."

A light knock sounded, and Parsons entered the drawing room. "The first of Lady Ariadne's callers are assembling downstairs, Your Grace."

"How many?" Mama asked the butler.

"Half a dozen, Your Grace, which means more will follow."

"Bring up the three who arrived first," Mama commanded.

Once Parsons left, Mama said, "Suitors usually spend about a quarter-hour when they stop by. The larger the arrangement they sent to you, the stronger their interest is in you."

Mama reeled off five names, stating those were the men who had sent the most expensive bouquets. "You are to be polite to everyone, naturally, but especially those five gentlemen. Do you understand?"

"I do," she said dully, knowing she was going to hate this afternoon.

And the rest of this Season.

Chapter Eighteen

Ariadne hugged Lia goodbye. "I am so glad you agreed to come to town with Tia. It has been wonderful having you here."

Tears misted her sister's eyes. "I wouldn't have missed it for the world." Lia paused, her eyes searching Ariadne's face. "I hope you will find your perfect match and that you enjoy every minute of the Season."

"Val will help me find the right gentleman," she said, with more confidence than she felt.

Tia came and threw her arms around Ariadne. "Thank you for everything. It was wonderful being in town and seeing you in all your splendor. I hope you will wed the most handsome man this Season and have many babes so Lia and I can spoil them."

She took the twins' hands in hers. "If I do wed, I would like for the two of you to come and spend Christmas with me and my new husband."

While Tia squealed her approval, Lia said, "That would be wonderful, Ariadne. We definitely would accept your invitation. As long as your husband would not mind. You will need to defer to him and his wishes."

"I will not wed a man who would begrudge me a visit from my beloved sisters," she said lightly. Kissing each of them again, she said, "Write to me. Give me all the news from home."

"We will," Tia promised, allowing Val to assist her into the carriage before he handed Lia up.

Both girls waved to them as the carriage set out and then turned from the square. Ariadne embraced her brother.

"Thank you again for persuading Mama to allow the twins to come. I enjoyed their company immensely and only wish Mama would have allowed them to remain in town longer."

She hesitated a moment. They had not been alone with one another this past week, but she wanted to talk to him about Mama and Papa.

As Val started inside, she tugged on his arm. "Walk about the square with me a few minutes," she urged.

They fell into step together. "What is it?" he asked. "You must have something to ask or confide. Have you grown fond of anyone in particular?"

"No, it is not that. Did you know . . . Mama ensnared Papa into marrying her?"

He startled. "What?"

Ariadne related the story Mama had shared with her.

"I have never heard any of this," her brother admitted.

"Neither had I."

"Why on earth would Mama share this with you?" he pondered. "It should have a been a secret she took to her grave with her."

Biting her lip, she revealed, "Because she thought it might be something I could do to Lord Aldridge."

"What?" her brother exclaimed.

"Despite my telling her that the marquess and I are not interested in a match between the two of us, Mama still believes wedding Lord Aldridge would be a good match for me. Naturally, I told her I would refuse to participate in such a scheme."

He began strolling again, saying, "I would not see either you or Julian unhappy. I am sorry the two of you could not come to an agreement, though. He is still spending his time with the wallflowers, and they are thrilled about it."

"Is there any particular girl he has called upon more than

once?" she asked, knowing she should not seem so interested in the marquess' actions. "After all, he is your friend and if he weds, you will be seeing his wife, too, when you socialize."

"Julian has been tight-lipped," Val revealed. "I have not pressed him about if he is wooing any particular young lady."

She sighed. "I just wanted you to be aware of what Mama had told me so that you could help me prevent any entrapment of Lord Aldridge from occurring."

He nodded. "It is good you shared this with me, Sis. Con and I have also warned Julian not to be alone with any lady. He understands the reasoning behind it. I do know he will be at the card party tonight at Lord and Lady Atterby's home."

Ariadne did not like hearing that. It had been easier to avoid the marquess at balls. He had not appeared at last night's musicale. She had seen him at a garden party two days ago, but only from the far side. They had never drawn close enough to even greet one another.

Tonight would be different. The possibility they might end up at the same table—even be thrown together as partners—was something she could not escape.

"You are escorting me tonight?" she asked, trying to keep the worry from her voice.

"I plan to do so. Mama and Papa are going to the theater with Aunt Charlotte and Uncle Arthur, so it will just be the two of us going to Lord and Lady Atterby's party."

"Aunt Agnes asked me to call upon her," Ariadne said. "I have not had a chance to do so yet. Might you walk with me to her house this morning? You could always have Tally come and act as my chaperone when I return home."

"Yes, I am happy to do so."

They returned inside so she could claim her reticule and bonnet. She told her maid where she would be and asked for Tally to come to Aunt Agnes' in an hour to see her home.

"We may talk longer, but you can wait in the kitchen and have a cup of tea until I am ready to leave."

"Happy to do so, my lady," Tally replied.

Val and she walked the few blocks to their aunt's, and her brother even came in for a few minutes before begging off for another engagement.

After he left, Aunt Agnes said, "I am so happy you made the time to visit with me, Ariadne. I only wish Verina and Justina were here with us."

"Would you ever consider bringing them to town with you?" she asked.

"No. They are settled into a nice routine in the country with their governess. I would hate to disrupt that. Once Verina is set to make her come-out in four years, though, I will certainly bring Justina with us. She would be lonely in the country without her sister. Her governess can always give her a few lessons."

"Why do you come to the Season each year, Aunt Agnes?" she asked, curious about her aunt's motives. "Are you searching for another husband and simply have not found one to your liking?"

Her aunt's laughter filled the room. "Oh, heaven's no, Ariadne. I adored Traywick. We were a love match from the beginning. The moment our gazes met, I knew he was the only one for me. He told me later he felt the same."

"That sounds quite romantic, Aunt," she said, a bit envious.

"Oh, your Uncle George was quite so."

A dreamy look crossed Aunt Agnes' face, and Ariadne could see she was lost in her memories. She sat silently, waiting. Then Aunt Agnes seemed to realize she had company and blushed.

"I hope you will find a love match yourself. It is what I wish for my three children."

"I doubt that I will, Aunt Agnes."

"Why?"

Suddenly, tears filled her eyes, and then Ariadne was sobbing. Her aunt came and placed an arm about her. "Cry it out, dear."

She did cry for several minutes before getting hold of herself. "I apologize for my outburst. Mama would be horrified that I displayed such poor manners."

"You have no need to apologize for feeling what you do. Has a young man broken your heart, my dear?"

"Yes," she admitted. "And no one else seems to draw my eye."

"Tell me about him. This gentleman. And why he hurt you so."

She took her time, leaving out Julian's origins, but telling her aunt how much she liked the marquess and how they had kissed.

"I never knew a man's kiss before. After sharing many with Lord Aldridge, I do not wish to know another one. But he has told me he has no interest in pursuing me. I cannot understand why he is willing to ignore the attraction between us."

"You think Val warned him off too sternly?" her aunt ventured.

"No. I sense there is more to it than that. He is distantly polite when I see him, but he does not seek me out. He has yet to sign my dance card. I do know he is interested in finding a wife this Season. He is eager for children and wishes to provide an heir. The previous marquess wed thrice and had no children to show for his marriages, so wedding quickly and getting an heir is very important to him."

She kept quiet about the fact that Julian was truly the son and rightful heir, though an unacknowledged one.

"Do you think you could be happy with another man as your husband?" Aunt Agnes asked.

"I . . . I am not certain. I suppose I shall have to try. Papa wishes me to become betrothed by summer's end. And Mama?" Ariadne shuddered. "She suggested creating a . . . situation with Lord Aldridge."

Aunt Agnes' brows shot up. "You mean she wishes for you to force the marquess' hand into wedding you."

"Yes," she said dully. "I am ashamed to even admit this to you."

"Well, she did it herself. It does not surprise me Alice would think to try it again with you."

Ariadne gasped. "You *know* about Mama and Papa?"

Aunt Agnes chuckled. "I am four years your mother's junior. Our mothers were close friends, however."

She thought back to what Mama had shared. "It was *your* mother who was with my grandmama when they discovered Mama and Papa alone together," she surmised.

"Yes. I overheard them plotting it together and was horrified by such a scheme. Your father had been courting your mother, but another pretty girl turned his head. She and your mother were the two beauties of their come-out group and bitter rivals. They both wanted to land a duke as their husband. Your papa must have had at least some feelings for your mother because he was caught kissing her."

"And Papa was honorable enough to wed Mama."

"He did. Later, Alice befriended me when I had my own come-out because our mothers were friends. She can be a bit overbearing, but she has always been nice enough to me. I did not want to do what she had resorted to, however. Thank goodness Traywick and I were a love match. And ironically enough, he was a cousin to your papa, and so that is how you and I came to be related."

"I told Mama in no uncertain terms that I would not connive to wed Lord Aldridge. I have plenty of callers who wish to woo me as it is."

Aunt Agnes looked at her sadly. "But none of them appeal to you as much as your marquess does?"

"No," she said flatly. "I have lost my appetite for the Season and its social swirl. Yet Papa expects me to wed. Val and Con are carefully reviewing my suitors. I suppose I will take their recommendation. Several of the eligible gentlemen courting me are quite nice. I never expected a love match, so I suppose I will have to make my mind up to be happy with one of them."

Pity filled her aunt's eyes. "I hope your Lord Aldridge will open his eyes and see what he is missing."

"I fear that will never be the case. He is a determined man. He will not change his mind. I worry because we are both to attend a card party this evening. It will be impossible to avoid him at such a small event."

"Be open to whatever happens," Aunt Agnes said. "And feel free to confide in me anytime."

She hugged her aunt. "Thank you. I could not burden Lia and Tia with this. They left only this morning for Millvale. And Val is good friends with Lord Aldridge. I cannot come between them."

Aunt Agnes patted her hand. "Come to me whenever you wish, Ariadne. I am happy to help in any way I can."

They talked another half-hour about upcoming events. Aunt Agnes revealed that she was a bit lonely in the country and enjoyed coming to town each Season in order to see her friends.

"You will be the same one day. You will visit with family and friends during the Season. It will be a time of year you will come to love."

"I hope so, because right now, I am not fond of it one bit!"

They laughed and embraced before she took her leave. The butler sent for Tally, and they walked the few blocks home.

Ariadne decided she was tired of moping around. Lord Aldridge had made it clear they were not meant for one another. It was time she got down to the business of deciding her own future.

And that meant becoming an active participant in deciding whom to wed once the Season came to a conclusion.

Chapter Nineteen

JULIAN STOOD STILL as Paulson tied his cravat. The valet stepped back a moment and then nodded his approval.

"You are set, my lord."

"Thank you," he said, dismissing the servant as he took a seat by the window.

He did not want to go to tonight's card party, but he had already replied to the invitation. Con also knew he was scheduled to go. That was before he learned Val and Ariadne would be in attendance. He should have realized they would be invited. Lord and Lady Atterby had only been wed two years and already had a son. Con told him it would be a younger crowd at the card party this evening. Julian had been eager to test his whist skills. But facing Ariadne in such a small setting would be difficult.

He had successfully avoided her ever since the first night of the Season. Feeling obligated to speak to her parents, he had taken time to stop and spend a few moments with Their Graces, along with her and Val. The deep yearning he had felt merely being a few feet from Ariadne told him he must stay out of her sphere.

Or disaster would occur.

They had been a part of the same group during the first dance. After that, he made certain he kept his eye on where she and her dance partner were in the ballroom and led his own partner far away from them. It was easier to avoid her presence at balls because of the sheer number of attendees. Tonight, however, Con had let him know there would only be about two dozen or so present. His greatest fear was being made to serve as her card partner. To have to sit across from her would be pure torture.

Maybe he could beg off. Send a note to Lady Atterby, saying he had taken ill. That would leave his hostess a man short, though, and he did not wish to do that. Julian told himself to stop behaving as a whining child and be the man he was.

Unfortunately, that was one who was desperately in love with Ariadne Worthington.

He refused to condemn her to a lifetime of being chained to him in matrimony. It was obvious from the first night of the Season how she attracted others to her. He didn't have to imagine the number of suitors she entertained after each at her father's townhouse because he only had to look out his window and see the steady group of men coming and going.

On the other hand, Julian had yet to call upon a single young lady. He had forced himself to dance at the different balls with various wallflowers, but he was afraid of giving any of them too much hope by calling on them the next day. Instead, he hid in his study, trying to read a book or look through reports Mr. Ross sent him regarding Aldridge Manor.

Determination filled him. He would go to this card party. He would even speak to Ariadne and act as if nothing was wrong—or nothing was between them. It was time to stop skulking about and get serious about the business of finding his marchioness. Once he did so, Julian knew he was too honorable to stray from her. Yes, it was better he found a marriage partner—and soon.

He came downstairs, having told Grigsby he did not need his carriage because the Atterbys lived only a quarter-mile away. Though his butler had frowned at the decision, he had not insisted on the carriage being readied for his employer.

Julian told his butler goodnight and left the townhouse, seeing the ducal carriage leaving the square. He steeled himself, knowing Ariadne and Val would already be present by the time he arrived at Lord and Lady Atterby's residence.

When he reached his destination, he was taken up to the drawing room. Lord and Lady Atterby greeted him. He liked the viscount, whom he had met at White's. They had had an interesting, amusing conversation. Atterby had a razor wit and was entertaining to be around. The viscount also had shared his political views with Julian, helping him to make sense of several issues which had puzzled him.

"Glad you could make it, Aldridge," Lord Atterby said. "Darling, this is the Marquess of Aldridge. My viscountess, Lady Atterby."

Bowing, he took her hand. "Your husband has been quite kind to me, my lady. Thank you for your kind invitation this evening."

"We are delighted to have you as a guest, my lord," the viscountess said. "I hope you enjoy card play. We will be playing whist this evening."

"I do," he said, not mentioning how new he was to the game.

He circulated around the room, speaking to those he knew, being introduced to a few others new to him. Finally, he reached Val and his sister, who were speaking with Con and Lady Alicia Smythe. Lady Alicia had been his first dance partner when the Season began. They had danced again a second time at another ball, where they had partnered for the supper dance. She was very plain but quite intelligent. Julian decided he would ask her to be his partner this evening.

And see if anything might come of it.

"Good evening, Lady Ariadne. Lady Alicia. Claibourne," he said, acknowledging Ariadne first because of her father's rank in Polite Society.

"Good evening," they replied as he took each lady's hand for an obligatory kiss, ignoring the sensation running through him when he touched Ariadne.

A bell sounded, and they turned their attention to their hostess, who had rung it.

"Thank you again for coming this evening. We will be playing here in the drawing room, taking a few breaks from card play throughout the evening. A buffet has been set up in the library, just a short way from here. I hope you will all partake of it."

He turned to Lady Alicia. "If you are not engaged to partner with someone this evening, my lady, I would like the opportunity to offer my services and pair with you."

Before she could reply, Lady Atterby said, "We will draw for our playing partners this evening." Her eyes twinkled. "That way, the best players will not team up and collect the prizes so easily. Tonight, the winners will receive a crystal punchbowl and engraved cane."

She indicated for a servant to hold each of the prizes up, and the crowd politely applauded. The butler then stepped forward with two small, velvet bags, handing one to his mistress. He crossed the room and gave the other bag to the viscount.

"Men will draw from the green bag. Ladies from the gold one. You will claim your number and match with your playing partner that way."

Julian glanced around the room. He thought the odds slim that he and Ariadne would draw the same number and relaxed a bit.

"Ladies, come choose your numbers from me. Gentlemen, you may report to my husband for yours."

Val slapped him on the back. "Let us go claim our numbers, Aldridge."

He followed his friend, moving in Lord Atterby's direction, and they joined the line forming in front of the viscount. Julian quickly counted and saw six other gentlemen in front of them.

"I would like that cane," Val said. "I hope I draw Ariadne's name. You know from experience how good she is at cards."

Val took his turn, and then Julian reached his hand into the velvet bag, drawing a slip of parchment, which he then unfolded.

His friend proclaimed, "Eleven. I am off to find my feminine counterpart. Best of luck to you, Aldridge."

Glancing at his own number, he saw the number seven.

As others began calling out their own numbers and circulating the room, he saw people pairing off. Then his eyes went to Ariadne. She nibbled on her bottom lip, causing a surge of desire to rush through him. His gut told him their numbers would be a match.

He began moving across the room, saying, "Seven?" to other unclaimed ladies. All shook their heads, so he continued on. Finally, he reached her.

"Do you hold the number seven, my lady?" he asked quietly.

She nodded. "I do, my lord." She scanned the room quickly and said, "If you wish, I will go and trade numbers with Lady Alicia. She has not found her partner yet."

Ariadne started to move away from him, but Julian clasped her elbow. She turned, a questioning look in her eyes.

"You do not need to do so. We can partner together this evening."

Relief swept through him when she said, "All right. If you do not mind."

He shrugged nonchalantly. "Why should I mind when I know I have been fortunate enough to be paired with the most talented strategist in the room?"

The apparent tension between them eased a bit, and they both chuckled at his remark. Julian added, "I hope I will not prove to be deficient, my lady. I know you are serious about your card play."

"We should discuss our tactics for play tonight," she said immediately, her competitive spirit revealing itself.

Quickly, she devised a strategy with him, and he readily agreed to follow her lead since she had far more experience at cards than he did.

"Thank you," he said as couples started moving toward the various tables in the drawing room.

"For what?" she asked, uncertainty in her eyes.

"I was unkind to you. You do not seem to be holding a grudge against me. For that, I am grateful."

Sadness filled her luminous eyes. "You were never unkind to me, my lord," she said quietly. "I merely had different expectations than you regarding our relationship. I am happy to remain a friendly acquaintance to you, especially because Val and Con think so highly of you. I hope your search on the Marriage Mart will prove fruitful."

She moved toward their hostess, and Julian followed, hearing Lady Atterby assigning them to table number four.

When they reached it, he saw Con already seated there. Across from him was Lady Alicia. Julian thought this an excellent sign. He was comfortable in Con's company, and he would still be able to visit some with Lady Alicia, spending time with her in a casual atmosphere.

Seating Ariadne first, he came and took the remaining seat at the table.

Con leaned across the table, saying, "We must conspire to win, Lady Alicia. Lady Ariadne is my cousin, and she is known for her skilled card playing. Aldridge is my good friend, and I would enjoy being the victor and lord it over him."

"I will do my best, Viscount Dyer," Lady Alicia responded. "I have been known to take more than a trick or two when playing whist."

"It sounds as if it will be a most interesting evening," Ariadne said. "Lord Aldridge and I cannot wait to trounce the two of you," she said confidently, then she began laughing.

Both Con and Lady Alicia laughed, as well, as the butler handed Julian a new pack of cards. He unsealed them and shuffled several times, glad for both the lesson Ariadne had given him and his additional practice of shuffling a deck. Turning to his left, he allowed Con to cut the deck before Julian dealt each player their hand.

Play was lively, and he could see Lady Alicia was an excellent card player. Con could be a little careless at times, but he saw how skilled his partner was and seemed to concentrate more when he saw they would be competitive as a team.

Julian and Ariadne took the first round by a single trick and only received a single point for their efforts. Con and Lady Alicia earned a point of their own the next round.

Though play was fierce, they all seemed to be able to concentrate on the cards in their hands and still banter. The more he learned about Lady Alicia, the more favorably Julian looked upon her.

Con and Lady Alicia tied the game, making it four points for all, meaning this last round would determine who won their match. It surprised Julian when they lost two easy tricks in a row. He tried to catch Ariadne's attention, but she focused intently on her own cards.

In the end, Con and Lady Alicia proved to be victorious. Con laughed heartily, thanking his partner, telling Julian he would make certain everyone at White's tomorrow knew he had bested his good friend at whist, thanks to Lady Alicia's remarkable play.

For her part, Ariadne turned to the other lady, saying, "You are quite the card player, my lady. I hope you and Con go on to win this evening's tournament and claim your prizes."

Julian said to Lady Alicia, "Congratulations, my lady, on your victory. I second Lady Ariadne's thoughts and hope you and my friend win the punchbowl and cane."

The two ladies rose, with Lady Alicia asking Ariadne if she wished to accompany her to the retiring room. Ariadne agreed, and the two of them left the drawing room.

Play was still going on with a few tables, but other guests were spilling from the room and heading to the library for refreshments. Julian accompanied Con there, where they ran into Val, who lamented his partner had no grasp of the game.

"We will be losing for the remainder of tonight," Val told them. "Still, my partner is fair of face. I have decided to concentrate more on her than the cards in my hand, so the evening will not be a total loss."

Julian excused himself, deciding to stretch his legs a bit. He still wondered why he and Ariadne had lost. They shouldn't have. She was too good a player to have made such mistakes, and their hands had been too strong that final round. He decided he would confront her and learn why she had deliberately thrown the game. He did not think her capable of being so petty, but perhaps she was angrier with him than she had let on.

Going down the corridor, he saw her heading his way. He stopped and waited for her.

"If you are looking for Lady Alicia, my lord, she has been detained. Someone stepped on the hem of her gown and tore it. A maid is now repairing it for her, so Lady Alicia will be delayed from joining us for a few more minutes."

"I was not searching for Lady Alicia, my lady. You are the one I wished to speak with."

"Oh!" she said, looking startled. "Why?"

"Why is the question I have of you. Why did you throw the match? I know you deliberately lost. You tossed our strategy to the four winds that final round. I would like an explanation from you."

She worried her bottom lip again, and he tamped down the instant desire which sprang to his loins.

"Because you favor her," Ariadne finally shared. "I have seen you dance with Lady Alicia. You even asked her to pair with you before Lady Atterby explained we would be drawing for partners. You like her."

Her answer dumbfounded him. "So, you chose to allow her to win for that reason?"

Nervously, she said, "I wanted Lady Alicia to shine in your eyes, my lord. She would make a wonderful Marchioness of Aldridge."

"So would you," he said roughly, causing her eyes to widen.

Looking quickly about, Julian saw no one else in the hall. He latched onto her wrist and pulled her into the nearby alcove which had caught his eye. The curtain fell behind them.

And his mouth came down on hers.

CHAPTER TWENTY

BEFORE SHE KNEW what was happening, Ariadne was kissing Julian. This kiss was even more unexpected than the first one had been. It proved fierce from the start, as he took charge of it.

And her.

His arms were about her now, crushing her to him, so there was no avenue of escape. Of course, escape was the last thing on her mind. She had dreamed nightly of being captive in his arms again, never thinking it could become a reality. She knew she should be sensible. Push him away. Scold him for trying to take advantage of her. Forbid him from ever speaking to her again. For once, though, she would follow her heart.

Damn the consequences.

She began kissing him back, her fervor equal to his. She had learned enough about kissing from the last lesson he had given her. Not only passion, but also confidence soared through her. His tongue swept into her mouth, sending a humming through her body. The familiar sensations began to grow inside her again, feelings only Julian Barrington brought to her.

He broke the kiss, and she murmured a protest low in her throat, needing more. His lips trailed down her throat, finding her pulse point, his tongue lapping at it, causing it to jump even more erratically. His mouth moved even lower, his tongue following the arch of the top of her breast, sending shooting desire through her. Ariadne whimpered, causing his mouth to return to hers.

Then voices sounded in the corridor, merely feet from them.

This was madness.

He broke the kiss, his lips hovering just above hers as they waited for whoever was nearby to move on. As the conversation grew fainter, Julian kissed her once more, a deep, lingering kiss which set her afire. Everything about this situation was wrong—but his kiss felt so right.

Ending it, his lips moved to her ear, and he whispered, "Let me leave first. Stay here for another minute or so. If anyone is present in the hallway, I will distract them so you can make your escape. Return to the retiring room. Make certain you look presentable before you come to the library."

She nodded in understanding, his lips grazing her earlobe, causing her breath to hitch. He released her, and his warmth left her. Ariadne wanted to cry out for him to come back to her. To hold her and kiss her again. To never leave her side. She remained silent, though, watching him slip from the alcove, leaving her in darkness again as she tried to catch her breath.

Why had Julian kissed her?

Despite telling Ariadne he no longer had an interest in her, it was obvious he had a great deal he needed to explain to her. A man did not kiss a woman like that for no reason. She determined she must speak to him. Alone. Try to understand why he had pushed her away and deny what existed between the two of them.

Hearing no voices, she composed herself, smoothing her skirts before parting the curtain slightly. As she glanced out, she saw no one to her right, where the retiring room was located, but to her left, Julian was engaged in conversation with someone she didn't recognize. Julian faced her and nodded for her to make her move. She supposed he had waylaid the gentleman he spoke with, maneuvering him so his back was to the alcove.

Quickly, she hurried down the hall and once more entered the retiring room, spying a maid clipping the thread and tying it off from where she had rehemmed Lady Alicia's gown mishap, which Ariadne already knew was no mishap at all.

"Lady Ariadne, are you all right?" asked Lady Alicia. "Your cheeks are quite flushed."

She fanned herself with her hands. "I found myself overheated in the library," she lied smoothly. "I thought to come and splash water upon my cheeks to try and cool down."

Hearing her words, a maid leaped into action, pouring water from a pitcher into a basin. Ariadne scooped some water into her hands and splashed it onto her cheeks several times, accepting a linen cloth from the maid to pat her face dry.

The maid handed her a hand mirror, and she caught a glimpse of herself, seeing her color was still high and her lips slightly swollen. Hopefully, it was not as noticeable now.

"Are you ready to return to the drawing room?" she asked her companion, slipping her arm through Lady Alicia's.

"I am," the young woman replied. "And eager to see who our next card opponents will be."

As they strolled down the corridor, she saw Julian and his companion were now gone.

"I wish I had not been so clumsy," Lady Alicia fretted. "At least there was a maid who could repair the hem on my gown."

Deciding to clue this woman in as to what she had observed earlier, Ariadne said, "I saw what happened, my lady, and it was no fault of yours. I believe Lady Eliza deliberately stepped on your gown and continued to hold her foot upon it as you moved away."

Lady Alicia looked puzzled. "Why would she do such a thing?"

Ariadne said, "I am not one who wishes to spread gossip, but I have heard some most unfavorable things about Lady Eliza. She is very competitive, as well as petty. I think she was trying to prevent you from returning to play in a timely fashion, meaning you and Con would have to forfeit your next match."

Her companion halted their progress, her eyes round and wide in surprise. "You truly believe she would do something so wicked?"

She nodded. "I witnessed it myself. While it is conceivable Lady Eliza could have accidentally stepped on your gown, the fact that she did not step away immediately but waited for you to move lets me know her action was intentional. I would do my best to avoid her in the future if I were you, my lady."

"Thank you for your advice, Lady Ariadne." She smiled ruefully. "It is not often I gain the attention of anyone. Surely, Lady Eliza does not think I am a rival to her."

"Who knows what lurks in her mind?" she asked as they entered the drawing room again. "Ah, there is Con. He looks a bit flustered."

Her cousin rushed to them. "I am glad you finally returned, Lady Alicia. Play is about to begin again. Lady Atterby has already assigned our table to us."

Ariadne watched the pair go to a table, seeing Lady Eliza already sitting at it.

After Con seated Lady Alicia, she glanced over her shoulder and smiled. Ariadne returned her new friend's smile, hoping Con and his partner would be victorious.

Glancing about the room, she saw Julian looking at her. It caused her breath to hitch, seeing him, finding him the most attractive gentleman in the room. Crossing to him, she joined the table, Julian rising to seat her.

Play began. Ariadne was determined to win every match after having given away the first one on purpose. The rest of the evening progressed. As she expected, she and Julian won every subsequent match. At one point between rounds, he escorted her to the library, where she drank some ratafia and nibbled on a tart and some cheese. She made a point of deliberately moving away from him, conversing with others. She found she liked a smaller social setting such as this as opposed to a ballroom full of guests, which could be a bit intimidating at times. Once again, she spent some time conversing with Lady Alicia, whom she liked very much. The young woman might be plain of face, but she was quick of wit, and her smile was contagious. If Julian truly wished to wed this woman, she would make a good companion to him and an excellent marchioness.

But why had he kissed her? Doing so had been incredibly dangerous for the both of them. They could have been discovered at any moment, even by another couple who might wish to avail themselves of the same actions in the alcove. Ariadne could not understand why he had taken such a risk, especially when he had had nothing to do with her since before the Season began.

What she needed were answers from him.

Play for the final match began, and Val and his vapid young lady were their opponents. The girl was quite pretty as her brother had mentioned, and Ariadne thought her neckline slightly too low, which definitely drew her brother's eyes. Julian and she took every single game in this final round, their opponents no challenge to them in the least.

Once play ended, she spoke with others as they finished up. After every table had finished their match, scores were tallied, and the guests awaited the results.

Their hostess rang her little bell again, and all turned their attention to Lady Atterby, who declared, "The winners of tonight's prizes are Lady Alicia and Lord Dyer."

Lord Atterby handed over the prizes to the winning couple as the others in attendance applauded their efforts. Ariadne noticed only Lady Eliza refrained from the gesture, which seemed petty on her part.

She and Julian made their way to the victors. She took Lady Alicia's hand and enthusiastically said, "I am delighted that you and my cousin won this evening."

"I was happy to make your acquaintance, Lady Ariadne. It is not often I experience such kindness."

Liking this woman very much, Ariadne asked, "Would you care to celebrate your win tonight by having tea with my family tomorrow afternoon?"

"Why, I would be honored to do so," her friend replied, her cheeks flushing. "Thank you for such a lovely invitation."

Ariadne turned her attention to Julian. "That invitation includes you as well, Lord Aldridge." She intentionally included him because she hoped at one point to separate him from the others so she might get answers to her questions.

Looking to her cousin, she said, "And you, too, Con. We will celebrate your win."

Val joined them, offering his hand to Con. "Congratulations, Cousin. You will have bragging rights at White's tomorrow."

She told her brother, "Con and Lady Alicia have agreed to join us at tea tomorrow." Smiling at her new friend, she added, "Please feel free to bring you parents, as well, to chaperone you."

Their group returned to the library for a final round of refreshments, Ariadne ignoring Julian the entire time. Only when they went downstairs did he move close to her, asking, "What are you up to, my lady?"

Giving him a benign smile, she said, "I could ask the same of you, my lord," she countered, noting the tips of his ears pinkened slightly at her words. "We look forward to your company tomorrow during tea."

Ariadne and Val stepped from the townhouse, her brother saying, "We will need to look for a hansom cab to convey us home, Sis, since Papa and Mama have use of the carriage."

"I am happy to drop you," a familiar voice behind them said.

Turning, she saw Julian smiling.

"Thank you, Julian," Val said affably. "That is most kind of you."

"We are practically going to the same destination," the marquess said. "I am always happy to help out my friends."

They stood together waiting for his carriage to be brought to them, the two men talking. Ariadne studied the marquess as they did so, trying to see if she might figure him out.

His carriage finally arrived, and she stepped forward quickly, allowing Julian's footman to hand her up. She didn't want him to touch her again because his touch confused her. The entire situation had her baffled, and Ariadne was determined to solve the mystery of where she stood with the Marquess of Aldridge.

Chapter Twenty-One

Julian couldn't believe that he had kissed Ariadne again. And not a mere peck on the lips. No, the kiss had started out fiery and only increased in passion from there. He could no longer lie to himself.

He loved her—and he was miserable without her.

Yet he refused to ruin her life. Ariadne was a special woman. He might have only met a small sliver of Polite Society since the Season began, but it was obvious she was unique. It was only fitting that she wed a man worthy of her. Already, thanks to his connection with Con and Val, he had met several gentlemen at White's and other social affairs. Julian had always considered himself a good judge of character, and he recognized a handful who stood head and shoulders above others. Those were the kind of gentlemen Ariadne needed to consider for her husband, not an undereducated dockworker who had only become a marquess because of a turn of good fortune.

The current situation he found himself in was one entirely of his own making. Julian had already told Ariadne he had no wish to pursue her. He had avoided her at social events. Yet he had done the unthinkable last night, dragging her into an alcove and kissing her senseless. It had not only been the absolute wrong thing to do, but he also knew it was dishonorable to trifle with her feelings in such an irresponsible manner. He was no different than the selfish blighters who toyed with a woman's feelings, only to discard her as rubbish.

Julian determined to apologize to her a final time—and then never speak to her again. It would likely mean cooling his friendship with Val and even Con, but things simply could not continue the way they were. He needed to get as far away from Ariadne as possible so he wouldn't be tempted to give in to his baser desires as he had last night. He shuddered to think about the outcry which would have occurred if anyone had discovered them together in that alcove. It had only been thanks to the voices he'd heard which had helped him cool his ardor and leave her before he took things further.

Still, he needed a wife. Though it would do a disservice to wed one woman when he was in love with another, he vowed to treat his wife kindly and respectfully. Of all the ladies he had met so far, the one who interested him the most was Lady Alicia. Where a majority of the wallflowers were painfully shy, Lady Alicia was spirited and intelligent. He had enjoyed being at her table for cards last night. It was her third Season to be out, and it didn't seem as if she had any prospects.

His mind was made up. Julian would offer for Lady Alicia. Con had even told him about something called a special license, an expensive way to wed, but one which allowed forgoing the calling of the banns and the three-week wait that process entailed. He would speak first to Lady Alicia and if she seemed willing to proceed, he would then go to her father and ask the earl for his daughter's hand. That settled, he would purchase the special license and wed as quickly as possible before retiring to Aldridge Manor for the remainder of the Season. Ariadne would be out of sight.

And hopefully, out of mind, both now and in the future.

Dreading today's tea, he would go anyway. It would give him an opportunity to spend additional time with Lady Alicia and also meet her parents. Hopefully, they could get to know him a bit, and his offer would not come as a surprise to them. Julian would pay special attention to Lady Alicia today. She was a very nice person and deserved better than what Polite Society had tossed her way.

He arrived at the same time Con and his parents did, finally meeting Lord and Lady Marley. They were accompanied by Con's aunt, whom he introduced as Lady Traywick. Parsons took the five of them upstairs to the drawing room.

"We are quite a large party for teatime this afternoon," Her Grace said after welcoming them. "Ariadne will pour out for you young people over there."

Julian glanced and saw a teacart already in place next to a grouping of seats near the windows. It would be easier to maneuver into a position to sit next to Lady Alicia in a smaller setting.

She and her parents arrived and were introduced to the duke and duchess. All three seemed in awe, being in a duke's drawing room.

Con said, "My aunt has designated the young people to sit over here, Lady Alicia." Taking her arm, Con led her across the room.

He had wanted to be the one who did so, but it would seem churlish to chase Con away at this point. Unfortunately, Val had followed them, leaving him alone with Ariadne.

"May I take you to tea?" he asked lightly, offering his arm.

She took it, and Julian felt the heady rush of her touch, as well as inhaling her vanilla scent.

As they crossed the room, she sternly said, "Do not leave today until we have talked."

"I do not think we have anything to talk about," he said, trying to put her off.

She halted, gazing up at him, fire in her eyes. "You do not get to kiss me the way you did last night and *not* explain yourself."

Her icy tone froze his blood. "What if I said I merely lost my head?" he asked, trying to make light of it.

"You owe me more of an explanation than that, my lord. And I will have it. Today."

She tugged on him, and they continued across the room until they had reached the others. Con and Lady Alicia settled on a settee together, while Val sat in a chair, his back to the windows. Reluctantly, Julian took a seat beside Ariadne on another settee.

Pouring out for them, Ariadne handed saucers and cups to everyone, with Lady Alicia saying, "You do that with such ease, my lady."

"Thank you," Ariadne said graciously. "Or rather, thank my governess. Miss Nixon not only taught me good penmanship and how to conjugate French verbs, but she also put me through many a practice of being a hostess. Miss Nixon said pouring out is a great art, not one to be underestimated, and we did so on many occasions until she was pleased with me. She is governess to my two younger sisters. Lia and Tia will make their come-outs next spring."

"Those are beautiful names, Lia and Tia. They sound so musical," Lady Alicia observed.

"They are actually named Cornelia and Thermantia," Val explained. "Our father was interested in history and insisted on unusual, historical names for all his children. Aunt Charlotte, Con's mother, did the same with her children, as did Uncle George with his. Aunt Agnes, Lady Traywick, is my uncle's widow."

Julian chose two sandwiches and a slice of cake and listened more than he spoke. He still felt odd at times in Polite Society, even amongst his two friends here, and he worried about making a faux pas, what his valet referred to as an embarrassing social blunder. He wanted to present himself in the best possible light so when he did offer for Lady Alicia, she would have no qualms in accepting him.

When they finished eating, Val said, "It is much too pretty a day to stay indoors."

He worried Val would suggest a drive through Hyde Park. It was a place Julian had avoided, knowing if he were seen there, his name would be coupled with any woman with him.

"How about a walk in our gardens?" Ariadne suggested. "I would appreciate a leisurely stroll in nature. I endured another dress fitting today at Madame Laurent's and then was busy for morning calls before tea."

"Excellent idea," Con said, coming to his feet and then assisting Lady Alicia to hers, something which Julian wished he could have been able to do. Instead, he offered his hand to Ariadne to assist her to her feet.

"I will tell Mama where we are off to," Val offered, heading toward the older people.

The four of them left the drawing room and went downstairs, exiting through a set of French doors, which opened onto the terrace.

"The gardens are this way," Ariadne said, leading them down the stairs of the terrace and to the garden's entrance.

By now, Val had caught up to them. He began talking with Lady Alicia, with Con moving to her other side. They set off down the pathway, leaving him with Ariadne.

"You are stuck with me, my lord," she said, no humor in her voice.

Forcing himself to behave as a gentleman, he slipped her hand through the crook of his arm and followed his friends. They were quite a ways ahead of them, though, and Julian could feel Ariadne deliberately keeping their pace to a crawl. He knew it was so they might speak privately. He owed her that much.

Continuing to move slowly, she said, "We are alone now, Lord Aldridge. I need for you to explain yourself. Your actions of last night. Do you know how frustrating it is to have you tell me in no certain terms that you have no interest in me and then avoid me entirely, only to have you kiss me with no warning? Your behavior is perplexing. Though your kiss was most welcomed," she added softly, gazing up at him.

She would never stop hounding him until she got the truth out of him, so Julian decided to give it to her.

"I am attracted to you, Ariadne. More than attracted. I have an intense physical desire for you. One which has caused me to behave in a very ungentlemanly fashion. For that, I apologize."

"Those same feelings are inside me, as well, Julian," she said earnestly. "I have not understood why you pushed me away in the first place, only that I am grateful I am not alone in these feelings." She hesitated. "I know ladies are supposed to refrain from such frankness, but I desire you, Julian. Your kiss transports me to the heavens. I feel as if I cannot live without it." She hesitated before adding, "Without you."

Guilt ran through him. "You cannot feel this way," he said harshly.

Anger sparked in her eyes. "And you cannot tell me how I may feel." She looked pleadingly at him. "Why are you fighting this, Julian? This thing between us cannot be denied. It is powerful. I have been so unhappy when I should be relishing my come-out. All I think about is you, though. You are the only person I wish to be with."

"Enough!" he said sharply. "We cannot be together, Ariadne. Do not continue to pester me this way."

Her cheeks flushed with anger now. "I am annoying you? Here I am pouring out my heart and soul to you, trying to let you know I understand the connection between us. That I want something permanent to come from it. Yes, I will say it, Julian, because you seem to be a coward and wish to ignore it."

Ariadne yanked her hand away, placing fisted hands on her waist. "I love you. I love kissing you. I love how it makes me feel. And I want more of it. More of you. Call me wanton, but I burn with desire for you."

He was too late. Her heart was engaged. This was going to prove messy, but she needed to hear him out.

Coldly, he said, "You need to listen to reason, my lady. With your head—and not your heart. I am not the one for you. I will never be worthy of you. I lack all the social graces necessary to be your husband. I have but two years of schooling because I was needed to earn money to survive. *Survive*, Ariadne. I labored to put a meager amount of food on our table, and it was never enough. I went to bed nightly with hunger pangs gnawing at my belly, listening to my mother cry herself to sleep because she could not provide enough for the two of us with her sewing."

He paused, seeing her eyes mist with tears. "I do not need or want your pity. You are a duke's daughter, and you should wed a man of good breeding. I am the grandson of a tailor, a working man, who tossed his daughter out when she became with child. I may possess a title now, but deep inside, I am still that barely educated, crude man of the docks, lacking in tact and social graces. You deserve a man who is polished in speech and manners. One who will never embarrass you. A man worthy of you.

"Because you are the most beautiful, wonderful creature in all of the *ton*."

She gazed at him, her astonishment evident. "That is why you are pursuing a wallflower," she said, understanding lighting her face. "You think to make one of them your marchioness and retreat from Polite Society." Then stubbornness tightened her jaw. "I will not have it, Julian. You are mine."

Before he could react, Ariadne had flung herself into his arms, wrapping her own around his neck, forcing his mouth down to hers. She kissed him, but Julian refused to yield, keeping his lips tightly together.

She broke the kiss and glared at him. "You better kiss me before I enter the nunnery."

"What the bloody hell are you talking about?" he asked, totally confused by her statement. "You are not a Catholic."

Grinning, she said, "Well, I suppose I will become one now. Because you are the only man for me, Julian Barrington. The only one I wish to kiss. The man I want as the father of our many children. If you deny me, then I will quit Polite Society. I will never wed. Never know the touch of a man. I will become a pious nun and spend twenty hours a day at prayer." She paused. "You are the only man I will ever want. My future is in your hands. Either I can become a very satisfied wife whom you make love to regularly—or the joints of my knees will become enflamed and painful because of all the time I spend on my knees in prayer."

A slow smile spread across his face. "You little minx," he said, his resolve to keep the woman he loved at a distance crumbling.

Ariadne frowned. "I am not certain I have ever heard that term. Is it good—or bad?"

"Shall we say it is not something any daughter of a duke should be called."

Her eyes lit with mischief. "Is it a wanton?"

"Yes," Julian said, sliding his arms about her waist. "But you are only to be a wanton in my bed. No other," he commanded, hoping she wasn't making a mistake in accepting him.

"I can agree to that," she said saucily. Then she frowned. "But I do not wish to be your mistress, Julian."

"I would never ask that of you, love." When her eyes widened hearing that word, he said, "Yes. You are my love. My one and only love. I will worship you until the day I die and even from beyond the grave."

He kissed her, hard and demanding. She yielded to him, opening, and he plundered her mouth, tasting her sweetness and innocence, joy filling his heart.

Ariadne broke the kiss. "Are you offering for me, Lord Aldridge?"

"I most definitely am, my lady."

"We should tell Val first," she insisted. "Then he can go with you to Papa. Papa has charged Val with approving my husband."

Taking her hand, he said, "Let us go find him—and share our good news."

They caught up to their companions, and Con grinned wickedly at them. "Do you have something to say, Aldridge? You look as if you do."

"I do." Looking to Val, he declared, "I am in love with your sister, my friend. We wish to wed as soon as possible." He did not think Ariadne would mind a quick engagement, especially after she had expressed her love for him.

Val looked at them, his smile broadening as he offered Julian his hand. "I am happy to welcome you into the family, my friend." Then he embraced his sister. "I assume this is what you want, Sis?"

"Most definitely," she said, her voice filled with happiness, her face radiant.

"My, a betrothal!" Lady Alicia proclaimed. "And so early in the Season. Why, you will be the first couple to announce your engagement. My congratulations to you both."

Julian turned to her, the woman he had thought he would wed. "I hope someday, my lady, you will find someone who loves you as much as I love Lady Ariadne."

Lady Alicia's eyes filled with tears. "We shall see, my lord."

"We need to go speak with Papa," Val declared. "Come along, everyone. Julian, I will have you wait in the study for us. Papa and I will be there shortly."

Val had Parsons take Julian to the study, where he paced nervously. He was filled with euphoria. A part of him was still uncertain that he was the right man for Ariadne, but his stubborn love would accept no one but him. For that, he was immensely grateful.

The door opened, and His Grace and Val entered, the duke looking stern, while Val grinned from ear to ear.

"Claibourne says you wish to speak to me about an important matter, Aldridge."

He bowed to the duke. "Yes, Your Grace. I have grown most fond of your daughter and wish to make her my marchioness." Julian swallowed, waiting, knowing this man could make him the happiest soul on the planet—or break him.

"My son tells me you are his first choice for Ariadne to wed," Millbrooke told him. "He claims you are a fine gentleman, one who will love my daughter and care for her always."

"Yes, Your Grace," he said resolutely.

The duke nodded. "Then you have my permission to wed my eldest daughter."

They returned to the drawing room, where His Grace made the betrothal announcement. Everyone congratulated them, welcoming him to the family. He thought how it had only been his mother and him all his life, but now he would be a part of a very large family.

Her Grace called for champagne, and while it was being brought, Ariadne quietly asked, "You mentioned you wished to wed quickly."

"I may have spoken out of turn," he admitted. "I should have first consulted you."

Her eyes shined brightly at him. "I would be happy to wed you tomorrow, Julian, but I have longed to wed at home. There is a small village near Millbrooke. Willowshire. I would like our wedding to take place inside the church there."

"I will purchase a special license tomorrow," he told her. "It is good for thirty days."

"Do so," she agreed. "I will help Mama work out the details." She beamed at him. "By this time next week, we should be man and wife."

Man and wife...

Julian decided he quite liked the sound of that.

Chapter Twenty-Two

THE NEXT EVENING, many well-wishers came up to Ariadne and Julian, congratulating them as the first betrothed couple of the Season. Val had seen to the announcement being placed in the newspapers, so it was the first thing most members of Polite Society saw when they perused the news. Mama had insisted upon going to Madame Laurent's to commission a wedding gown, but Ariadne vetoed that idea, showing her mother one of her new gowns which she wished to wear for the ceremony.

She had also informed her mother that Julian would seek a special license and that the wedding would occur at Willowshire. When Mama protested, her father stepped in, saying he had already agreed to the plan and that it would be a very exclusive list of guests who would be invited to the ceremony. That mollified Mama, who insisted upon leaving for the country immediately to put the wedding breakfast together after she composed a guest list, which her husband approved. Invitations were delivered, and the ceremony would take place the next Wednesday morning. The rest of the family would follow her mother to Millvale in a few days.

Ariadne was pleased that her uncle and two aunts would be in attendance as well as Con. Val and Con would stand up with Julian, while she had written a letter to the twins, asking them to stand by her side on this special day. She also insisted that Mama invite Lady Alicia and her parents, telling Mama that she was good friends with Lady Alicia and anticipated remaining so.

Val had gone to Julian's townhouse and scoured his wardrobe, declaring Julian must have a new coat, vest, and trousers made up for the wedding.

"My sister's gown is an iced blue, so faint in color that you have to look twice," Val told her betrothed. "I think if you are dressed in a dark gray coat and pale gray trousers, you would look well together. And of course, you will need a matching top hat."

"I want to go with you," she said. "After all, I have visited the tailor's before."

Con accompanied them, and they arrived at Mr. Dalglish's shop the next morning shortly after it opened. Again, she had an odd feeling as if she recognized the tailor from somewhere and couldn't seem to shake it.

Dalglish congratulated them after they shared their good news, and he was already working on pieces for Julian which would be perfect for their wedding.

"I shall move your order to the front of my line, my lord," the tailor told them. "It will be my top priority. In fact, you may return for a fitting tomorrow. Everything will be close to being done by then."

Con signaled Val and Julian. "Come look at these and see what you think."

The trio of men left to look at some fabrics, leaving her with Mr. Dalglish. This was the closest she had ever stood to the tailor, and as she smiled at him, it was as if lightning struck her on the spot.

He seemed familiar because he had a look of Julian about him.

She recalled how Julian had shared with her that his mother was the daughter of a tailor. Could this man be related to her betrothed?

Eager to find out, she asked, "When did you become a tailor, Mr. Dalglish?"

"Oh, I trained under my uncle for several years. Originally, this was Uncle's shop. He left it to me in his will, with the stipulation that I would care for my aunt, his wife. I lived with them since I was a boy because my parents died close together, leaving me an orphan. My uncle assumed the care of me, and shortly afterward, I began apprenticing with him."

Trying to recall the name Julian had used, she asked, "What was your uncle's name, Mr. Dalglish? Was he also a Dalglish?"

"No, my lady. My aunt was the Dalglish. She married Mr. Watts, my uncle."

Hearing it, she knew Watts was the name which Julian had told her he had gone by. That meant Julian and Mr. Dalglish were related—and that Mr. Dalglish's aunt was Julian's grandmother.

Ariadne needed to make certain she was absolutely certain before dragging her fiancé into this, and so she asked, "Did your aunt and uncle have any children of their own?"

Mr. Dalglish looked uncomfortable. "Yes. A daughter."

"Was she asked to leave home because she became with child?"

The tailor gasped. "How did you know this, my lady? It happened many years ago, far before you were born."

She glanced to Julian and then back to the tailor. "Because, Mr. Dalglish, my husband-to-be is her son."

His eyes cut to Julian. "Lord Aldridge is . . . no, it can't be!"

Julian turned, frowning, and headed toward them. She knew Mr. Dalglish's raised voice had attracted Julian's attention.

"Is something wrong?" he asked, gently taking her elbow, looking from Ariadne to the tailor.

Val and Con now wandered over, concern evident on their faces, as well.

"My lord, Mr. Dalglish trained under Mr. Watts."

She paused, letting Julian absorb her words. His mouth moved, but no words came out.

"Mr. Dalglish came to live with Mr. and Mrs. Watts when his parents died. He knew your mother."

Pain filled her beloved's eyes. He turned his gaze to the tailor. "Is this true?"

Dalglish sighed. "It appears so, my lord. My mother and Mrs. Watts were sisters. I came to live with the Watts when my parents died. They had a daughter, but my uncle tossed her onto the street when he learned she would bear a child out of wedlock."

"It . . . seems . . . we are related then," Julian said.

The tailor looked at Julian with sympathy. "Your grandfather died several years ago. I inherited his shop and customers." Dalglish hesitated. "But your grandmother is still alive."

"Alive?" Julian echoed.

"Would you care to see her, my lord? She is upstairs."

Panic filled Julian's eyes. Ariadne reached for his hand, feeling how cold it was.

"You need to see her, Julian. If only this once," she encouraged.

"No," he refused. "She did not want my mother. She did not want me."

Dalglish spoke up. "That wasn't the case, my lord."

"What do you mean?" Julian pressed, anguish in his voice.

"My uncle was a hard man," the tailor admitted. "He expected perfection from everyone. He was an excellent tailor who worked long hours, creating the perfect wardrobe for men of Polite Society. That need for flawlessness consumed him, even in his personal life. Uncle was the one who threw your mother out. My aunt never wanted that to happen. I remember how distraught she was. She wept for days after it occurred."

Ariadne squeezed Julian's hand. "See? She would want to know you are alive, Julian."

"You think so?" he asked hoarsely.

"I know so," she said firmly.

Uncertainty clouded his eyes. "Will you come with me?"

"Of course, my love." Glancing to Val and Con, she said, "We will return shortly."

"We will wait for you in the carriage," Val told her as she and Julian followed Mr. Dalglish through a set of curtains and then ascended a staircase.

The tailor opened the door at the top of the stairs and then turned to them. "She has been bedridden for the last two years. Her health is now failing, and she is very weak."

"I understand," Julian said.

"Wait here," Dalglish said, crossing the parlor and disappearing.

Ariadne and Julian stood silently, their fingers entwined, until Dalglish appeared again.

"I told her who you are, and she wants to see you."

They let Dalglish take the lead, and he entered a bedchamber. Ariadne saw the woman in the bed, looking old and frail. She had the same pale blue eyes as her grandson, though, and tears spilled down her cheeks as they approached the bed.

Reaching out, the old woman took Julian's free hand, kissing it over and over. "I am so happy," she repeated several times. "I never wanted your mother sent away, but I was powerless to do anything."

Ariadne released Julian's hand, and he perched on the bed beside his grandmother.

"Tell me about my girl," she pleaded. "Was she a good mother?"

"She was the best mother a boy could have," he shared. "We did not have many material possessions, but I always knew how much I was loved."

Julian talked with his grandmother for several minutes, telling her a few stories about his growing up and how his mother supported them with her sewing.

"She was a talented seamstress. Better than her father. Oh, I am so sorry about everything." The old woman smiled. "But look at how you are dressed now. Your father must have claimed you."

Only Ariadne saw Julian stiffen slightly as he said, "I am the

Marquess of Aldridge now, Grandmother. If there is anything you need—medicine, a doctor—I can see you get it."

She shook her head. "I haven't long to live. The doctor has told me this much. I can die peacefully now, knowing you have gained your rightful place in the world." Her eyes closed, "I am tired. Will you come again?"

"Of course, Grandmother," Julian replied. "I am to wed Lady Ariadne next week in Kent. I promise I will come and visit you before I leave town."

"Do that," she mumbled, falling fast asleep.

Dalglish guided them from the bedchamber, and in the parlor, Julian said, "I meant it. Whatever you need is yours. If you want to move her into my townhouse, I am agreeable to it. You may come yourself, Mr. Dalglish."

"Thank you for the kind offer, my lord, but this is the world I know. I have a skill and am good at it. I like being useful. I fear the doctor would tell you not to move her. The last time he came, he told me she only had a short time to live."

She spoke up. "Would you like us to postpone the wedding?"

Her betrothed shook his head. "No. I refuse to lose any time with you. This may sound callous, but you are my future, Ariadne. She is my past."

Dalglish said, "She would want you to be happy, my lord. I say wed your lady love. My aunt will be happy because you are."

"May I see her again when I come for my fitting tomorrow?"

"Of course, my lord," the tailor replied.

The next day when they arrived at the tailor's shop, a clerk greeted them, saying, "Mr. Dalglish's aunt passed away during the night, my lord. He asked that I see to your fitting, but he would like to speak to you before you leave the shop."

Ariadne's throat thickened with emotion, knowing how hurt Julian must be to have found his grandmother, only to lose her so quickly.

He turned to her. "Do not worry about me, love. It was enough to see her and know the truth."

They spoke with Dalglish once Julian's suit had been fitted, and the tailor said he had arranged for the funeral service to be held the following afternoon.

Ariadne, Val, and Con accompanied Julian to the service and burial, delaying their departure from town by a day. She was thankful they had not already left for Millvale and was proud to stand by Julian's side as he said goodbye to his grandmother.

When they left for Kent the next morning, her betrothed saw them off, saying, "I am grateful I was able to meet my grandmother. She reminded me of my mother in many ways."

She took his hand. "You will see her—and your mother—in our children," she promised.

He kissed her softly before she boarded the carriage. "You are a balm to my soul, Ariadne—and the light of my life. I look forward to speaking my vows with you."

Chapter Twenty-Three

Julian looked out over Millvale as his carriage headed up the lane toward the main house. The ducal estate was breathtaking. Kent was so green this time of year, showing off the estate's natural beauty. Hopefully someday, he could go about the property with Val and its steward and see more of it. He would only be here a short time, however. Once he wed Ariadne, she would accompany him back to Aldridge Manor and he would introduce her to his own country seat, its staff, and his tenants.

The carriage rolled up to the house and came to a halt, and Val said, "You are definitely getting the royal treatment, Julian."

He glanced out the window and saw the entire family, including the Duke and Duchess of Millbrooke, waiting to greet him. Stepping from the carriage, his gaze met that of his betrothed's. Her smile radiated all her love for him. Knowing he must observe protocol, however, he went first to Their Graces and acknowledged them.

"It is good to have you here, Aldridge," the duke told him.

"We are most happy about the engagement," Her Grace added.

Ariadne stepped forward, and he took her hands, bringing them to his lips and kissing them tenderly. "How are you, my love?"

"Better, now that you are finally here," she said, her eyes conveying more than her words said.

Her sisters came up on each side of her, and Lady Tia asked, "May we call you Julian now, my lord?"

"You will not, Thermantia," Her Grace said sharply, causing her daughter's face to fall.

Intervening, he gave the duchess his most charming smile. "I did not have siblings, Your Grace, and I always yearned for them. With your permission, I would be most happy if your daughters addressed me informally, as Julian. It would mean a great deal to me."

Since the request came from him, he saw the duchess soften. "If it is truly what you wish, Aldridge."

Nodding, he confirmed, "It is, Your Grace." He turned and took Lady Tia's hands. "Call me Julian," he encouraged, kissing her fingers. He did the same with her twin, who told him, "It is nice to add you to our family, Julian."

These two, who resembled one another so much in the face, were very different. Julian thought both, however, would be quite successful when they made their come-outs next Season.

Val led his parents into the house. Julian took Ariadne's hand and slipped it into the crook of his arm.

"How are the arrangements for the wedding coming along?" he asked.

"Everything is set for tomorrow morning's ceremony, as well as the wedding breakfast afterward."

"I passed through Willowshire on our way here and saw the church where we will wed."

"I hope you do not mind us marrying here instead of in town," she said. "I did not want hundreds of people to be present at something which I believe to be a private matter between the two of us. We do have several guests which have come down from town, though. The church will be filled for the ceremony with them and the villagers."

Inside, Her Grace asked, "Would you care for tea, Aldridge, or would you prefer to rest in your room after your travels?"

"Actually, Your Grace, I believe I will stretch my legs after having our journey to Kent. Perhaps Lady Ariadne might show me your gardens." He thought that would give them time alone.

"I would be happy to do so, my lord," she said, leading him through the house and out the back.

They went through the vast gardens, Ariadne asking him several questions about Aldridge Manor. They had decided they would spend a week at his country estate before returning to town and the remainder of the Season.

"After all," she told him, "I have some very pretty gowns I would still like to wear, and we can enjoy the social events now we have found one another."

They reached a large gazebo and took a seat upon a bench inside it, where Julian hoped to steal more than a few kisses from his fiancée. He noted, however, that she appeared nervous, something he had never witnessed before.

Licking her lips, Ariadne said, "We must discuss something serious, Julian. I was so taken by your proposal that I should have shared things about myself before we agreed to wed." She swallowed. "Things that might make you change your mind."

Panic surged through him. This creature was perfection. He feared she was the one who had reservations about him and would now give him some excuse as to why they should not wed.

"I know we both want children," she began, slipping her hand into his. "I am thrilled to be your marchioness and want to always make you proud of me."

She fell silent, and he said, "Speak your piece, Ariadne. I need to know what is in your heart," he told her, worried his own was about to be shattered.

"I wish to fulfill my traditional role as a wife and mother, but I need to be more than that, Julian."

She had avoided looking at him but now met his gaze, and he saw tears swimming in her eyes. Concern filled him.

"What is it, love? What disturbs you so?"

"When I came to town this year, I found I was moved by those I saw in poverty, especially the children on the streets.

From my father's grand carriage, I have seen the poor ragamuffins on the street. I have felt tremendous guilt spending lavishly on gowns. My hats and slippers. I do realize those in trade depend upon the business of the *ton* for their livelihoods, so I have no quarrel with having an extensive wardrobe.

"But I must do more, Julian. To help those in need." She swallowed. "I even went to St. George's and asked what I could do. The curate sent me to Oakbrooke Orphanage, where I met with a Miss Crimmins. I tried to volunteer my time and teach the children living there, but she was dismissive of me."

Ariadne sighed. "I need to make a difference, Julian. I know you will give me pin money through our marriage settlements, and I will give as much of it as I can to this orphanage and other places which help those in need. Especially children. But I also want to donate myself."

She bit her lip. "If this upsets you, I understand if you choose to break off our engagement, but I had to let you know that I want to be more than a beautiful ornament which others admire. I must make a difference, or I will not be able to live with myself."

He took her in his arms, kissing her tenderly. "You are truly a woman who speaks to my heart, Ariadne. The first thing I thought of when I gained my title and fortune was how I might use some of my new wealth to do good for others. You know of the extreme poverty I was raised in. I, too, agree that the Marquess and Marchioness of Aldridge can be more than members of Polite Society. That we can aid the poor of London."

Tears spilled down her cheeks. "Oh, Julian, your words assure me that I am marrying my soulmate."

She kissed him fervently, and their kisses went on for some time. He couldn't believe his good fortune. That this heavenly creature was as beautiful inside as she was on the outside.

Together, they would have an enduring marriage, one filled with love, respect, and purpose.

JULIAN ALLOWED PAULSON to fuss over his cravat until the valet thought it perfect.

"There, my lord. You're ready now to wed your lady love."

He decided he must thank this servant for all he had done to make Julian's entrance into a new world a smooth one.

"I would not have gotten as far as I have without your help, Paulson," he told the servant. "You, more than anyone, prepared me for entering Polite Society. I would not have had a chance with Lady Ariadne had it not been for your guidance and advice."

The valet looked pleased. "You have made a wise choice with Lady Ariadne, my lord. Your servants and tenants will adore her as much as you do."

He left the bedchamber, going downstairs, where Val and Con lingered in the foyer.

"Ready to be caught in the parson's trap?" Con quipped.

"I do not look upon marriage as a trap, Con." He grinned. "Because I am wedding the most wonderful woman in the world."

Val patted Julian on the back. "From the start, I thought the two of you were meant to be. I am glad you worked out whatever differences you had. The carriage is waiting to convey us to the village. Shall we go?"

Once they left Millvale, it was a mere two miles to the church. Already, several carriages stood outside the building, and he supposed they belonged to various guests waiting inside. They entered the church, and he saw the flowers decorating it, courtesy of Lia and Tia. Lia had told Julian last night after dinner they had done so and it was the twins' wedding gift to the couple. He would have to make certain he complimented both of them on their efforts.

They met briefly with the vicar. Julian produced the special license, and the vicar said, "You could have wed at Millvale with this, my lord."

"It was important to Lady Ariadne to speak her vows within these four walls," Julian replied. "She grew up worshipping here. The place means a great deal to her."

The vicar had them wait in the anteroom for a few minutes, and then he returned, saying, "Lady Ariadne's carriage is approaching, my lord. You may come and take your place near the altar."

He, Val, and Con returned to the front of the church. Every pew was filled with guests of Their Graces, along with various villagers, and the walls and rear were lined with servants from Millvale. He found his heart pounding as he focused on the door where Ariadne would step through.

Val left his side, moving down the aisle, and Julian saw his friend went to his mother. The duchess entered the church looking regal, as always. He wasn't overly fond of the woman but would be polite to her since she was Ariadne's mother. Val escorted Her Grace to a seat in the front pew and then claimed his spot beside Julian once again.

The vicar nodded, and the church doors were opened wide. Ariadne's sisters joined them at the front of the church, both smiling encouragingly at him.

Then his betrothed appeared in the doorway on her father's arm. The pair made their way slowly down the aisle. Julian was aware of the murmur within those present, the guests obviously speaking of the bride's appearance. She was a vision of loveliness.

And she was all his . . .

Their gazes met as she came down the aisle, their eyes never leaving one another's as the duke brought his eldest daughter to Julian. His Grace surrendered the bride to her groom, and Julian thread his fingers through hers, squeezing them reassuringly.

They spoke their vows, making promises to one another that Julian knew they would keep, unlike most members of Polite Society. Both Val and Con had spoken of how many men within the *ton* took on a mistress, but Julian knew he would be ever faithful to this woman.

The vicar announced them as man and wife, and he kissed his bride for longer than he should have, but he was so happy to know they were two who had become one.

They signed the registry and departed for Millvale, where the wedding breakfast awaited them. For the next two hours, they ate their fill and then circulated about the room, greeting their guests. Julian was familiar with many of those in attendance, having met them at various social affairs since the beginning of the Season. He knew the Duke and Duchess of Millbrooke had only invited a handful of the most noteworthy members of the *ton* to their daughter's wedding, and now he was a part of this exclusive group.

While the guests still made merry, the family accompanied the bride and groom outside to say their goodbyes to them. Ariadne hugged everyone, and he couldn't help but be proud as Lia and Tia affectionately embraced him. He had never had anyone but his mother to claim as family, but he knew his wife's family would now become his, too. He had asked Dalglish to come down for the wedding, being his only living relative, but his cousin told him it was the height of the Season and he had too many orders to fill. He'd thanked Julian profusely for the invitation, and Julian had understood why Dalglish could not attend. He wondered if they would have a relationship and was curious to see what their future might hold.

He handed his wife into the carriage, warmth filling him as he thought of her in that role. Julian then gave a wave and climbed into the vehicle, sitting next to Ariadne and slipping an arm about her.

"It is done," he declared. "We are husband and wife. The Marquess and Marchioness of Aldridge."

"Thank you for opening your heart to me, Julian," she said. "There was a time when I feared I had lost you forever. I know you felt I deserved better than you, but let me tell you that I am the fortunate one in our union."

Ariadne framed his face with her hands and kissed him softly.

Then grinning at him, she added, "And I am eager to explore the marriage bed with you as soon as we reach Aldridge Manor."

Chapter Twenty-Four

Ariadne felt someone nudging her. She opened her eyes, blinking several times, realizing she had fallen asleep in the carriage. Lifting her head from Julian's chest, she asked, "Are we almost there?"

"Yes. We are approaching my lands now. I wanted you to be able to see them with me this first time when you caught sight of your new home."

It struck her that home was no longer Millvale. From now on, she would reside with her husband either here in Surrey or at his London townhouse. Though she loved her new husband deeply, a wave of sadness crossed through her. She would never again be in the bosom of her family, being able to go down the hall and jump into bed with Lia and Tia or share late night confidences with Val over a game of chess.

Still, she was incredibly happy about the choice she had made. Becoming Julian's wife made her happier than she could imagine. She could not wait to spend more time with her new husband.

Especially in bed.

His kisses had been addicting, and Ariadne knew there was so much more to come between them. Thanks to Val, she had a much better idea of what to expect. Once she understood more about coupling with her husband, she would share what she could with her sisters, not wanting them to go completely unprepared into their own marriages.

As they passed the rolling grassland, Julian pointed out things to her. Their carriage arrived at the main house, and she instantly fell in love with her new country home as they disembarked. She was a bit taken aback at the two long lines of servants waiting for them, though, and tried to compose herself. She would be their mistress and wished to make a favorable impression upon them.

A couple stepped forward. "My lord, my lady," said the man. "I am Briscoe, your butler, Lady Aldridge. This is Mrs. Briscoe, who serves as housekeeper."

"Thank you for such a warm welcome," Ariadne replied. "It was thoughtful of you to assemble the servants so that I might meet them. Shall we go down the line and do so?"

Briscoe introduced everyone to her, and she made certain to say something to each servant.

The final person they came to was a young man who looked to be between her age and Val's. Deducing who he weas, she said, "You must be Mr. Ross."

"Aye, my lady," the steward said. "My father is employed by yours. Lord Claibourne recommended me to Lord Aldridge, and here I am."

"It is good to have someone so capable in charge of the tenants," she said. "It will allow Lord Aldridge and me to come and go freely, knowing Aldridge Manor is in good hands."

"We can meet tomorrow afternoon, Mr. Ross," Julian said. "I will send word to you when."

"Yes, my lord," the steward replied deferentially.

As the Briscoes led them into the house, Ariadne told her husband, "I was afraid you were going to want to meet with Mr. Ross first thing in the morning."

Julian cocked one brow. "Why meet with a steward when I can have all the attention of my wife?" His wicked grin caused her belly to flip crazily.

Mrs. Briscoe halted and faced them. "I know you have had an unusually busy day, my lord. Would you like a light supper brought to your rooms?"

"Yes, Mrs. Briscoe. That would be delightful."

She saw Tally starting up the stairs and called her over, saying, "This is my maid. Tally has been with my family a good number of years, but she agreed to come with me once I wed."

"See to unpacking Lady Aldridge's things, Tally, and then come to the kitchens. Supper will be waiting for you, and then I will take you to your own room."

"Yes, Mrs. Briscoe," her maid replied, heading up the staircase.

"Let me show you your rooms and then we can go to mine for supper," her husband said.

They went to a large suite, where Tally had a footman opening Ariadne's trunk. She had left most of her things at her father's townhouse, and Mrs. Parsons was going to pack them and have them delivered to Julian's townhouse. She took the time to remove her gloves and hat before continuing on.

Julian showed her the door which connected her bedchamber to her dressing room. A bathing chamber, which they would share, came next. Finally, they entered his dressing room and then bedchamber. She glanced at the large bed, wondering if she were to come to him or he to her own bed. Though she had the rudiments down of what lovemaking would be like, it was still foreign territory to her.

He discarded his own coat and undid the knot of his cravat, sliding it from his neck. Julian wore only his shirt and vest, and she wondered if things would always be so casual between them when they were alone. It was rare for her to see Val without his coat, and she couldn't recall a single occasion when Papa had not been fully dressed.

"Hopefully, Mrs. Briscoe has supper for us now," he said, guiding her through another door to his own sitting room. It contained a settee and two chairs, along with a small table and two more chairs. The Briscoes awaited them.

Her husband seated her, and Briscoe delivered two covered

plates to the table, lifting the covers from them. Mrs. Briscoe poured wine for them, and the butler placed the crystal goblets next to the plates.

"I am sure you would like a bit of privacy now, my lord," Briscoe said. "Please ring if you require anything else."

"We won't for the rest of the night," he assured the couple. "Pass that along to Paulson and Tally, as well."

Their butler and housekeeper exited the room, and Julian picked up his glass. "A toast to the loveliest bride England has ever seen."

She picked up her own glass. "To the most handsome marquess I know—and a day I will never forget."

They clinked their glasses together and took a sip. The light meal was just what Ariadne needed to revive her. Cold chicken. Cheese. Bread. Fruit. She ate sparingly, though, as nerves began to flit through her, the unknown still to come.

"I would like to propose something to you, my love," her husband said.

"Another proposal?" she teased. "After all, I did go ahead and wed you."

"I talked to Paulson about this first and would now like to broach the subject with you."

"Hmm. Now you have me most curious, Lord Aldridge. What do you and your valet propose?"

Julian slipped his hand around hers. "You have seen your rooms. They are large, with plenty of space for your wardrobe." He hesitated. "But they are also far from me."

Ariadne's heart beat more swiftly. "Yes?"

"Though Paulson assures me it is not custom, I am the marquess, after all. I should have the final say in matters, but it is your household to command, my love."

He brought their joined hands to his lips and kissed her fingers. "What would you think of using your rooms as a place to dress or a quiet respite during the day—but sharing my rooms at night?"

His words surprised her. Her parents had always kept to their separate rooms. Of course, there had to have been at least three occasions over the years when they had coupled in order to produce their children. Still, what Julian intended was far from the norm.

And she liked it.

"I would be happy to share your bed each night, Julian," she told him. "Whether it is to sleep . . . or do other things a married couple does in a shared bed."

Kissing her hand again, he asked, "Are you ready to explore those very things now, my sweet marchioness?"

With conviction, she said, "Absolutely."

He rose, their hands still joined, and led her back into the bedchamber. Pulling her into his arms, he kissed her long and slow, her body against his, his heat and scent overwhelming her. Julian deepened the kiss, and Ariadne lost herself in it, thankful he didn't rush her into lovemaking. As his hands moved slowly up and down her back, his actions told her they had all the time in the world, and no one would interrupt them.

"Shall I play Tally's role tonight?" he teased after ending the kiss.

His hands went to her hair, and Julian began removing the pins from it. Her tresses spilled to her waist. He set aside the pins and ran his fingers through her hair, causing her scalp to tingle pleasantly.

"Another time, I will brush it for you," he promised. "But we have more to do tonight."

Leading her to a chair, he knelt before her, removing her slippers and then reaching under her gown. Soon, her slippers and stockings were gone, and Julian caressed her calves lovingly, causing a tender ache within her.

"You may have to give me a little direction for the rest," he said lightly, bringing her to her feet and turning her so he could unbutton the myriad of buttons along her spine. One by one, each layer came off, until she stood bare before him. It surprised

Ariadne that she felt no shyness. No embarrassment.

What she did feel, however, was impatience.

His gaze lovingly took her in. "You are a marvel to behold, my love."

"Then allow me the same pleasure, my lord," she said, her voice low and seductive.

Ariadne's fingers unbuttoned his vest, removing it. He now stood in his shirt and trousers, and she was eager to see what was under them. Slowly, she unbuttoned the three buttons of his shirt and lifted it over his head, tossing it aside. Her eyes roamed his chest, broad and muscular, covered in a fine matting of dark hair. She placed her palms against his bare skin, running them along it, delighting in the muscles moving beneath her fingertips.

"Help me with my boots," he asked, taking a seat.

She removed them, though it took a bit of effort. Quickly, he ridded himself of his trousers and stood before her. She was dumbstruck by his body, so perfect that it made her teeth ache.

"Come," he said, holding open his arms in invitation.

She walked into them, placing her own about him, pressing her face to his chest, inhaling his cologne and the musky scent that was all Julian.

"Mine," she whispered, in awe of that fact.

"Mine," he repeated, caressing her, his hands moving down her spine and squeezing her buttocks. "Mine," he said again. "You are mine, and I am yours. Shall we see what each other is like?"

He led her to the bed, which was already turned back. Surprising her, he swept her from her feet and gently placed her on it. Joining her, they soon were a tangle of limbs. Heat rose within her as he touched her everywhere. Kissed her everywhere. Her heart slammed against her ribs, and she was afraid it might very well pop through her chest.

Lazily, his finger glided along the curve of her breast, back and forth, before sliding to her erect nipple. He tweaked it playfully, sending a jolt of pure, hot desire through her. His mouth followed, and he feasted upon it, his teeth grazing the nipple, his tongue working her into a frenzy.

His mouth returned to hers for long, drugging kisses, but she was aware of his hand stroking her belly, moving lower. Then his fingers danced along the seam of her sex, gliding back and forth, causing her core to beat violently. When he pushed a finger inside her, Ariadne almost came off the bed, the sensations starting to overwhelm her.

"Relax, love," Julian encouraged. "Enjoy."

She fell back against the pillow and gave into the pleasure. A second finger joined the first, the caresses intimate and long. A rhythm began, a drumbeat within her, building to some unknown climax. She began gyrating under his hand, panting, having to break their kiss because her sole focus was on that beat. The blood rushed to her ears, the sensations crazy now. She felt as if she were balancing on a cliff, about to fall over. Fall apart.

And then his thumb pressed hard against her, moving in a circular motion. Ariadne whimpered, her head tossing back and forth, her body no longer hers, but his. Then a cascade of pleasure rushed through her quickly, and she met his hand, moaning, laughing, rocking. Her body quivered, shaking as pure pleasure enveloped her.

Then it ended, leaving her limp. Unable to speak or move.

Her husband, wearing a very satisfied look, kissed her. Ariadne wrapped her arms about him, holding tightly, never wanting to let this man go. She felt him touch her again, but his hands cradled her face. Something hard pressed against her now.

"What is that?" she managed to ask.

"My cock. It is hard for you, love. It wants to be inside you."

"Oh, I know that part. Val explained it."

He chuckled. "Your *brother* told you about lovemaking?"

"Well, Mama refused to answer any of my questions. Where else would I turn?"

He mused, "Indeed," and then kissed her deeply.

Julian moved slightly, and his hands left her face. "This might sting a bit, but the pleasure will outweigh any pain."

"I am ready," she said stoically.

With one thrust, he broke through her maidenhead. It did sting, but she liked the fullness of him within her. Ariadne shifted.

And liked that feeling even more.

Slowly, Julian began to move in and out of her, almost like a dance, and she wrapped her limbs about him, allowing him to drive more deeply into her. Soon, they were flying, and all those lovely sensations built again, spilling from her. He also made a noise and then called her name over and over, making her feel free and alive.

Her husband collapsed atop her, breathing heavily. She kissed his neck and then licked him, causing him to groan.

He rolled, taking her with him, so they faced one another. Still joined intimately, he stroked her face tenderly.

"Our first time making love," he said.

"Our first time tonight," she corrected playfully.

Julian groaned again. "We will go at it again, sweetness, but it takes time for a man to recover."

Propping her elbow onto the pillow, she rested her head in her hand. "I will think of something to do in the meantime. Maybe you would like me to do to you what you have done to me," she playfully mused aloud.

Leaning over, she swiped her tongue across his nipple several times, then lazily circled it. Her husband laughed. Then moaned. Then grabbed her, kissing her possessively.

Oh, yes. This exploring was going to be ever so much fun.

Chapter Twenty-Five

Ariadne stepped from the carriage, confidence soaring through her. They were headed into a ball, the first event they had attended as husband and wife since their return to town yesterday afternoon. She had found that all her clothes and other personal items had been transferred from her father's townhouse to her husband's. Tally moved things about a bit to her liking, but Ariadne felt settled into her new home in town. She would still have to send for a few things she'd left at Millvale, but there was no rush regarding those items.

The week with Julian at Aldridge Manor had been spectacular. She had enjoyed touring the countryside and meeting Julian's tenants. They had also gone into the village of Alderton and visited with some of the merchants, as well as attending church services on Sunday. She had learned the names of most of the household staff, and she and Julian had gone riding several times. He had not known how to do so when he first inherited his title, and his head groom had given him lessons, explaining how important riding skills were to get about the countryside. If he had not shared this with her, Ariadne would never have guessed because her husband looked quite at home on horseback.

They had shared walks and intimate dinners. He had asked her to play the pianoforte for him each night after dinner and had even taught her two naughty songs which he had learned while working on London's docks. After a bit of practice, she could now play both, adding chords to the jaunty tunes' melodies.

More importantly, they had grown accustomed to one another in the bedroom. The first night alone, Ariadne had learned more about lovemaking than she had ever known existed. Each time they came together, they discovered new things about one another. What pleased their partner most. How tender those times were after they had made love and lay in each other's arms before falling asleep.

She was happy her husband had suggested that she remain the entire night with him each night. Already, she was used to his large body protecting hers, even in sleep. His heat kept her warmer than the bedclothes ever had, and she was finally getting used to sleeping nude. She would keep that to herself, however, since she thought it was likely they were one of the few couples in Polite Society who did so. However, when Tia and Lia found husbands of their own?

Ariadne would highly recommend they follow the same practice.

She and Julian had already discussed having the twins come and stay with them over the Christmas holidays. He had been enthusiastic in his response and even mentioned if she wished to invite Val or any of her other cousins, they would be more than welcome at Aldridge Manor during the holiday season.

They entered the receiving line and greeted their hosts and their daughter, who was also making her come-out this Season.

As they entered the ballroom, Julian asked, "Were your parents supposed to host a come-out ball for you?"

"Yes. It was planned for mid-June. Mama said the other mothers get together and discuss when their daughters' debut balls are to be held so one does not conflict with the other."

He smiled ruefully. "I hate that you missed out on yours. Perhaps we should hold a ball in your honor to celebrate our marriage."

"That would be lovely. I could plan everything myself and not have to agree to what Mama would have planned."

"I see your parents now. We should discuss it with Their Graces. Come along, Wife."

She and Julian approached her parents. Papa nodded brusquely, but Mama was all smiles, thanks to her daughter having been the first girl of the Season to wed.

After the formalities, Julian said, "Your Graces, I regret that Ariadne did not get to experience her own come-out ball. Would you mind if we took that date on the social calendar and held one to celebrate our marriage?"

"Oh!' Mama said, fanning herself. "What a lovely idea, Aldridge, but you should let His Grace and I host it. You will not have to do a thing."

Julian smiled at her mother. "I would not think of doing so, Your Grace. You planned a most wonderful wedding and breakfast for us. You must be exhausted after that. We will assume the responsibility—and cost—of the ball."

That perked up His Grace's ears. "Let them do as they wish," he told his wife. To Julian, he added, "We will happily attend, Aldridge."

"Then it is settled," Ariadne said. "Thank you so much."

She danced with her husband and a few other gentlemen, each of them expressing regret that she had exited the Marriage Mart early. They joined Lady Alicia and Val for the midnight supper. Her brother shared quietly that both he and Con were making a point of dancing with Lady Alicia at every ball. Because of it, her dance programme was filling regularly. Val assured her that while neither he nor Con were interested in wooing her, their attention had brought other gentlemen into Lady Alicia's sphere, and he hoped she would find a suitor who would offer for her by Season's end.

After supper ended, Ariadne yawned. Julian leaned over, stroking her cheek. "We are more used to country hours after this past week."

"Do you think we might go home now?" she asked. "While I have enjoyed the dancing, I see no point in continuing to do so for several more hours." Smiling slyly, she added quietly, "Not when I could be home in bed with my marquess."

"We are leaving," Julian announced, shooting to his feet. "It was good seeing you," he told Val and Lady Alicia.

"We must say goodbye to our hosts," Ariadne reminded him. "Especially because we are leaving quite early."

"Do you truly believe they would miss us?" he asked, his eyes gleaming at her. "And if they do, surely our excuse is that we are newlyweds."

"All right," she said, laughing, letting him lead her down the staircase and to their carriage, where they kissed the entire way home. It did not take them long since the streets were clear of traffic.

"We should leave balls early every time," he murmured into her ear, nibbling on her lobe. "How nice for it to only take a handful of minutes to arrive home and not an hour or more. It gives us that much more time to spend awake in our bed."

His words caused a frisson of desire to run through her.

Tally readied Ariadne for bed, and she went through the series of connecting doors until she reached her husband. He sat on the bed, pillows propped behind him, not a stitch on.

Climbing from the bed, he said flirtatiously, "You are overdressed for this evening's activities, Lady Aldridge. Allow me to take your robe and night rail."

Quickly divested of her garments, Julian pulled her into bed, their passion instant, their coupling fast.

She lay in his arms afterward, trying to slow her breathing and racing heart. "I think that was my favorite dance of the evening, my lord," she said seductively.

"Perhaps we will dance again when we awaken, love," he said, gathering her into his arms, both of them falling asleep immediately.

TRUE TO HIS word, her husband made sweet love to Ariadne before they rose for the day. They separated for a few minutes as they washed and dressed for the day and then met up in the sunny breakfast room. She had told him how her parents never breakfasted together, and he had replied that her parents were fools to miss out on spending such precious time together. Ariadne reminded him that her parents were not a love match. She was too ashamed to tell him how her mother and grandmother had ensnared her father in a trap so that Mama could claim a duke for her husband.

As breakfast concluded, Julian told her, "We have an appointment this morning with the vicar of St. George's. Mr. Charleston is expecting us at ten o'clock."

"Whatever for?" she asked.

"To begin our purpose," he replied solemnly.

Excitement filled Ariadne. Once Julian had shared with her how he, too, wanted to help the downtrodden of London, they had talked over ideas about where to start. She had no idea he had taken that first step, especially with them only having arrived back in town recently.

On the way to Hanover Square, she asked, "Do you have an idea what we should address first?"

"The future is always dependent on the children of the present," he said thoughtfully. "I think Oakbrooke Orphanage is where we should start."

Wrinkling her nose, Ariadne said, "I hope you will have better luck with Miss Crimmins than I did."

He took her hand, raising it to his lips and kissing it tenderly. "You might have been a duke's daughter when you spoke with her, but you now have the power of your husband behind you, love."

She smiled. "I did not know I was wedding a champion."

He brought her hand to his cheek. "I will always champion you, Ariadne."

Her confidence rose. She believed she could accomplish

much good with Julian's backing. His title and wealth would open doors previously closed to her. Together, she hoped they would prove to be a formidable team.

They entered the offices at St. George, and Ariadne saw Mr. Rogers, the curate. She couldn't help but ask, "Do you recall meeting me, sir?"

"Yes, my lady," he said sheepishly. Looking to Julian, the curate asked, "Are you Lord Aldridge?"

"Yes. Lord and Lady Aldridge to see Mr. Charleston."

"One moment," the curate replied, vacating the room.

"See how he cowed, Julian?"

"I never want to use my position to harm anyone, but if mentioning my title gives us an advantage, I will not refrain from doing so."

Mr. Rogers appeared again. "Mr. Charleston will see you now, my lord. My lady."

The curate led them down a long corridor and indicated a room for them to enter. Seated at a desk was the vicar of St. George's. Ariadne recognized him from the Sunday sermons she had attended since coming to town.

Rising, Mr. Charles bowed. "Lord and Lady Aldridge. It is good to see you. Please, have a seat.

They took the two chairs in front of the vicar's desk, while he sat in the one behind it.

"What might I do for you?"

"Lady Aldridge is extremely interested in assisting the poor," Julian began. "In particular, the children of Oakbrooke Orphanage."

"Yes, Mr. Rogers told me he had directed her to the orphanage. It is the largest one our congregation supports."

"Nothing came of my wife's previous visit to the place," Julian said bluntly. "She was sorely disappointed." He then stared at the vicar, who began to look quite uncomfortable, and Ariadne had to stifle a giggle.

"I would see this remedied," Julian said firmly. "Who owns

the building?"

"Why, St. George's does, my lord," Mr. Charleston replied.

"And I assume you pay for the staff, including Miss Crimmins' salary? As well as feed and clothe the children who live there?"

"Yes, through the poor tax, my lord. Mr. Rogers explained all this to Lady Aldridge."

"Did Miss Crimmins share how she refused my wife's help?"

Color sprouted on the vicar's cheeks. "Miss Crimmins was happy to receive a donation. In fact, she told me that a Lord Claibourne, Lady Aldridge's brother, made a substantial contribution after her visit to Oakbrooke."

"How many teachers are on staff?"

"I am not certain, my lord," responded the vicar. "I would have to see."

"I would like to take on Oakbrooke Orphanage," Julian announced calmly, as if he were ordering a cup of tea.

Shock filled the vicar's face. "My lord, it is quite ambitious to handle everything associated with running such a large orphanage. Why, we at St. George's—"

"I will buy the building outright from the church," Julian said, causing Ariadne to smile as she watched Mr. Charleston squirm. "Then St. George's will be free to support the poor in other places. Once I obtain ownership, I will be responsible for everything within its four walls. St. George's may use its resources elsewhere."

"Do you truly wish to take on such an expense, Lord Aldridge?" the vicar questioned. "It is not as if it is a one-time occurrence, and you can move on from your responsibilities."

"I know what I am getting into," Julian said impatiently. "How much for the building?"

Mr. Charleston named a price. Julian countered, saying his solicitor had checked into the value of other places in the neighborhood.

"You wouldn't be trying to fleece a marquess now, would

you, Mr. Charleston?"

The question hung in the air, and she saw the vicar quickly reconsider.

"The price you offered is perfectly acceptable, my lord."

Julian rose, offering Ariadne his hand, and she did the same. "Then have St. George's solicitor come to my solicitor's office this afternoon at two o'clock. We will complete the transaction then." He gave the solicitor's address.

"I must speak to the bishop first," Charleston protested. "Possibly the archbishop, my lord. I need more time."

"Oh, I have already written to the archbishop. He is well aware of my plans."

This was news to her, and she tried to maintain a face which gave away nothing.

"We will see you and your solicitor at two, Mr. Charleston," Julian said, smiling benignly at the vicar.

In the carriage, she asked, "Is it true you have written the bishop?"

"Once you told me of your desire to aid the poor and your experience at Oakbrooke Orphanage, I wrote to my solicitor and the archbishop, telling them both of my desire to do my Christian duty and see to the orphans living at Oakbrooke. The sale of the building will go through, Ariadne. In fact, I am so certain that we are now going to see Miss Crimmins."

"She is odious."

"You will be the one to decide if she stays or goes."

"Me?"

"Yes, my love. We will take on this endeavor together, but I believe you should make the decision regarding Miss Crimmins' fate."

They arrived at Oakbrooke, and Julian escorted her inside. They were met by a woman who introduced herself as Miss Darnell.

"How may I help you, my lord? I am a teacher on staff here."

"I am Lord Aldridge, and this is Lady Aldridge. We are the

new benefactors of Oakbrooke and will be in charge of all aspects in running the orphanage, from staff hired to what is taught to providing decent clothing and tasty meals."

"Does Miss Crimmins know about this?" asked Miss Darnell, her brow creased with worry.

"She is about to hear the news from me," Julian replied. "How long have you been teaching here, Miss Darnell?"

"Seven years, my lord."

"Do you enjoy your work?" Ariadne interjected.

Miss Darnell's face softened. "Very much indeed, my lady. I feel as if I were born to teach, especially the orphans at Oakbrooke."

"And your thoughts regarding Miss Crimmins?" she asked. Seeing how nervous the teacher appeared, Ariadne added, "Please, be frank. We are evaluating the staff of the school and will be deciding who should remain. Your honesty is vital."

Miss Darnell took a deep breath and expelled it. "Miss Crimmins and I do not see eye to eye on numerous matters, my lady. The courses taught and the manner in which material is communicated to students." She hesitated and then added, "And discipline." Her mouth tightened.

"You believe Miss Crimmins to be heavy-handed," Ariadne guessed.

The teacher took a moment to gather her thoughts and then said, "While I am in favor of exercising discipline, it must be done for a reason. And practiced with love. These children have lost everything. They must see that it is not only their physical needs which are met. Shelter. Clothing. They must see they are cared for as individuals."

She glanced to Julian, and he nodded approvingly. "We are quite impressed by you, Miss Darnell. How would you like to be in charge of running Oakbrooke?"

Without hesitation, the woman said, "Only if I could spend some of my time in the classroom, Lady Aldridge. I love what I do and these children. While I am organized and would do a thorough job as an administrator, I need to be with the pupils at least a part of every day."

"Do you have time to give us a tour of the facilities?" Julian asked.

Miss Darnell checked the watch pinned to her blouse. "If it is a quick one, my lord. I can show you everything now, but I am certain you will want to come back and observe things at greater length, including some of the classes being taught."

They followed Miss Darnell about Oakbrooke, seeing things they liked and others they would change. Some, immediately. Some, gradually.

Julian offered the teacher his card. "We would like to discuss matters with you at greater length, Miss Darnell. Be thinking about the staff you wish to retain and how many additional positions need to be filled. If the food is good or—"

"It is barely edible, my lord," Miss Darnell said passionately.

"Then note we need to hire a decent cook and scullery maids," he continued. "Also think about what is taught and how you wish it changed. You will prepare the model for teaching, as well as be the model for your staff."

"I believe practical training is important," the teacher said. "Once our students have decent reading, writing, and maths skills, we could train them for service. They could be maids. Footmen. We could also prepare them to work as a clerk in a shop or on the land, teaching them about farming and how to look after livestock. I want to give all our students practical skills and then see ways they can become gainfully employed."

"Write it all down, Miss Darnell," Julian encouraged. "When you are ready to present everything to us, please come to the address on the card."

Miss Darnell studied them, tears in her eyes. "Thank you, my lord, my lady. These children need so much. I believe you will give them a way out of poverty and hope for their future."

"What is going on?" a voice cried.

Ariadne turned and saw Miss Crimmins headed their way.

"You'd best be on your way, Miss Darnell," she warned, knowing a confrontation was at hand, and the teacher fled up the stairs.

Coming to stand before them, Miss Crimmins said, "I remember you. The idealistic young lady who thought she could lark about and teach for a few hours and make a difference." Looking at Julian, she added, "I suppose this is your brother. The one whom you bullied into making a donation."

"No," said Julian firmly, his voice full of authority. "I am Lady Aldridge's husband, the Marquess of Aldridge. I have bought this building, and my wife and I will be responsible for every aspect of it. Your services are no longer required, Miss Crimmins."

"What . . . why . . . you cannot do that!"

"I can—and have," her husband said. "You have a day to pack your things and leave."

"I will speak to Mr. Charleston about this, my lord," Miss Crimmins said, her face turning beet red.

"You may call upon him, but it will do you no good. You must seek employment elsewhere."

The headmistress whirled, hurrying away.

"You realize things will be in turmoil by tomorrow," Ariadne pointed out.

"We may have to give up some of our social engagements and late nights for a bit," he said, slipping his arms about her, a satisfied smile playing on his sensual lips. "I fear we shall need to be here first thing tomorrow to right the chaos. Are you willing to forgo some of the social activities?"

"Let me think." She pretended to ponder a moment. "Listening to gossip about people I do not know or care to hear about. Staying out until dawn. Or standing with my husband and making a difference in the lives of so many children." Ariadne brightened. "I choose Oakbrooke.

"And you."

"I thought you might, Lady Aldridge." Julian threaded his fingers through hers. "We should go home and enjoy the rest of our day because tomorrow—and the tomorrows after that—are going to be quite busy."

In the carriage, Ariadne covered his face in kisses. "Oh, I am so glad to have married you, Julian Barrington."

Her husband smoothed her hair. "Not half as happy as I am for having married you, my love."

Julian kissed her, and Ariadne knew they had a bright future ahead of them.

Epilogue

London—December

JULIAN BOUNDED FROM the carriage and handed down Tia and then Lia. He signaled the footman to stand on the other side of the stairs as Ariadne descended them. She took the hand of each of them and eased her way down. She was in her sixth month of increasing, and Julian worried about her constantly, while she reassured him everything happening was perfectly normal.

She had been violently ill every morning for the first couple of months. They had to place chamber pots in every room she entered and even kept them on the landings of the staircase. Ever since then, however, his beautiful wife had boundless energy and glowed with good health. The doctor told them she would begin to slow soon, but for now, Julian found it hard to keep up with her sometimes.

They entered Oakbrooke Orphanage, and he couldn't help but feel a bit of pride at what they had accomplished at the school since they had claimed ownership of the facility. Proving true to her word, Miss Darnell was both efficient and organized. Moreover, the new headmistress was caring toward her staff and nurturing toward the orphans.

It had been Ariadne and Miss Darnell who had hired additional staff for the school, which was woefully underfunded and lacking in teachers and adult supervision. Ariadne had insisted they hire former governesses who had a reasonable amount of teaching experience. The interview questions she and Miss Darnell had devised allowed them to sort through and find the type of teachers they wished for the orphanage to have.

Miss Darnell welcomed them, taking the twins to one of the classrooms to help out for the morning, while he and Ariadne went to another one. Julian stood in the rear of the room, watching his wife read a story to a group of children gathered about her. She changed her voice with each character and read with such animation that her joy proved contagious. He saw the smiles on the faces of the children and knew they adored her as he did.

Changes had been made to what the students were taught, and a wonderful cook had been hired. In speaking with a few of the older students, he had seen how thin and frail many of them were and suspected they were malnourished. Now, however, with their talented cook and plenty of food, these orphans thrived physically. With the help of their caring staff, he knew they also thrived socially and emotionally.

Julian had learned the names of every child in the building since he and Ariadne had spent so much time at the orphanage. They split their time between town and Aldridge Manor. Thankfully, with his country estate so close to London, this was easy to do. As predicted, his tenants and staff in the country worshipped Ariadne. She was the epitome of what a marchioness should be.

They had discussed future endeavors to become involved with, but his wife cautioned him not to take on too much, saying she wanted Oakbrooke Orphanage to be a beacon of light and example to other orphanages before they began new projects to aid the poor. She asked him for a year in which to stabilize things and make certain everything to keep Oakbrooke running was secure, and then they would tackle a new challenge, such as feeding or clothing those on the streets or others in need, such as Julian and his mother had been.

While the orphanage consumed a great deal of their money and time, he knew both were well spent. Julian pictured many of these children working for them or other family members down the line, be it as house servants, stable lads, or tenants. His cousin had agreed to take on a couple of boys as apprentices in his tailor shop, and Julian and Ariadne had plans to talk with other shopkeepers, as well, trying to secure good futures for these orphans.

Ariadne finished reading the story, and the children clapped enthusiastically, begging for another one. He was tapped to read the next one and did so. Much to the delight of the children, he added sounds to the story he read, encouraging them to do the same. They assisted him in knocking on doors, tapping their feet, and even chattering like magpies.

Miss Darnell came to the doorway, signaling it was time for the assembly. The children ran to line up without being told to do so and marched from the room in an orderly fashion. Unlike her predecessor, Miss Darnell used discipline lightly. Because of that, very few children stepped out of line. Those who did proved to be contrite and rarely caused trouble after a first incident.

He went and slipped an arm about his wife's waist. "Are you happy, love?"

She stroked her belly. "I did not realize just how happy I could be, Julian. You. The babe. These children at Oakbrooke. It is as if I am living in a dream."

He kissed her softly. "It is no dream, my darling. You have made a difference in the lives of these orphans, but more importantly, you have made all the difference in my life."

Her palm cradled his face. "I am grateful every day that we are husband and wife."

Julian kissed her again and then said, "Come. They will not start the assembly without us."

They went to the dining hall, which was the only place in the building large enough to have the entire population gather as a whole. Lia and Tia motioned to them, and they joined his sisters-in-law at a table in the rear. He loved these two young ladies as if they were his own flesh and blood, and he was happy his wife would help launch them into society next spring.

Julian marveled that by that time, he would be a father. Having grown up with no father in his life, he fully intended to be an active participant in his child's life. He had heard enough from Ariadne and Val about what their childhoods had been like, and how they could go days without seeing their parents in the country, much less the months they had been left with servants while the duke and duchess attended the Season in town. Ariadne was in agreement with him that they would never be separated from their children and that their family would come to town each year and remain until the Season ended.

Ariadne had told him they would only attend a handful of events in future years. She even planned to wear gowns more than once, which would set tongues wagging, but she didn't care. His lovely wife said she would rather spend money on their orphans than on herself, but she made certain that people such as Madame Laurent and his own Cousin Dalglish would be hired to sew clothes for these children. They had already engaged the services of the pair this autumn, and both modiste and tailor had been grateful to have such a large amount of business come their way during a slow time of year for them. Children grew rapidly, and Dalglish and Madame would be kept busy making new outfits for the Oakbrooke Orphans.

Miss Darnell addressed everyone, and Julian thought again what a treasure they had in her. The woman was a dedicated headmistress and had also become a dear friend to the two of them.

"We have a special treat awaiting all of you. The Christmas season is upon us, and Lord and Lady Aldridge wanted to celebrate it with you. They have gifts they wish to distribute now to everyone. My lord?"

He rose from his seat and said, "We will be giving out the gifts now, and Lady Aldridge and I want to wish each of you a most happy Christmas."

The children cheered. He doubted a single one of them had ever received any kind of present. He certainly never had.

Until Ariadne Worthington came into his life—and she was a present who would give and give as the years went on.

Helping Ariadne to her feet, he motioned for Lia and Tia to join them. They began calling out names, handing over packages wrapped in brown paper and tied with string. Each child was to receive a new pair of shoes, along with something to wear, as well as a book and an item to play with, based upon their age. Ariadne had chosen every single book, gearing it toward the interest of that particular child, as well as deciding what toy should be gifted to them. He watched as children opened their packages with glee, finding everything from dolls to tin soldiers to blocks and spinning tops.

To a child, they all came and thanked their benefactors, awarding hugs and kisses in gratitude.

The last orphan to approach was Joseph. Although he tried his best not to play favorites, this boy reminded Julian so much of himself at that age. When the time came, he fully intended to take Joseph into their household.

"My lord, my lady, you have been so generous to us since you took over," the boy said, blinking back tears. "I hated it here before you came. I was going to run away and live on the streets. Any place had to be better than here. You changed that. You make me want to learn more about reading and writing, and I want to better myself, all thanks to you."

Ariadne wrapped her arms about Joseph, stroking his hair. She released him, and Joseph turned. Julian also embraced him, telling Joseph, "Keep up with your studies. There will be a place for you with Lady Aldridge and me when you are ready to leave Oakbrooke."

Tears of gratitude spilled down the orphan's cheeks. "Thank you, my lord," he said fervently. "Thank you for changing everything."

"It is time for another treat," called Ariadne, and the kitchen staff brought out trays of baked goods from Gunter's.

As the orphans ate their sweets, Julian and the others distributed guineas to the employees, from the teachers to the kitchen and cleaning staffs. His wife had discussed it with Miss Darnell, and the two women had agreed it would be better to give the teachers and other workers coin to spend on whatever they wished.

He slipped his arm about his wife's waist and looked on at the animated children, who were laughing, eating, and talking about the gifts they had received.

"I think it is time we depart," he told his wife.

She motioned to her sisters, and the twins joined them.

"Thank you for allowing us to come with you today," Lia said. "It was wonderful to get to meet these children."

"They are so kind and loving," Tia added. "You are doing wonderful things for them, and they are so appreciative of your efforts."

"It is time for us to leave," Julian said. "You will need to pack because we will depart tomorrow morning after breakfast for Aldridge Manor. We have our own Christmas to celebrate there," he declared.

Julian had been happy to ask the twins to spend Christmas with them. He knew how much Ariadne loved her younger sisters and how little attention the three had received from their parents. His wife would watch over these young women as they made their come-outs next Season. Hopefully, they would find men they loved.

Julian had come to understand that marriage contained many layers, but for him, the most important aspect was love.

As Tia and Lia headed for the carriage, he gazed into his wife's sky blue eyes. "Do you know just how happy you have made me, Ariadne Barrington?"

Her radiant smile warmed him as much as the sun of a summer day. "You couldn't possibly be any happier than I am, my darling husband."

He bent and kissed his precious wife, knowing each day shared with his marchioness would be one filled with love.

About the Author

USA Today and Amazon Top 10 bestselling author Alexa Aston lives with her husband in a Dallas suburb, where she eats her fair share of dark chocolate and plots while she walks every morning. She enjoys travel and sports—and can't get enough of *Survivor* or *The Crown*.

Her Regency and Medieval historical romances bring to life loveable rogues and dashing knights. Her series include: *The Strongs of Shadowcrest, Suddenly a Duke, Second Sons of London, Dukes Done Wrong, Dukes of Distinction, Soldiers and Soulmates, The St. Clairs, The de Wolfes of Esterley Castle, The King's Cousins, Medieval Runaway Wives,* and *The Knights of Honor.*